She loved him—
no question about it

Not so much because of his tenderness in bed but because of the way he smiled afterward, the pleasure he took in bringing her pleasure, because of his immeasurable generosity.

His generosity out of bed, too. He had accepted her into his home, welcoming her even after she'd given him grief for so long about how she didn't want his help. He hadn't criticized her, hadn't stood in judgment of her. He had simply been there, ready for her, willing to give whatever she was willing to take.

He knew who she was; he knew her capabilities. He wasn't aiming to control her, to dominate her. He only wanted to be a part of her life.

She wanted that, too—more than anything.

ABOUT THE AUTHOR

Judith Arnold can't remember ever not being a writer. She wrote her first story at age six and pursued a successful career as a playwright after getting a Master's degree from Brown Univerisity. Judith, who now devotes herself to writing full-time, also pens novels under the pseudonym Ariel Berk. She and her husband and two young sons recently moved into their dream home in Massachusetts.

Books by Judith Arnold

HARLEQUIN AMERICAN ROMANCE

*KEEPING THE FAITH SUBSERIES

HARLEQUIN TEMPTATION

Don't miss any of our special offers. Write to us at the following address for information on our newest releases.

Harlequin Reader Service
901 Fuhrmann Blvd., P.O. Box 1397, Buffalo, NY 14240
Canadian address: P.O. Box 603,
Fort Erie, Ont. L2A 5X3

LUCKY PENNY

JUDITH ARNOLD

Harlequin Books

TORONTO • NEW YORK • LONDON
AMSTERDAM • PARIS • SYDNEY • HAMBURG
STOCKHOLM • ATHENS • TOKYO • MILAN

Published May 1990

ISBN 0-373-16342-8

Prologue

Ordinarily on Sunday, Tom Barrett read the *New York Times*. His routine was to leave the apartment at sunup, take a brisk jog through the park along the East River and then detour to First Avenue on his way home to buy some fresh pastries and the newspaper. By eight-thirty or so he was showered, dressed and relaxing in the cozy, sun-filled breakfast nook of his kitchen, sipping hot coffee, nibbling on a croissant and boning up on the state of the world.

The first week of June hadn't been ordinary, however. Feeling achy and exhausted, he'd left the office early on Monday, and by Tuesday he was running a fever and suffering from dizzy spells and bouts of nausea. Days blurred one into the next; his greatest challenge was trying to keep down the steaming chicken broth his neighbor from across the hall was kind enough to bring him. His secretary rescheduled the week's appointments; his partners sent him an obscene get-well card and a bouquet of helium-filled balloons. His mother threatened to fly to New York and nurse him back to health but, expending his last ounce of strength, he managed to talk her out of it.

At last, on Sunday, the fever broke. He woke up feeling clear-headed, refreshed and ravenous. To celebrate his survival, he showered, got dressed and took a leisurely stroll over to First Avenue, intending to pick up a newspaper and splurge on a couple of apple turnovers.

The corner newsstand had already sold out its supply of the *Times*. "It's almost noon," the vendor pointed out. "You usually get here much earlier."

In truth, Tom didn't mind forgoing the paper. For his first day of genuine consciousness, he figured he would be better off immersing himself in the sort of tabloid trivia the *Times* never published: color comics, gossip, horoscopes, recipes and advice columns. So he purchased one of the other Sunday editions, sauntered down the block to the bakery and headed back to his apartment building.

He read the comics while his coffee brewed, and the sports pages with his first turnover. Searching for a crossword puzzle, he thumbed through the "Living" section. Somewhere between Erma Bombeck and Dave Barry he noticed a column called "Penny-Wise—by Penny Simpson."

Penny Simpson.

Forgetting the crossword puzzle, he pored over the article, which contained miscellaneous housekeeping suggestions and answers to questions, none of which seemed particularly relevant to Tom's life. At the bottom of the article an address—a post-office box in Orangeburg, New York—appeared, along with an invitation for readers to send in their questions, comments and helpful hints. It was signed: *Cheers! Penny.*

Penny Simpson.

Impossible. She would never write a newspaper column. Although she'd been smart and capable, her only ambition in life had been to get married, to be a wife, to raise a family. That was all she'd ever wanted— and she'd wanted it too much to wait for Tom.

Lowering the newspaper section and closing his eyes, he envisioned her as she'd been when he had first fallen in love with her—bewitchingly pretty and smelling of jasmine. He pictured her dressed in jeans and a pastel-pink blouse, her golden-blond hair pulled back in a wavy ponytail and her lips spread in a warm, welcoming smile. He recalled her hushed, slightly breathy voice, the feel of her arm around his waist, the flash of light that brightened her blue eyes whenever she saw him.

Tom would have married her. He had hoped to and planned to. But not until he'd finished his schooling. How many working-class hicks from western Iowa got the opportunity he'd been granted, to attend Harvard University on a scholarship? As much as he'd loved Penny Simpson, he hadn't been willing to sacrifice his education for her. And so he'd flown home during his school's Christmas vacation one year and learned that she was engaged to someone she'd met at State. Since Tom wouldn't marry her, she'd gone out and found herself someone who would.

Ancient history. What had been had been. He and Penny had both grown up. They weren't the same people anymore. He shouldn't even have been thinking about her. It was just such a shock, seeing her name in print. He had so recently returned to functional condition; he'd only just emerged from the delirious netherworld of the flu. He was overly sensitized to things. Everything seemed too vivid and sharp; everything called upon his emotions in unexpected ways.

He reread the entire article, searching for proof that, whoever the author was, she couldn't possibly be *his* Penny Simpson. He absorbed the words, in the process learning that reheating leftover rice in a vegetable steamer made the rice plump and juicy; that home-made Play-doh concocted out of flour, water, cream of tartar, oil and salt was cheaper than the store-bought variety; that you should never clean a computer monitor's screen with the spray-and-wipe glass cleanser you use on your windows; and that buttoning cotton shirts before placing them in the clothes dryer reduced the amount of wrinkling.

Just the sort of stuff a devoted homemaker like Penny Simpson would have cared about.

He tried to banish her from his thoughts. He shoved aside the "Living" section and continued his search for the crossword puzzle. Yet while he solved it, while he read the "Personalities" feature and wondered who in heaven's name all the celebrities so breathlessly mentioned in the articles might be, his mind insistently drifted back to Penny. He daydreamed about her sunny smile and her glossy hair and her whispery voice and the way he'd felt in her arms. He reminisced about the way he had let himself imagine a future for her and himself. He recalled the many nights he'd spent alone in Cambridge, fantasizing that someday he'd return to Carroll with his Ivy League diploma and a law degree and claim his bride and buy a big brick house and sire a tribe of daughters and sons with sunny smiles and glossy hair just like their mother's.

He wasn't still in love with Penny. Curious, that was all. Curious about whether she had, in fact, written the column. Curious about whether, after having spent her youth dedicating herself to the prospect of becoming someone's wife, she'd suddenly developed a hankering for a career.

Curious about whether she still smelled of jasmine, whether her eyes were still as clear and blue as a prairie sky.

Curiosity, he swore to himself, was all it was.

Chapter One

"Dear Penny: You know how when you bake an empty pie crust you've got to put something heavy on the dough to keep it from losing its shape? Well, I've found the perfect thing to weigh down my pie crusts is buckshot from my husband's rifle. The weight holds the dough in just the right shape."

"And the lead does wonders for your brain," Jodie mumbled, glaring at the sheet of paper in Helen's hands. Helen usually read the "Penny-Wise" mail aloud to Jodie, sparing her the torture of having to decipher the less legible letters. "Where do these crackpots come from?" she groaned. "Is it just me, or is the world really insane?"

"I'm sure it can't be you," Helen said dryly. In the six months since she'd signed on as Jodie's assistant, she'd learned not to take her boss's ravings too seriously. "I assume this one's a no-go?"

Jodie nodded and turned her attention to the tote bag beneath her desk. Somewhere within its cluttered interior was a waxed-cardboard container of marinated beef and broccoli, and Jodie was starving. She propelled her swivel chair backward, bent over and poked through the canvas bag, shoving aside her wallet, a month-old grocery list with two expired supermarket coupons clipped to it, an unsharpened pencil with gold letters reading Montoya—The Tune-Up Specialist embossed on its side, the ring of toy pistol caps she'd confiscated from her nephew three days ago and a folding umbrella. With a triumphant hoot, she grasped the wilted brown-paper bag at the bottom and pulled it out. She wheeled her chair back to her desk and pried open the container's flaps. Even cold, the beef and broccoli smelled delicious.

Helen was skimming the next letter in the stack. Most of the people who read the syndicated "Penny-Wise" column each Wednesday and Sunday in their local newspapers undoubtedly assumed that Penny Simpson worked inside a cozy, shingled house filled with spotless carpets, frilly curtains and the redolence of goodies baking inside brick wall ovens. They would undoubtedly be shocked to learn that Penny Simpson actually tested housekeeping tips and techniques and wrote her column in a flat-roofed granite-walled building virtually indistinguishable from all the others in the West Hudson Industrial Park in Rockland County. Her readers would also be shocked to learn that Penny Simpson was not a plump, rosy-cheeked, silver-haired grandmother in an apron but rather a frazzled thirty-one-year-old named Jodie Posniak, with short dark hair, a degree in English and a penchant for strange earrings, brightly colored stockings and take-out Chinese food.

"What's that one about?" Jodie asked, waving her plastic fork at the letter Helen was perusing.

"This one may be a keeper," Helen announced before reading.

"Dear Penny: The other day I cut myself pretty badly in the bathroom and I used a sanitary pad as a compress to stop the bleeding. It really worked. From now on I'm going to keep a sanitary pad in my first-aid kit."

Jodie almost choked on her food.

"I think it sounds like a good idea," Helen remarked. "You might advise people to use the ones that come individually wrapped. They'll stay cleaner longer in the first-aid kit."

"Oops—nicked my finger. Pass me a Kotex," Jodie muttered sarcastically, then speared a chunk of marinated beef and popped it into her mouth. "Come on, Helen, what's wrong with using a Band-Aid?"

"You'd use a pad on a cut that's too big for a Band-Aid."

"If it's that big, you ought to get stitches."

"And you can use the sanitary pad as a compress until you get to a doctor."

"Right." Jodie grimaced. "And if you get a nosebleed, you can use a tampon."

"All right," Helen sighed. "It's a no-go." She placed the letter on the reject pile on top of the buckshot letter. Eighty percent of the mail the "Penny-Wise" column received wound up on the reject pile. The remaining twenty percent included useful hints from readers and legitimate questions regarding household difficulties. Down the hall from Jodie's and Helen's offices was what Jodie called her "laboratory"—a vast, vaulted room containing an industrial kitchen for testing recipes as well as a conglomeration of home furnishings for experimenting with cleaning and repair techniques. After sorting through the mail each morning, Jodie spent much of her day in the laboratory, finding out what worked and what didn't.

"Don't sulk," Jodie warned Helen, who continued to gaze longingly at the letter about sanitary pads.

"I'm not sulking. I just thought it was a good idea."

"That's why I'm Penny Simpson and you're not," Jodie teased. For six years she had held the job Helen now had, as the right-hand woman to the original Penny Simpson. When the original Penny Simpson had retired a little over a year ago, she had anointed Jodie her successor. Jodie was reasonably certain that Helen aspired to become the next Penny Simpson, but Jodie was in no hurry to hand over the reins—or the name.

Even though she herself was arguably the most inept housekeeper in the universe, Jodie adored being Penny Simpson, that omniscient mythical goddess of home and hearth who bestowed her abundant wisdom on beleaguered housekeepers throughout the country. She loved knowing that millions of readers from Key West to Nome, San Diego to Bangor and just about every town in between opened their newspapers twice a week and learned that, if applied immediately, salt could remove red wine stains from carpets, that if you were making potato salad, you should boil the potatoes with the skin on and it would slide right off once the potatoes were the right consistency for the salad, and that a plastic squeeze bottle full of water was a handy item to keep at the table when you were feeding small children.

Jodie didn't think her millions of readers wanted to read that sanitary pads made good compresses for cuts. "What's the next letter?" she asked Helen.

"A request for you to run the granola recipe again."

"I ran it last January. Put that letter on hold. Maybe I'll run it again in a few months."

Helen placed the letter in a separate pile. Glancing up, she watched Jodie spear a piece of broccoli. "What are you eating?"

"Szechuan beef and broccoli."

"You can't eat that for breakfast!"

"I'm not. I'm eating it for dinner. I never got around to having dinner last night."

"That's not healthy," Helen chided her.

Jodie grinned. It occurred to her that Helen was much better suited to be the nation's ultimate homemaker. Although six years Jodie's junior, Helen appeared older. She always dressed conservatively; her wavy blond hair was always neatly pinned back from her pretty round face with tortoiseshell combs, her posture was ramrod perfect and her pencils were sharpened. She was without question the most uncreative person Jodie had ever met, but she made a damned good assistant.

"What's not healthy?" Jodie asked her as she swirled a sliver of meat through the soy-laden sauce that had accumulated at the bottom of the container. "Eating this at nine-thirty in the morning or skipping dinner?"

"Both. Why didn't you eat dinner last night?"

"Why do I feel like I'm talking to my mother?" Jodie shot back. At Helen's reproving look, she explained, "It was a hellish night, that's why. I spent two hours at the lawyer's office figuring out what to do about that idiot who's suing me over the spinach soufflé recipe we ran last year."

"You mean the woman whose soufflé collapsed when her husband's boss came to dinner? I didn't know she was suing you."

"Technically, she's suing Penny-Wise, Incorporated and the syndication company. But the real target of the suit is me. This bozo is incredible. She claims she prepared the soufflé when her husband invited his boss to dinner. When she served the thing it collapsed, and a week later her husband was fired.''

"But surely not because of the soufflé."

"If his choice in a wife is any indication, he probably got fired for lacking brains. Anyway, her suit claims the mortification of serving the boss a bad dinner led to her husband's losing his job, and it's all my fault because I failed to specify in the recipe that you've got to bake soufflé in a soufflé dish. She's demanding fifty thousand dollars—lost wages and mental anguish. The lawyer warned me, though—she's vindictive. She's really after me."

"Why?"

"Why?" Jodie shrugged. "How should I know? Maybe because I've got a job and her husband doesn't. Maybe because my soufflés come out better than hers."

Helen rolled her eyes.

"The world is insane," Jodie summed up, kicking off her shoes and tucking one green-stockinged leg under her other knee.

"Just because the world is insane doesn't mean you shouldn't eat dinner at dinnertime. You're too thin as it is."

Jodie scowled. Talking to Helen *was* like talking to her mother. "I would have eaten this last night," she defended herself. "I stopped at House of Cheng and bought it on my way home from the lawyer's office, with every intention of eating it as soon as I got to the house. But the place was a disaster. Lynne had locked herself inside my bedroom and was having one of her sob fests, and the kids were tearing the rest of the house to smithereens. When I told them to stop trashing the place, Peter had the gall to lecture me on the fact that *trash* is a noun and not a verb. Nine years old and he's already got a mouth on him like you wouldn't believe.''

"How long are you going to let them stay with you? It's been nearly a week already."

Jodie shrugged. "Lynne's my sister and Hank's a jerk. I can't throw her out in the street, can I?"

"And in the meantime, you can't eat a decent dinner."

"The day they sign a divorce decree," Jodie promised, "I'll eat a dozen decent dinners in one sitting—and Hank can foot the bill. Let's hear the next letter."

"Dear Penny,
I noticed your column in the newspaper recently. Are you *the* Penny Simpson from Carroll, Iowa? If you are, please get in touch.

Sincerely,
Tom Barrett"

Jodie put down her fork and reached across the desk. "Let me have a look at that," she said.

Helen pursed her lips. "Jodie, we're supposed to be working. This isn't a real letter. It's from someone who's got your pseudonym mixed up with a Penny in his past."

Ignoring Helen's protests, Jodie plucked the letter out of her assistant's fingers. It was handwritten in bold script on heavy cream-colored stationery. Printed across the top of the page was Black, DeLucca, Stone and Associates, Attorneys at Law, followed by a midtown Manhattan address and telephone and telefax numbers.

She reread the brief message silently. She wasn't *the* Penny Simpson—not even the original Penny Simpson had actually been Penny Simpson; she'd been named Penelope Entwistle. "Penny Simpson" had been a bland, euphonious name she'd conjured up back in the 1960's, when her column first began to appear in a few local weeklies. To be sure, Penny Simpson sounded like the sort of name that would belong to someone living in some small midwestern town. Jodie wouldn't be surprised to learn that there were hundreds of Penny Simpsons in Iowa.

Please get in touch, Tom Barrett had written. A basic wish, plainly stated, lacking in sentiment. Yet Jodie sensed something hidden behind the simple words, something personal, vital, pulsing with emotion. She wasn't sure why, but she suddenly felt an inexplicable sympathy for this Mr. Barrett, whoever he was.

"Can we get back to business?" Helen broke into her ruminations. "I have at least twenty more letters here."

"This *is* business," Jodie argued. "The man's a lawyer. If Penny-Wise's legal counsel can't fend off the lady who's suing me over her soufflé, I might want to retain another lawyer to defend me in court "

"Now, Jodie," Helen reprimanded, addressing her boss as one would a recalcitrant child. "You're facing a 5:00 p.m. deadline for your next column, you're supposed to come up with a solution for the problem of flatware rusting in the dishwasher, and you're scheduled to have lunch with three executives from the syndication company—which, I might remind you, pays your legal fees."

Jodie sighed and tossed the empty carton and the plastic fork into the garbage pail beside her desk. "Very well, Mother," she said with mock obeisance. "Let's get back to work."

But even as she listened to Helen read the next letter, Jodie couldn't keep her thoughts from straying back to Tom Barrett's note. *Please get in touch,* he'd written— leaving so much unsaid. She knew, just knew, that something significant had occurred between him and *the* Penny Simpson back in Carroll, Iowa.

Maybe Jodie had a hyperactive imagination. But she simply couldn't close her mind to the unvoiced emotion in Tom Barrett's modest letter. She sensed that he'd been carrying a memory of Penny Simpson around with him—for years, perhaps—and then he'd accidental- ly happened upon a "Penny-Wise" column on the women's page of a newspaper and his past had come back to haunt him. His heart had swelled with senti- ment. True love: Jodie was certain of it.

How thrilling it would be to have some man sending blind, groping messages out into the unknown in search of her. How exciting to be thought of as *the* Jodie Posniak, as if there had never been any other woman in the entire world. How romantic to have a Tom Barrett in her life, wondering whatever became of her, where she was, how she was faring, whether she still remem- bered him with fondness.

Helen's voice cut through her ruminations.

"Dear Penny,
How can you tell when the tank of your gas grill is low on fuel? We're always running out of propane in the middle of a barbecue. Why can't manufac- turers put a meter or something on the tank?"

"Too expensive, probably," Jodie opined. "It's a valid question, though. Put it on the keeper pile. We'll do a column on how to time your gas use. A full tank is supposed to give you a certain number of hours of grilling time, right?''

"We can get the figures from the grill manufacturers," Helen concurred, placing the letter on a third pile.

Jodie glanced at the letter and smiled wryly. Forget about Tom Barrett and his long-lost Penny. When it came to broken relationships, the gas-grill letter said it all: you could be cooking away, enjoying the feast until suddenly, without any warning, the fuel runs out and the party's over. The man—call him Tom—leaves Iowa, the woman—call her Penny—vanishes and the flame dies. That was reality, that was life. That was love as Jodie knew it.

And the "Penny-Wise" author had no handy answer for how to deal with it.

HELEN FOUND JODIE on her hands and knees in the laboratory, sliding a hot iron over a wet towel that had been spread across a remnant of carpet. "What are you doing?" she asked.

"Trying to rejuvenate the pile," Jodie explained, turning off the iron and shrugging the stiffness out of her shoulders. "Someone sent me a letter saying this would work."

She'd received the suggestion nearly a month ago, but as usual she was behind in testing the recommendations that arrived in the mail. In the nine days since she'd gotten the letter about running out of propane gas during barbecues, she still hadn't gotten around to telephoning the gas grill manufacturers to work out an easy formula for calculating the tank's capacity—and that had been a good idea for the column. Attempting to revive carpets with a steam iron didn't seem like nearly as good an idea, but Jodie had been in a quirky mood, so she'd shut herself up in the laboratory for a half hour and given the wet towel treatment a whirl.

She stripped away the towel and uncovered the life-less pile underneath. "So much for that brainstorm," she observed with a weary sigh.

"There's someone here to see you," Helen announced, reaching down and helping Jodie to her feet.

"Who?" Jodie asked as she smoothed the creases out of her modified miniskirt. She was wearing a light-weight cotton sweater the same charcoal color as the skirt, as well as peacock-blue stockings, red canvas espadrilles and silver scarab earrings. It wasn't the sort of outfit she wore when she was expecting visitors.

"He said his name is Tom Barrett," said Helen.

"Tom Barrett?" Jodie's eyes grew round.

"Isn't he that fellow you heard from over a week ago, asking you whether you were from Iowa?"

Jodie nodded vaguely.

"What's he doing here, Jodie?"

"You should have asked him," Jodie remonstrated. "That's your job."

"No—I mean, what's he doing *here*? How did he know where you worked? Did you tell him?"

Jodie wondered the same thing. "No. Of course not," she said. She didn't like readers to know where she worked. If they ever did, they might storm the industrial park, brandishing mildewed shower curtains and pots of lumpy gravy and beseeching Jodie's aid.

"You must have told him something," Helen pointed out, frowning sternly. "You wrote him a personal response. That's against policy, Jodie."

"I'm the boss. I set the policy."

"Fine, boss," Helen said with a withering look. "I hope your policy includes dealing with correspondents who barge in uninvited. I'm not going to entertain him."

Jodie tuned out Helen's self-righteousness. She was secretly rather pleased that Tom Barrett had shown up, even if he was interrupting her work day. Long after she should have forgotten his wistful letter, she had continued to think about it. A day after she'd received it she'd sent him a response, regretfully informing him that Penny Simpson was merely her pen name and wishing him luck in his search for *the* Penny Simpson. She'd felt she owed him that much; if she hadn't written to him, he might have spent the rest of his life wondering.

"What does he look like?" she asked Helen, running her fingers through her cropped black hair and trying to recall whether she had any lipstick in her tote bag. "Is he old or young?"

Helen shrugged. "Youngish."

"Good-looking?"

"Kind of, I guess."

Jodie smothered a curse. Helen was an able assistant, but when it came to men her powers of observation were sorely deficient. She had once described Don Johnson as "okay"; she complained that Bruce Springsteen's chin was too big and that Paul Newman had funny eyes. Not sure what to expect of Tom Barrett, Jodie unplugged the iron and accompanied Helen down the hall.

At the door to her office, Jodie whispered, "Give me a minute and then send him in."

"All right." Helen checked her watch. "It's quarter to five. Do you want me to come rescue you in fifteen minutes?"

"Only if I scream," Jodie said.

"I'm leaving at five, no matter what," Helen warned. "I'm having dinner with my Aunt Louise tonight, and she hates it when I'm late."

"Fine. Leave at five," Jodie said. "If it looks as if I'm going to have to scream, I'll do it before then."

With a bemused smile, Helen vanished into her own office across the hall from Jodie's.

Jodie raced around her desk and dived underneath it to fetch her tote bag. She rummaged through its disorderly contents in search of anything—makeup, a comb, a more reputable pair of shoes—with which she might improve her appearance. She had no reason to worry about the sort of impression she'd make on Tom Barrett. No matter how she fixed herself up, she was never going to resemble his Penny Simpson.

On the other hand, it wouldn't hurt to make herself more presentable.

A quick glance at her cherry-red espadrilles caused her to wince. She pulled them off and shoved them into the tote, then straightened up at the sound of her door opening. "Jodie? This is Mr. Barrett," Helen announced, stepping aside to admit Jodie's unexpected guest.

Helen deserved a point for describing the man as "youngish." She lost ten points, though, for describing him as "good-looking kind of, I guess." As far as Jodie was concerned, the man was gorgeous.

A bit too straight-arrow, perhaps, she conceded as she took in his neatly styled dark blond hair, his impeccably tailored gray suit, his maroon silk necktie and his buffed cordovan loafers. Given his ritzy attorneys-at-law stationery, Jodie couldn't blame him for grooming himself in a fashion befitting the high-priced lawyer he undoubtedly was.

Her gaze rose from his shoes back to his rectangular face. He had a strong, dynamic jaw—if Helen considered it too large, that was her problem—and a narrow nose. His eyes were a gentle hazel and were set deep beneath his high brow. They scrutinized her with an intensity that contradicted his diffident smile.

"How do you do?" he said politely, remaining in the doorway.

Jodie circled her desk to usher him in. His gaze dropped to her long legs and unshod feet covered with the bright turquoise stockings, and he seemed to shrink back a step. Jodie could sense more than see Helen's smirk. Helen was always chiding her about her bizarre taste in hosiery.

"Thank you, Helen," she said pointedly. "Is there anything else?"

Helen dutifully took her cue. "I'll just finish opening the afternoon mail," she said. "Remember, I'm leaving promptly at five." With that she was gone, closing the door behind her.

Jodie extended her hand to Tom Barrett, who recovered from the sight of her stockings in time to give her a courteous handshake. "I'm Jodie Posniak," she introduced herself.

"Yes, I know." His hand engulfed hers, his fingers long and his palm smooth and dry. "I'm Tom Barrett. I'm sorry to barge in on you like this."

"That's all right. I was just trying to resuscitate some carpet pile. Any interruption would have been welcome. Please have a seat." She gestured toward a chair in front of her desk, then scampered to her own swivel chair and sat, hiding her garishly clad legs beneath the well of the desk. She folded her hands on her blotter and smiled expectantly.

"I appreciated the note you sent me," he began. He leaned forward slightly in his chair, with his knees apart. He had a tall, thin build, with disproportionately long, lanky legs. "I—um—" he tapped his fingertips together "—I was just getting over the flu when I wrote that letter asking you whether you were from Iowa. I've since learned that your column appears in newspapers all around the country, but I had never seen it before. I felt pretty foolish." He smiled apologetically. "According to my secretary, you're famous the world over."

Jodie shrugged. "Penny Simpson is famous," she corrected him. "It's a name that appears on a column. And it's not so strange that you'd never heard of me. Ninety percent of my readers are women. Eighty-five percent of them bake their own muffins. Forgive me if I'm wrong, but going strictly by appearance, I don't think you fit the demographics."

"I like muffins," he said, then smiled. "I don't bake them, but I do like them."

"They're actually pretty easy to bake," she told him. "We ran a recipe a few weeks ago for oatmeal muffins—very healthy, and delicious, too. You really ought to read my column, Mr. Barrett. I mean, *I* don't fit the demographics, either, but I can bake a darned good muffin if I have to."

He gazed at her for a moment. Perhaps she was only imagining it, but he seemed to relax a bit in his chair. "Why," he asked, "would anyone ever *have* to bake a muffin?"

Jodie laughed, and Tom joined her. He had a disarming, almost boyish smile, not the sort of smile Jodie would have associated with a hotshot New York City lawyer. When she reminded herself that a hotshot city lawyer was, in fact, what he was, her defenses rose, protecting her against the thawing effect of his grin. "Oh, God," she groaned, disgusted at having been duped so easily. "You're working for *her*, aren't you?"

"Who?"

Jodie struggled to recall the name of the law firm representing the woman who was suing her. Had Tom been sent here as a spy? Had he been hired because of his natural charm and his terrific looks?

"You know who," she muttered. "That dimwit who thinks it's my fault her husband got the ax."

His smile disappeared. "I beg your pardon?"

"The one with the soufflé."

"The soufflé," he repeated, his frown deepening.

His confusion seemed genuine. He might simply be a superb actor, but Jodie honestly didn't want to believe ill of him. Besides, the woman couldn't really hope to learn anything useful by hiring someone to perform espionage.

"How did you even find me?" she challenged, not yet ready to trust him. "The column's address is a post-office-box number."

"I knew you were located in Orangeburg, so I drove up here and asked around. Someone at a gas station told me I'd find your headquarters in this industrial park. I must say I was surprised. This place looks like a factory."

Jodie nodded, silently allowing that anyone with a bit of moxie would be able to find her office without too much effort. "We rent part of the building. The rest of it is used by a consumer research firm for testing products. Why are you here, Mr. Barrett?" she pressed him.

If he expected the question, he lacked a ready answer for it. "I'm not exactly sure," he confessed. "When I saw your name—I mean, your pen name—in the newspaper, well, it reminded me of someone I used to know. I don't know why I thought it would be fun to get in touch with her and see what had become of her after so many years, but . . ." He smiled again, pensively. "The letter you wrote me was so kind. You didn't know who I was or what I wanted, yet you took the time to write something personal. It was a sensitive note, and—" he smiled sheepishly "—I wanted to meet the woman who sent it."

Sensitive? What had Jodie written that was so sensitive? As far as she could remember, she'd informed him of her real name and the nature of her column and said something along the lines of, *Your Penny must have been someone special. I wish you the best of luck in finding her.*

"You were right," he said, evidently reading her bewilderment. "Penny Simpson was important to me at one time and . . . well, you lose touch with people and years pass and you get to wondering."

"You must have really loved her a lot," Jodie said without thinking, then pressed her hand to her mouth in chagrin. "I'm sorry."

Tom didn't seem embarrassed by her tactless remark. "I did—past tense. It was years ago. Now I'm only curious about what's become of her. Recovering from an illness can make you reflective. You think about your life, your past. . . . You realize it's all right to take chances sometimes. Writing to someone I thought was Penny Simpson was an impulsive thing to do, and I'm not usually an impulsive person. Coming here was impulsive, too. I guess my curiosity got the better of me." He paused, his gaze circling the room before coming to rest on Jodie. "I'm sorry for taking you from your work—"

"Oh, no, don't apologize," she said, hastening to mollify him. "This has been the highlight of my day." She laughed so he wouldn't misconstrue her statement.

"Most of the time my big thrills around here have to do with discovering a shortcut for making frozen yogurt or a better way to remove grease stains from hardwood floors or something. Getting an unexpected visitor—especially if it's a lawyer who *isn't* here to serve me papers—is nice."

"Oh?" His golden-brown eyebrows arched high. "Are you being sued?"

Jodie pulled a face, then laughed again. "I'm afraid so. One of my readers seems to think I'm responsible for her husband's losing his job."

"Really?"

"It's a long story, Mr. Barrett," Jodie said. "Not worth going into. Suffice it to say that when you're famous the world over, you tend to make a few enemies along with all the fans. Then, when something goes wrong—a recipe doesn't turn out right, for instance—you become a convenient scapegoat. People take out their rage on you. Or, in this instance, they use the legal system to try to extort money from you."

"We live in a litigious society," he lamented.

"As a lawyer, you should know." She leaned back in her chair, assessing him. "So, have you satisfied your curiosity? Are you glad you came all this way from Manhattan?"

"It wasn't so far. Only a half hour's drive. And yes, I'm glad I came."

"Am I anything like your old Penny Simpson?"

Her candor seemed to amuse him. "Not that I can tell," he answered. "She would never wear stockings like yours."

Jodie considered fabricating some excuse for her brassy stockings—that she'd borrowed them from her sister, that she was using them for an experiment on how to dye synthetics—and then she discarded the idea. She was never going to see Tom Barrett again. She didn't have to pretend to be something she wasn't. "I like bright stockings," she said simply.

He opened his mouth and then shut it. His lips skewed upward into a grin. "So do I," he said, rising to his feet. "I've taken up too much of your time already, Ms. Posniak. I really—"

Before he could finish, the door whipped open and Helen rushed in, her usually placid demeanor wrought with tension. "I just found this in the mail, Jodie," she declared without preamble. "I think you should read it." She thrust a creased sheet of paper at Jodie and then turned to Tom Barrett. "Forgive the intrusion," she said belatedly.

Startled by Helen's uncharacteristic lapse in manners, Jodie took the paper. She offered Tom a shrug, then lifted the letter and read:

Dear Penny:
Write a will. Your days are numbered.

Chapter Two

He watched as all the color drained from her face. She had clear, peach-toned skin and angular features—delicately defined cheek bones, a sharp nose and chin and eyebrows that arched high above dark, playful eyes. That was the word for Jodie Posniak: *playful*. From her borderline-punk hairstyle to her loud blue stockings, she seemed to be the sort of woman who attacked life with vigor and spirit.

But as she scanned the letter her secretary had handed her, the sparkle faded from her eyes and the curve of her lips flattened into a taut, grim line. After a couple of seconds, she lowered the letter and produced a bogus smile. "Another day, another crackpot," she said with false cheer. "Forget it, Helen."

"Forget it? You should report this to the police!"

"Don't be so melodramatic." Jodie appeared to have regained her composure. Her smile looked less forced and her cheeks lost their waxy pallor. "This is meaningless. It's not worth losing any sleep over."

"Jodie—"

"Forget it," Jodie said, cutting her off. She folded the paper along its creases and dropped it into the wastebasket next to her desk. "It's five o'clock, Helen. I think I hear your aunt a-calling."

The secretary glared at her, then shook her head. "Why can't you take anything seriously?"

"If something is serious I take it seriously. This—" Jodie gestured toward the waste basket "—isn't serious."

"How can you be so sure? You *are* being sued, after all. Obviously there are people out there who aren't exactly in love with Penny Simpson."

"Oh, He-e-e-len," Jodie called, disguising her voice and echoing the syllables as if she were shouting from a distance, "this is your Aunt Lou-we-e-e-eze. Dinner's getting co-o-o-old...."

"Have it your way," Helen snapped, pivoting on her heel. "But don't expect me to identify you when they fish your body from the river." She stalked out of the office, slamming the door behind her.

Jodie released a long, tremulous breath. Turning toward the wastebasket, she glimpsed Tom and flinched. Apparently she had forgotten he was in the room.

"What did the letter say?" he asked gently. It was none of his business, but she was growing pale again, her smile waning and her eyes becoming opaque.

"Nothing," she said hastily, then issued a feeble laugh. "Just your run-of-the-mill death threat. But really, it's nothing to get worked up about. When you solicit mail for a column that appears in newspapers all across the country, you're bound to get lots of dillies."

Tom crossed the room and pulled the letter out of the basket. When she didn't stop him, he took the liberty of unfolding it and reading its nasty message. The letter was typed on plain white paper. "Where's the envelope?" he asked.

Jodie shrugged. "Helen's office, I guess."

"We ought to get it and check the postmark."

"We ought to throw the damned thing out and forget about it," she argued, although Tom detected a distinct quaver in her voice. She was standing less than a foot from him, eyeing the paper in his hand and gnawing on her lower lip. He realized that she was taller than he'd thought—perhaps five-foot-seven or eight—and marvelously leggy, a fact her above-the-knee skirt emphasized to splendid effect. Her shoulders were narrow, her hips slim, her breasts attractively small. For a brief, illogical moment Tom found himself trying to visualize what she'd look like naked. The picture his imagination conjured was spectacular—those long legs, that soft, tawny skin...

"Why don't you want to tell the police about this?" he asked, willfully dismissing the fantasy.

She folded her arms across her chest and scowled. "I'm Penny Simpson, remember? Famous everywhere except in certain offices of Black, Beluga and Associates—"

"Black, DeLucca," he corrected her.

"Whatever. If I go to the police with this, it'll be publicized all over the place. I don't want that kind of publicity. It goes against my image. Penny Simpson is the Happy Housekeeper, the ally of overworked women all over the nation, the symbol of peace and warmth and security. She's baseball, Mom and apple pie rolled into one."

"With a few oatmeal muffins thrown in for good measure," he said, gazing at her. The panic in her face—the panic she was trying so hard to deny—tugged at him, making him want to take responsibility for her, to shield her from harm. "Does Penny Simpson's wholesome image include cockroach earrings?'' he asked as his vision narrowed on the bug-shaped blobs of silver adorning her earlobes.

She reflexively reached up and touched her earrings, refreshing her memory of which ones she was wearing. ''They aren't cockroaches,'' she told him. ''They're scarabs.''

''Call them whatever you'd like—I still wouldn't want them in my kitchen.''

''Have you got a roach problem? The best way to get rid of roaches is by mixing boric acid with sugar and—''

''Ms. Posniak,'' Tom interrupted, extending the letter toward her, ''*this* is the problem you ought to be focusing on.''

''This is nothing more than a crank sounding off,'' she insisted, taking the letter, giving it a sidelong glance and then tossing it onto her desk. ''It's time to close up here, Mr. Barrett, so—''

''Can I see you home?''

''What?''

He didn't want to come across as paranoid, but the world was a dangerous place, full of deranged people. Every newspaper that carried Jodie's ''Penny-Wise'' column also had occasion to carry gruesome stories about car bombings and lunatics with semiautomatic weapons and religious fanatics calling for the murder of anyone who dared to disagree with them. ''I just want to make sure you get home safely,'' he said.

She peered up at him, evidently perplexed. ''That's really not necessary.''

''Humor me,'' he implored her.

She gazed at him for a minute longer, her eyes profoundly dark and piercing, her lips twitching as she considered and discarded various rebuttals. At last she capitulated with a shrug. "If you really want to," she said.

"I really want to," he confirmed, meaning it. He was surprised at how much he wanted to make sure this feisty, funny woman got home in one piece.

He waited patiently while she made a halfhearted attempt to straighten out her desk. She donned a pair of rope-soled canvas shoes of a nearly blinding red hue, lugged a suitcase-sized tote bag out from under her desk and marched through the door ahead of him.

She started down the hall, but he clamped his hand over her shoulder before she could get far. His fingers curved around the gracefully shaped ridge and he found himself imagining her body again, wondering whether she was married or otherwise attached, wondering why he should find himself attracted to a woman so unlike the demure, cosmopolitan women he usually dated. Wondering whether it would be out of bounds to invite Jodie out for dinner.

His touch made her gasp. She must be frantic, he thought, jumpy and nervous. She might even think that Tom was the person who'd sent the death threat, that he'd come up to Orangeburg deliberately to be with her when she received it, to savor the perverse thrill of witnessing her dread before he snuffed out her life. That she'd allowed him to remain with her after her secretary had left the building indicated that she was much too trusting. Anyone—even an alleged attorney from New York City—could be a murderer in disguise. He suspected that that very realization had just entered Jodie's mind and that she was presently berating herself for her stupidity—or saying her prayers.

"The envelope," he explained quietly, withdrawing his hand and angling his head toward her secretary's office. "Go get it."

"Oh," she said in a small voice. He loitered in the corridor while she ducked inside the office. When she returned to him she was carrying an envelope. "I think this is it," she announced. "Postmarked Philadelphia."

"Do you know anyone in Philadelphia?" he asked.

She frowned. "I know people everywhere. Not that it matters. This whole thing is just someone's idea of a sick joke."

She put the envelope in her tote and he pulled it back out before it got lost within the bag's cluttered interior. "Save it," he said, once again ignoring the voice inside his head reminding him that Jodie Posniak's problems were none of his business. "Put it in your office with the letter. It could be important evidence."

"Evidence?" She seemed momentarily gripped by terror and the laughter with which she tried to shake off her fear sounded painfully hollow. "You mean, for the police to make their case after I'm murdered?"

"For the police to track down whoever sent you the letter—*before* you're murdered. If you don't get any more threats, fine, but if you do, you're going to have to have them investigated. You know that."

Her gaze met his. He was moved by the transparent emotion in her eyes, the glistening veneer of tears failing to conceal the stubborn courage that burned within her. Her eyelashes were dark and thick, her lids naturally shadowed. A slow smile played across her lips as she appraised him. "Something tells me your specialty is criminal law," she guessed.

He shook his head. "Taxes," he informed her, dismayed by how unexciting that sounded. "Even a tax lawyer knows you should never be careless with evidence. Go put it on your desk, Ms. Posniak."

Her gaze lingered on him for a minute more and then she turned and entered her own office with the envelope. "Call me Jodie," she shouted over her shoulder.

He smiled. "Call me Tom."

She returned to the hallway and they walked down to the front door. The evening sky was glazed with late-June sunlight; the warm air held the summery scent of newly cut grass. A uniformed security guard was checking the locks on the building across the road, and Jodie waved to him before strolling with Tom toward the gravel parking lot that abutted her building. "See?" she whispered. "I've got Mr. Molloy there to keep me safe."

The presence of a security guard didn't reassure Tom. After all, he'd gotten inside Jodie's office without interference from the guard. If he could do it, any of Jodie's readers could.

When Jodie halted beside an aged, somewhat battered Plymouth Horizon, he blocked her hand before she could open the door. "Hold on a second," he said. He circled the car, inspecting the windows and the dashboard, then squatted down near the rear bumper and surveyed the car's underside.

"What are you looking for, a bomb?" she asked.

"That's right."

She laughed. "You're as bad as Helen."

Helen, he recollected, was Jodie's solemn blond secretary. "Maybe she and I simply want you to stay alive," he noted, straightening up and dusting off his trousers. "I'm parked over there," he said, pointing across the lot to the silver Acura standing in one of the spaces reserved for visitors. "I'll follow you."

"This really isn't necessary," Jodie argued, although he sensed from her grateful smile that she was flattered by his solicitousness, and perhaps even a bit relieved. And if there happened to be a husband or a boyfriend waiting at home for her, well, it would be better for Tom to find out before he asked her to be his guest for dinner.

They got into their cars and cruised out of the lot, along the central artery of the industrial park and onto a public roadway. Tom took in the array of stickers on the Plymouth's rusting bumper: a parking permit, an advertisement for Epcot Center, a sign reading Seatbelts Save Lives and another reading Recycling Saves the Planet. She drove aggressively through the rush-hour traffic, weaving from lane to lane and braking at the last minute whenever she came upon a red light. Tom might have assumed that she was trying to get rid of him—except that she'd smiled so enchantingly when he had insisted on following her home.

As soon as they got off the main thoroughfare and onto a snaking rural route, Jodie floored the gas pedal, indicating that, her bumper stickers notwithstanding, she was perilously willing to risk her life—as well as the planet's. It took all of Tom's concentration to keep up with her as they sped along the twisting lane, hurtling past houses and stretches of forest. The road climbed and dipped, and Jodie greeted each hill and turn by accelerating. If not for her masterly control, her ability to slow down just before any of the road's curves sharpened to a critical extent, he might have worried that her brakes had been tampered with.

Eventually she veered off the road onto a short un-
paved driveway and halted. Tom stopped behind her,
caught his breath and climbed out of his car. He
smothered the impulse to lambaste her about her driving; he didn't want her equating him in her mind with
her prissy secretary.

Instead, he directed his attention to the house at the
end of the driveway. It was a farmhouse style reminis-
cent of the architecture of his hometown. The front
porch was broad and in need of paint; the yard
appeared not to have been mown since the spring thaw;
the distressed bricks in the chimney clearly hadn't been
added as an architecturally stylish statement. A station
wagon was parked in the detached garage, and Tom
braced himself for the likelihood that whoever owned
it lived with Jodie and was of the male persuasion. He
was even more disheartened by the sound of a child's
shrill giggles spilling through an open window.

"Well, I'm still alive," Jodie announced cheerfully
as she shut her car door.

Tom sensed that was his cue to leave. He opened his
mouth to bid her goodbye, then closed it. Jodie had a
family. Tom didn't belong here...and yet her gaze
seemed so inviting, so utterly friendly, he couldn't bring
himself to leave.

As if she could read his thoughts, she said, "Would
you like to come in for a minute?"

To meet her husband and children, he thought
glumly. "I don't know—"

"Why don't you come in and have something to
drink? I'll make you a fruit smoothie," she went on,
beckoning him up the uneven slate walk to the porch.
"Somebody sent 'Penny-Wise' a recipe that's incredible. You pour a cup of OJ in the blender, then add

chunks of cantaloupe, banana, peeled apples and pears and blend it until smooth. It's like a high-fiber low-calorie milk shake. Want one?''

Before Tom could answer, the screen door swung open and a sturdy boy of about nine or ten darted out, followed by a girl of six or so. The boy was armed with a toy pistol—at least Tom hoped it was a toy—that he fired at random over his shoulder. The girl, with dark, beribboned pigtails streaming back from her head, was screeching. ''Gimme it, Peter! Gimme back my Boglin!''

The boy responded with maniacal laughter and a flurry of make-believe shots from his pistol.

Tom watched the youngsters until they disappeared around the side of the house. ''Your children?'' he asked.

''My sister's,'' Jodie told him, stepping into the house and holding the screen door open for him. ''She's moved in with me. Temporarily, she says, although it's been a couple of weeks already.''

Not a husband, not Jodie's own progeny. Tom's mood brightened considerably.

Jodie nudged the carpet runner adorning the hardwood floor of the entry hall with her toe, smoothing the wrinkles. Then she set her tote bag down on an ancient-looking chair that stood next to an equally ancient-looking mail table, and waved Tom into the kitchen. The room was large, the appliances old and the cabinets stripped down to bare oak. Several had been recently varnished, and a can of polyurethane and a paintbrush stood on a square of newspaper in a corner of the room, no doubt waiting to be applied to the remaining cabinets. Two empty pots stood on the stove, and a loaf of bread and a jar of strawberry preserves lay on the round center table, which was covered with a quaint checkered cloth. The curtains featured a dinosaur motif.

Tom wasn't sure what he'd expected to find in the kitchen of the nation's Happy Housekeeper, but it wasn't dinosaur curtains on the windows.

"Would you like a fruit smoothie?" Jodie offered again, as she shoved up the sleeves of her sweater and stepped out of her shoes.

"No, thank you."

"What can I get you? Milk, coffee, soda—"

"Jodie?" A woman's voice reached them from another room, followed shortly by the arrival of the voice's owner. Tom easily identified her as Jodie's sister, thanks to the strong resemblance between the two women. Both had wide-set dark brown eyes, smoothly sculpted cheeks and pointy chins, narrow shoulders and long, tapered fingers. There were differences, though: Jodie's sister was an inch or so shorter than Jodie and a few pounds heavier. Her hair, the same black color, was longer and wavier. In her acid-washed jeans and knit jersey, she made a substantially less flamboyant impact than Jodie. Her face lacked the lovely animation that even a death threat hadn't completely erased from Jodie's luminous brown eyes.

As a matter of fact, Tom acknowledged as he assessed the woman, Jodie's sister looked as if she hadn't smiled in ages.

She was sizing him up, and Jodie made the introductions. "Lynne, this is Tom Barrett, a—a friend of mine. Tom, my sister Lynne Duryea."

"How do you do?" he said politely, shaking the woman's hand and trying not to look too pleased that Jodie had introduced him as a friend.

Lynne returned the handshake and then flopped onto one of the chairs near the table. "It's been awful, Jodie. Hank called twice today. He begged me to come back."

Jodie opened the refrigerator and gave its contents a leisurely inspection. "What did you say?"

"I said I was happier here."

Jodie contemplated a bottle of raspberry-flavored seltzer for several seconds, then replaced it on the shelf and shut the door.

"I could go back to him, I guess," Lynne muttered. "If I had to, if you insisted. You must be sick of me."

"I've been sick of you since the day I was born," Jodie teased. "You and the kids can stay here as long as you want, and you can tell the bastard I said so."

"I did," Lynne related, permitting herself a timid smile. "He said you were a—" she shot Tom a quick look and edited herself "—a meddlesome witch. He said if it weren't for the fact that you were willing to put all three of us up, I would have gone back to him by now. But I can't, Jodie, you know? He's crazy if he thinks I would."

"If you can't, you won't." Jodie lifted the conic lid of a tacky ceramic cookie jar, which was shaped like a clown, poked inside and pulled out a couple of chocolate-chip cookies. She extended one to Tom, who declined with a shake of his head. For the second time that afternoon he felt as if he were eavesdropping on Jodie's personal conversations.

She didn't seem to mind, though. This time she obviously hadn't forgotten that he was in the room, and she hadn't asked him to leave so she and her sister could confer privately. As awkward as he felt about listening, he was gratified that she felt comfortable enough in his presence to engage in a fairly intimate conversation with Lynne.

"Have you made anything for supper?" Jodie asked

"Made anything?" Lynne glanced at the pots and scowled. "Was I supposed to make something?"

"Well, I was at work all day. The least you could have done was cook dinner."

Tom realized that this was the perfect time to ask Jodie out—except for Lynne sitting just a few feet away, looking addled and forlorn. Jodie might have no compunctions about discussing her sister's marital difficulties in front of him, but he was reserved enough not to want to risk rejection in front of an audience.

Lynne didn't seem to be in any hurry to leave the room. Not wishing to lose the opportunity, Tom took a deep breath, edged closer to Jodie and murmured, "Maybe we could grab a bite to eat somewhere."

Unfortunately, Lynne overheard. "Hey," she said, brightening. "That would be fun. We could go to Burger King."

"I think Tom was talking to me," Jodie said, silencing her sister. She cast him a winsome smile. "I'd like that. This house is too chaotic. Penny Simpson's always writing about the importance of order in a person's home. I wish to God I took her advice." Still smiling, she stepped back into her glow-in-the-dark red shoes, gave her sister a wave and pranced out of the kitchen. Tom issued Lynne a brief farewell and hurried out after Jodie.

"I'll drive," he offered as soon as they were outside. It had been scary enough tailing her in his car; the prospect of being her passenger was even more horrifying than a death threat.

Jodie's smile expanded. "Is this a date?" she asked.

He wasn't accustomed to such bluntness from women. But then, given Jodie's irreverent way of dressing, he ought to expect that her personality would be equally irreverent. Once she was settled in her seat, he closed her door and circled the car to the driver's side. He started the engine, then glanced to his right. He liked having Jodie beside him. He liked seeing her dark, radiant eyes, her elfin profile, the weird silver bug earrings, the sleek line of her jaw and her long legs extending beneath the glove compartment.

"Sure, why not?" he answered. "This is a date." He started the car, then asked, "Where should we go? What's a good restaurant in the area?"

She meditated for a moment, then asked, "Do you like Chinese food?"

Fifteen minutes later—Jodie would have driven the distance in under ten, Tom estimated—they arrived at a cozy restaurant specializing in Szechuan cuisine. Although the bar was doing a lively happy-hour business, the dining area was fairly empty and he and Jodie were promptly seated. The prices on the menu would have seemed low to him even if he weren't used to the inflated prices of Manhattan's better restaurants. "What do you recommend?"

"Everything," Jodie said grandly. "It's all delicious."

"Why don't you order for us?" he suggested.

Jodie appeared delighted by the prospect. She quickly rattled off a bunch of dishes to the waiter, then handed him her menu.

Tom waited until the waiter had filled two glasses with water and departed. Then he presented Jodie with an amiable smile and said, "All right—explain to me why the Happy Housekeeper lives amid such chaos."

She returned his smile. "First you've got to promise never to go public with the truth about Penny Simpson," she demanded. "It would destroy my reputation."

"I promise," he said.

She searched his face for proof that he meant it, then relaxed in her seat. "I didn't become Penny Simpson as a home-economics major or anything," she explained. "As a matter of fact, when I was a kid, I used to make fun of my mother for clipping the original Penny Simpson's hints out of the newspaper. It all seemed so repulsively domestic to me. I, of course, was going to be liberated from all that household drudgery." She flashed him a self-deprecating grin. "After I finished college, I got a job doing research for a professor who was an expert on consumer movements. She had me codifying the syndicated 'Penny-Wise' columns because they were filled with consumer tips, strategies for saving money and outwitting big business and so on."

"How on earth does a column about ways to reheat leftover rice teach its readers to outwit big business?" Tom asked.

"The more leftover rice you can use, the less rice you have to buy. 'Penny-Wise' frequently prints recipes for expensive prepared foods so people can make their own inexpensive imitations. The original Penny Simpson came up with a lot, but I've worked out a few specialties, myself. I've got a dynamite granola recipe, for instance, and a do-it-yourself pancake mix that you can make in bulk and store indefinitely. Lately I've been analyzing those powdered instant dessert coffees—I've got a couple of them psyched out and I'll get the rest of them in time. And, of course, there's the do-it-yourself roach killer, various cleansers and the like. The original Penny Simpson won her audience by finding them ways to save time and money. And given that women never have enough of either, that's important. Women earn less money than men do; when they're married and work, they still wind up doing most of the housekeeping. 'Penny-Wise' has probably done more for women than affirmative action, in terms of making their lives a little easier.''

Her fervent speech impressed him. "So, you went from researching Penny Simpson to becoming her?''

"I came to Orangeburg to interview her for the professor and wound up accepting a job as her assistant. We worked well together and she taught me everything she knew. When she retired I took over.'' Jodie sipped some water and chuckled. "I can write a fine column, but that doesn't mean I follow all my own recommendations. I spend eight hours a day figuring out ways to keep house. I'm not going to keep house in my free time, too.'' She paused while the waiter served their hot-and-sour soup, then added, "Of course, my house is in worse shape lately because I've got Lynne and her kids staying with me.''

"Lynne's left her husband, I take it," Tom surmised. Since Jodie and Lynne had discussed Lynne's situation in front of him, he felt safe in commenting on it.

Jodie confirmed his guess with a nod. "She and Hank have been fighting for years over whether she should take a job. She wants one. The kids are old enough now that they don't need her to be available every minute of every day. But Hank hits the ceiling every time Lynne mentions the possibility of working.'' Jodie tasted her soup, then continued, "When Lynne and Hank were living in Houston, she had nowhere to run during their fights. Now they're living back East, and when Hank started in on her, she had a place to come to.''

"I see."

"It probably sounds like a sordid soap opera to someone from Iowa."

"As a matter of fact," Tom revealed, "husbands and wives have arguments in Iowa, too." He tasted the soup and winced at its extreme sourness. A few beads of sweat popped out on his brow as he manfully swallowed the broth.

"This is more than an argument," Jodie said. The soup's pungent flavor seemed to have no effect on her. "I think Lynne's going to divorce him. It's high time, too."

"You don't like your brother-in-law much," Tom said before forcing down another scathing mouthful of soup.

Jodie scowled. "He's much too domineering. He insists on being in charge all the time. I can't stand that kind of controlling behavior."

"Maybe he has a good reason for not wanting his wife to work," Tom proposed gently. Although he viewed society from a modern perspective, he could understand a man's desire to provide for his family and to have his wife at home, taking care of the children. Maybe it was reactionary—and, given the economics of the day, maybe it was a financial impossibility in most households—but he could understand the yearning. His mother had had to take a job when his father had died, and he'd often dreamed of being able to support her, as well as his own family, once he was a lawyer and returned to Carroll and married Penny.

Wisely, he kept his thoughts to himself. Jodie was shaking her head; he could guess she wouldn't take kindly to such old-fashioned sentiments. "I'll tell you why Hank won't let Lynne get a job. He wants to be the boss. He knows that if she starts earning money she'll deserve a say in how it's spent."

"It sounds like a difficult situation," Tom said in a tactful, lawyerly tone. "Has your sister retained legal counsel?"

"Not yet. Are you interested?" Jodie asked, then corrected herself. "I forgot—you're a tax lawyer."

"One of my colleagues specializes in divorces," he told her. "But there's no reason for her to hire someone from the city. I'm sure there are plenty of competent attorneys close by." He dabbed his face with his napkin, attempting to dry off the sweat without Jodie's noticing.

"Just in case—does Black, Beluga charge high fees?" Jodie asked.

Tom didn't bother to correct her. Jerome DeLucca, the divorce specialist, happened to be a huge man, well over six feet tall and at least two hundred fifty pounds, most of it centered in his midsection. Referring to him as a breed of whale seemed comically appropriate. "We charge Manhattan fees," he explained to Jodie. "Everything costs a lot there, including lawyers."

"How'd you wind up in Manhattan?" Jodie asked. "It must have been quite a culture shock for a midwestern native like you."

"It was," he admitted, spotting the approaching waiter and smiling at the prospect of having his bowl of soup cleared away. His relief was short-lived, however; although the soup was removed, several platters of food, potentially just as spicy, took its place on the table. At least the fried rice looked safe, he thought, helping himself to a heaping mound of it.

"What made you settle in New York, then?" she questioned him.

"A good job offer," he replied automatically, then reconsidered. The position at Black, DeLucca had been an excellent one, but his decision to move to New York City after completing his legal studies had been based on more than the fact that an ambitious tax lawyer was smart to locate himself near the sort of major clients one found primarily in bustling financial centers. When he'd first dreamed of becoming a lawyer, he'd had no particular inclination toward tax law. Quite the contrary, he'd pictured himself becoming a general legal practitioner in a modest midwestern town, like Carroll.

"You wanted to get away from Iowa, huh," Jodie hazarded, piling her plate with an assortment of food and then digging in.

"I suppose I was ready for a change."

She scrutinized him intensely, then smiled. "And you wanted to put some distance between you and Penny Simpson."

Startled, he lowered his fork and took a bracing drink of water. He scrambled for a way to contradict her without sounding defensive, but before he could say anything the urge to equivocate vanished. Jodie had been frank with him about herself. He wanted to be just as frank with her. "Actually, there was already plenty of emotional distance between us by then," he said. "She got married right after our sophomore year of college."

"Did you attend the wedding?"

"No." He ate some fried rice as he reminisced. "We'd been high school sweethearts. You can't build a lifelong relationship on puppy love. I certainly didn't plan my career based on how many miles it would put between me and her.''

"Why did you come here?" Jodie inquired, leaning back in her chair and studying him. "I mean to Orangeburg. I'd already written you that I wasn't the Penny Simpson you used to know. Why did you come?"

He lowered his fork and returned her thoughtful gaze. Her question was one he'd asked himself many times since he'd made the decision to take off from work early that afternoon and drive north in search of the author. Part of it, as he'd already told her, was that the note she'd sent him had been both sweet and surprisingly perceptive. Part of it was an irrational, mildly manic eagerness to embrace life, to take chances, to celebrate his survival of what had been a truly wretched case of the flu. But still, there had been more to it than that.

"I'm not really sure why I came," he admitted.

Jodie smiled. "Did you expect that I'd be something like your Penny?"

"I don't know what I expected. You're nothing like her, though."

"Of course I'm not," Jodie declared. "For one thing, I'm a lot older. I bet you still remember her the way she was in high school."

He considered Jodie's charge and concurred with a grin. "I guess I do. Lord only knows what she's like now."

Jodie nibbled on her food. "I can't imagine wanting to get married in college. My sister got married right after she graduated, and look at her now."

"Not all marriages are bad," Tom pointed out. "My parents had a wonderful marriage until my father passed away. And my grandparents have been happily married for fifty-seven years."

"Fifty-seven? Wow." Jodie nudged her plate back and sighed. "My parents are approaching their thirty-sixth anniversary, but it's been a pretty stormy thirty-six years. I don't know—I suppose some people can pull it off. There was a time I thought I'd get married, but now..." She shrugged and shook her head. "I don't think I could stand having someone watching over my shoulder all the time."

Tom comprehended that she was speaking from personal experience, even though he couldn't begin to fathom what that experience might have entailed. His definition of a good relationship had little to do with people watching over each other's shoulders. "Do you think some ex-boyfriend could have sent you that death threat?" he asked.

Jodie erupted in a loud laugh. When Tom didn't join her she grew sober. "I doubt it," she said. "My most recent ex-boyfriend's idea of solving a disagreement was to vanish into thin air, not stick around and fight. A death threat takes a certain degree of passion, don't you think?"

What Tom thought was that Jodie struck him as the sort of woman a man would be more than willing to stick around and fight for—or fight with. Her clothing was lusty, her laughter effervescent, her mind quick, her eyes alluring and her attitude refreshingly uninhibited. He wouldn't necessarily apply the term "passionate" to himself, and yet within moments of meeting Jodie he'd been undressing her in his mind.

"It couldn't have been Jeff," she decided. "I'm sure it's one of my readers. You wouldn't believe some of the nuts I hear from," she continued. "People send me recipes for tadpole stew and advice on how to fall off a roof without breaking your neck. People write to tell me I'm a discredit to feminists, to ask for political endorsements or to request that I hang up my apron and move to Antarctica. People who are unable to take out their rage on their husbands or parents or kids take it out on me instead. I'm used to it."

She nearly had him convinced. He wanted to believe she wasn't in any danger. But the same people who expressed their rage on paper could also express it by stalking a household-tips columnist, couldn't they?

"Maybe you shouldn't be used to it," he admonished her gently. "Tell the police about the letter, okay?"

She bristled visibly. "Don't be so protective," she flared. "I didn't ask you for advice, did I?"

"I just don't want anything to happen to you," he explained.

"Welcome to the club. I don't want anything to happen to me, either."

"It's just that you seem a little bit cavalier about the letter—"

"So you're going to take over and protect me, huh?" Her eyes shone with anger. "Tell me, Tom, what should I do? Lock myself up in the house? Buy a shotgun and an electric fence? I have every intention of living my life normally—"

"Normal and careful aren't mutually exclusive," he observed. "All you have to do is take a few precautions."

"Like what?" she snapped. "Avoiding dinner dates with strangers? Fine." She stood and tossed down her napkin.

He hadn't meant to insult her; he couldn't even think of what he'd said to ignite such fury in her. "Please, Jodie," he said, scrambling to his feet. "At least let me pay the bill."

She glowered at the half-consumed food on the table, her arms crossed and her eyes blazing. "You ought to ask for a doggie-bag while you're at it," she grumbled.

In spite of her lacerating anger, Tom found himself grinning. Jodie, he recognized, was above all a practical woman. Practical people didn't waste food, and they didn't go out of their way to put themselves in dangerous positions. She was too damned stubborn to let anyone—whether a tax lawyer from New York or a potential assassin—get the better of her. Her anger, however irrational, would save her.

Never had Tom been so pleased to be the target of a woman's wrath.

Chapter Three

You're scared. a voice whispered inside her. *You're pet-rified. Admit it.*

She stood on the sidewalk outside the House of Cheng, next to Tom's fancy import car. He was still settling the bill, and the polite thing would have been for her to wait inside the restaurant until he was done. But something had snapped inside her and she'd had to get away from him until she calmed down.

Tom Barrett wasn't just a terrific-looking guy—he was genuinely nice. Unlike most of the men she met, she'd gotten through the better part of a dinner with him without once feeling that his primary interest was himself or that his primary goal was to get her into bed. He seemed bright and courteous and generally quite charming—until he'd started patronizing her. Until he'd all but come right out and said, "You can't take care of yourself, so I'll take care of you."

She *could* take care of herself. She'd been taking care of herself all her life—and taking care of her older sister and even, on occasion, her parents when they lost control of themselves during their frequent quarrels. She ran her own life and didn't answer to anyone. And she sure as hell wasn't going to run her life according to the

maniac who had sent her that stupid letter. She wasn't
going to answer to anyone by taking precautions and
begging the police for protection.

Oh, God, she was scared. She'd managed to put her
fear out of her mind while she and Tom had talked
about other things—her career, his long-lost love, her
sister and his grandparents—but then he'd gone and
spoiled everything by wagging a figurative finger at her,
accusing her of not handling this silly problem as he
would have her handle it.

It wasn't like her to suffer from anxiety. She was
strong, sturdy, perpetually optimistic. She was proud of
her independence. No one, not even some lunatic from
Philadelphia with a typewriter and a postage stamp, was
going to rob her of that independence. And no one, not
even a good-natured, heartbreakingly handsome tax
lawyer from Manhattan, was going to make her fearful
and then offer himself up as her gallant protector. She
didn't need Tom Barrett to save her life.

He emerged from the restaurant carrying a white paper bag. "Here," he said, extending it to her.

"No, you keep it," she countered, a halfhearted attempt to make up for her earlier brusqueness. "You
paid for it, after all."

He eyed the doggie bag apprehensively, then pressed
it into her hands. "To tell you the truth, Jodie, it was a
little bit too spicy for me."

"All right. I'll eat it for breakfast tomorrow."

He grinned—the same cocky grin he'd given her after
she'd lost her temper in the restaurant. Mingled with her
annoyance was the unhappy recognition that Tom had
one of the most beautiful smiles she'd ever seen. His
teeth were straight and white—all that wholesome milk-
fed Iowa living, she supposed—and the lines bracket-

ing his mouth curved in beguiling symmetry. His eyes actually seemed to twinkle, and Jodie wasn't in a twinkling mood.

He unlocked the car's passenger door for her, and she stubbornly refused his hand as she took her seat. After closing the door behind her, he sauntered around to the driver's side and got in. The faint citrus scent of his after-shave blended with the aroma of the car's leather upholstery and the peppery fragrance of the leftover Chinese food in the bag on her lap. "Do you own this car?" she asked, exerting herself to be congenial. During the trip to the restaurant she'd noticed that Tom drove extremely conservatively. She imagined, however, that a car like this would perform spectacularly on the back roads outside town.

"Of course I own it," he answered, pulling away from the curb. "Did you think I stole it?"

She hadn't expected sarcasm from him, but she deserved it. "It's just that most people I know from New York City don't own cars," she explained. "If they can't get a train out of the city, they'll rent a car."

"I like having my own car," he said. "When I was a child I lived in a town even smaller than Carroll. A person's vehicle represented survival, communication, connection and entertainment all rolled into one. I went through seven years of higher education and another seven years of New York living without a car, and I always felt trapped. The apartment I'm living in now is roomy and it's got a decent view of the East River, but I still get a little claustrophobic every now and then. I like the freedom of knowing I can get wherever I want, whenever I want."

"That's a pretty expensive freedom in New York," Jodie remarked.

"Worth it, though."

She shot him a quick glance. A roomy East Side apartment with a river view, and a car. It dawned on her that tax lawyers must earn scads of money.

"Did anyone ever tell you you drive like a maniac?" Tom inquired.

She attempted to stifle the fresh burst of indignation his criticism provoked. "Did anyone ever tell you you're as overbearing as a mother hen? Believe it or not, I have somehow managed, without any assistance from you, to stay alive for thirty-one years. As Penny Simpson I've received countless letters from crackpots, and as Jodie Posniak I've received a grand total of one speeding ticket—for going forty miles an hour in a thirty-mile-an-hour zone. And if you ask me, this car is wasted on you."

Instead of being insulted, he laughed. "I didn't ask you," he noted.

"Turn left at the light," she muttered crossly. She wasn't sure why she was feeling so grouchy, other than the fact that Tom was right and she was wrong. "I'm sorry," she said, staring at the road ahead. "I'm just . . . in a touchy mood."

"Perfectly understandable."

"I'm usually much nicer."

"You're usually not operating under a death threat."

"Please don't keep reminding me."

He sent her a compassionate look, then steered around an S-shaped curve in the road. "Do you think you'll be safe in your house?" he asked.

"Of course I will," she said with feigned confidence. "The twerp sent her charming little message to my post office box. My readers don't know where I live. And besides, Lynne and the kids are at my house."

"Ah, yes. I've witnessed your nephew's skill with a gun. I'm sure he'll be able to defend you."

"That's my driveway up ahead," she said, refusing to respond to his mocking.

He pulled onto the gravel driveway and stopped the car. A lamp had been left on in the living room, filling the windows with a golden glow that illuminated the sagging porch. A light was also on upstairs in the room the children were using as temporary living quarters. Judging by the hour, Jodie figured that Lynne was getting them ready for bed. The house was tranquil, the sky darkening to a velvety night blue and the air alive with the chirring of crickets and the rustling of leaves shifting in the breeze.

Tom swung open his door and Jodie climbed out, as well. Given his generally chivalrous behavior, she assumed he would escort her to the front door. But beyond that she didn't know what he expected, if anything. "Tom," she said as they strolled along the slate walk, "I—um—I'm sorry I bolted from the restaurant like that."

"It's okay," he assured her, cupping his hand around her elbow and ushering her up the steps to the porch. "You're a little overwrought—I understand."

"No," she argued, frustrated by his unflappability. "You don't understand." She broke from him and paced a few steps away. "I don't like to be babied, Tom."

He looked perplexed. "Was I babying you?"

"You were lecturing me on what I was supposed to do, how I was supposed to handle this ridiculous letter. *I'll* decide what I'm supposed to do about it, Tom. Not you, not anyone but me."

He regarded her for several long minutes. The amber light coursing through the windows washed over his face, emphasizing the lean angularity of his features. She entertained the inane thought that if her homicidal correspondent was going to slay her in the near future, she wouldn't mind experiencing a final, tragically doomed but unspeakably beautiful romance with Tom before she met her Maker.

That peculiar notion was quickly dashed by his words. "Maybe you're not quite rational about it, Jodie. I'm no psychologist, but it seems to me that you're denying the truth in the hope that the entire incident will fade away. That's not going to happen, though, and—"

"And so, lucky me, I get to have you take care of me," she retorted sardonically. "No way, Tom."

"Is it a crime to let someone give you a little sensible advice?"

She shot him a swift look. Despite his benign question, she discerned a challenge in his attitude. His chin was raised defiantly and his eyes were hard and piercing in the dim light. "When you start taking advice from someone else," she answered heatedly, "they take over. When you seek help from someone else you wind up helpless, and I have no intention of letting that happen."

He continued to measure her with his sharp gaze. His voice, however, was muted when he asked, "Are we talking about someone specific?"

"I don't know who you're talking about," she countered. "I'm talking about men in general. They just love to come in and take over and be heroes. If you insist on carrying your own weight and not being dependent on them, it offends their male pride. Well, I've got my pride, too.''

"The fellow who vanished into thin air," he guessed, ignoring her lofty explanation. "What exactly did he do to you?"

Jodie felt her cheeks grow warm; she thanked the darkness for hiding her blush from Tom's perceptive gaze. Jeff hadn't actually vanished into thin air, although he might as well have. He'd left her because, as much as she liked him and enjoyed his company, she hadn't needed him the way he'd wanted to be needed. She earned a comfortable living, did her own household repairs, solved her own problems. She'd spent her entire life seeing how her mother's inability to take care of herself bound her to Jodie's father and how Hank was now trying to keep Lynne dependent on him by denying her the opportunity to hold down a paying job.

"What he did," she said slowly but firmly, "was refuse to accept that I could take care of myself."

Tom opened his mouth to speak, then rethought his words, mulling them over, weighing them as he scrutinized Jodie across the shadowed porch. "Considering the way you're handling this death threat, I can see why he'd feel that way."

"Go away!" she yelled, waving wildly toward the porch steps. "I don't need to listen to this!"

"That's your opinion," Tom said his lips twisting in a wry smile. Still, he showed enough respect for her anger to move toward the steps.

"Anything else you want to criticize me about before you leave?" she roared. "Don't you want to remind me to lock the door before I go to sleep? If you don't remind me, heaven knows whether I'll remember."

Again he exercised restraint, mulling over his words before he gave voice to them. "Don't forget to lock the door..." was all he said, his smile taking on an amused quality.

Before she could think of a suitable comeback, he'd reached his car and climbed in.

She turned and stormed into the house. The sound of his motor revving in the driveway was overtaken by Lynne's lilting voice, which drifted down the stairway from the second floor as she read a Dr. Seuss book to her children. Jodie hesitated at the foot of the stairs, listening, hoping the familiar rhymes would anchor her back in reality.

They didn't. She felt disoriented and incomplete. She should have thanked Tom for dinner and for his well-intended concern. She shouldn't have lashed out at him just because she'd felt smothered by his solicitousness, just because the last man she'd been involved with had been turned off by her independence. Tom had meant well; she should have accepted his kindness for what it was.

That was the problem, though—no matter how prettily veiled, it was a typical macho approach to things: a woman is threatened and therefore a man must take over, protect and advise and defend her and prove to her how much her survival depends on him.

Forget that. Jodie could survive just fine without any interference from Tom Barrett.

Sighing, she trudged into the kitchen and placed her doggie bag in the refrigerator. The telephone rang and she hurried across the room to answer it so the ringing wouldn't disrupt Lynne's quiet time with her children.

"Hello?"

She heard only silence on the phone, so ominously long it caused an icy shiver to run down her spine. She tried to calm herself with the understanding that whoever had sent her the threatening letter couldn't possibly have obtained her home phone number—a hollow consolation at best.

"Hello?" she said again, forcing strength into her voice.

"Hi, Jodie," came a rumbling response. "Put the wife on, would you?"

Hank. Jodie let out her breath and sagged against the counter. She detested the way her brother-in-law referred to Lynne as "the wife," as if she were an inanimate object. "Can't you even say please?" Jodie scolded.

"Okay," he said with spurious contrition. "Pretty please, Jodie, would you put Lynne on?"

"She's busy."

He lapsed into another lengthy silence. "Listen, Jodie, enough is enough. I want her back in New Jersey."

"I'm not holding her here against her will. She's free to go back to you whenever she wants to. Obviously, she doesn't want to."

"If you weren't standing in the way she'd want to, all right. You're pumping her full of your self-reliance junk and you've got her head all twisted around. Why can't you stay out of it, huh?"

"I'm not in it."

"You're letting her live with you, aren't you?"

Jodie exhaled. She was too edgy about her own plight to waste valuable mental energy on her brother-in-law. "All right, hang on," she muttered, feeling traitorous. "I'll go see if Lynne wants to talk to you."

Lynne didn't want to talk to Hank. When Jodie went upstairs and informed her sister of the call, Lynne wrinkled her nose and emitted a tiny sound of disgust. Then she realized the children were listening and yielded with an exasperated groan. "I'll take it downstairs," she told Jodie. "Would you finish reading *Fox in Socks* to the kids?"

Jodie picked up the book, sat on the edge of Sarah's bed and stammered her way through the pages of rhythmic tongue twisters. Some small part of her brain remained detached from Sarah's round, wide-eyed face, Peter's restless twisting and writhing in his sleeping bag on the floor and the doggerel she was reading to them about Slow Joe Crow and Tweetle Beetles. Even as she read she couldn't stop thinking about everything that had happened that day: Tom's unexpected invasion of her office, the letter, her chilling insight that he himself might have written it and her more profound insight that she was attracted to him. And her understanding that if she attempted any kind of relationship with him he would try to protect her.

She didn't want protection. She could take care of herself. She was Penny Simpson, the symbol of domestic peace and security. Only a sicko would try to hurt her.

The world, unfortunately, was teeming with sickos.

Ignoring the frisson of panic brought on by that thought, she plowed through the children's book, stumbling over the more diabolical tongue twisters. When she reached the last page and looked up, she found Sarah dozing on top of her blanket and Peter busy constructing a card house on the worn carpet beside his sleeping bag. "Bed time," she informed him brightly, rearranging Sarah on the bed and pulling the blanket up over her.

"Who'd you have supper with?" Peter asked as he knocked down his unfinished card structure.

"A friend."

"Yeah? Your boyfriend?"

"No," Jodie said, gathering up the playing cards and snapping a rubber band tightly around the deck. "When I've got a boyfriend, Peter, you'll be the first to know."

"My dad says when you get a boyfriend it'll be a cold day in hell," Peter related. "Was that him on the phone?"

"Yes."

"Can I talk to him?"

"He wants to talk to your mother, Peter. Let them work it out, okay?"

Peter scowled but crawled back inside the sleeping bag. Jodie plumped the pillow beneath his head, then kissed him good-night. He made a retching noise and screamed, "Yuck! Don't kiss me!"

"Sorry," Jodie apologized with a grin. She kissed Sarah, who was too deeply asleep to object, and shut off the light.

Stopping in her bedroom to kick off her espadrilles, she noticed that she'd never gotten around to making her bed that morning. It was a good thing she hadn't invited Tom inside....

Good God. Why was she mentally associating Tom with her bed? She barely knew the man, and she was never going to see him again. How could she even think of him in the context of her bedroom?

Irritated with herself—and with him for having been so damned attractive—she left the bedroom. At the top of the stairs she listened for Lynne's voice. All was silent downstairs—no shouting or weeping. Not knowing what she'd find, she headed down to the kitchen.

Lynne stood at the counter next to the refrigerator, unrolling the top of the doggie bag. Jodie smothered the protest that sprang to her lips at the sight of her sister raiding her beloved Chinese food stash. If anyone needed the pick-me-up of a little Szechuan cuisine, Lynne did.

"What did the bum want?" Jodie asked her.

Lynne glanced up. "You don't mind if I eat this, do you?"

"Go ahead," Jodie said magnanimously. "What did Hank want?"

Lynne pulled a fork from the drying rack beside the sink. "It's too awful to talk about," she said, then gobbled some chicken and proceeded to rehash her phone conversation. "He said I'm an ingrate and an idiot and I'm trying to emasculate him. And he also said it's all your fault. He had some really colorful words for both of us, Jodie."

"My fault, huh." Jodie flopped onto a chair and grunted a colorful word of her own. The truth was she welcomed Hank's vitriol. At the moment, it was the most familiar thing in her life.

"That was the pleasant part," Lynne warned her, setting down the fork and grimacing. "When he got tired of cursing you, he said that if I'm so hell-bent on getting a job it must mean I have no interest in being a mother, and if I press ahead with a divorce he's going to demand full custody of the kids."

"Custody! For crying out loud! The guy balks when you ask him to drive Peter to the dentist."

"He's much too selfish to be a good father. Even he knows that." Lynne's eyes filled with tears. "He just wants to make my life hell, that's all," she complained in a tremulous tone. She lifted a forkful of chicken, then thought better of it and pushed aside the food. "He said that if I don't go back home he's going to get himself a shrewd lawyer and make sure I never get a cent out of him, on top of which he's going to take Sarah and Peter away. Jodie..." She released a sob. "I don't know what to do. I can't bear the thought of using the kids as a weapon. It's not fair to them. But if Hank goes through with this—" She fought valiantly against the urge to cry. "I'd almost rather go back to him than let him use the children in a tug-of-war."

"Those aren't your only options," Jodie pointed out. "What you've got to do is get yourself a shrewd lawyer, too."

Lynne mulled over Jodie's suggestion. "You think I should risk a court battle? What if I lose? I might lose the children, and—"

"If you get a superior lawyer, you won't lose. You might even avoid the court battle altogether. Hank's only trying to blackmail you, Lynne. He doesn't really want custody of the kids, and he's not stupid enough to think any judge would rule in his favor. But with a top-notch lawyer you can avoid all that. You can get Hank to agree to a fair settlement. You haven't got a job yet—which means he ought to be required to give you alimony, to say nothing of child support. You need a lawyer to work all that out for you."

Lynne's eyes shimmered with gratitude through their glaze of tears. "You don't happen to know any good lawyers, do you?" she asked.

"Tom," Jodie said instantly. Then she rolled her eyes and laughed. "Scratch that idea. He's a tax lawyer."

"But he's good?"

"He seems like an ethical guy. But he doesn't do divorces. My syndication company hired a local firm to represent me against that ninny who's suing Penny Simpson," she noted. "Maybe they've got a divorce lawyer on the payroll."

"You told me those guys are a bunch of hacks. I don't want hacks, Jodie—not when the stakes are this high."

Jodie didn't want Lynne to settle for second-rate legal representation, either. Jodie loved her niece and nephew, and she couldn't bear the possibility of their being taken from her sister. Lynne needed the most reliable, most trustworthy attorney to counsel her through her divorce.

It wouldn't be Tom. It couldn't be. But... "Tom has a partner who handles divorces," she revealed. "I can't vouch for Tom's legal expertise, let alone his partner's. And you've got to remember, they're based in Manhattan. They're going to charge a fortune."

"If they're good it would be worth every penny," Lynne declared vehemently.

"But—"

"Please, Jodie, please ask Tom if his partner will see me. If the lawyer's sharp enough, maybe he'll be able to work out a settlement where Hank has to pay all legal costs. You know Hank can afford it, Jodie. When he accepted the transfer from Houston he got a huge raise."

"All right," Jodie said, trying to squelch her misgivings. "I'll call Tom tomorrow and see what I can find out about his partner."

"Thank you!" Lynne swept across the room, hauled Jodie out of her chair and gathered her in a crushing hug. "I love you, Jodie! I appreciate this so much!"

"Yeah? Then keep your cotton-picking hands off my ginger chicken," Jodie muttered, wriggling out of her sister's embrace and moving to the counter, where she folded down the flaps of the carton containing her left-over dinner and returned it to the refrigerator.

"Could you call him tonight?"

"Don't be silly," Jodie said quickly, unwilling to admit that the thought had crossed her mind, too—for reasons not entirely related to her sister's marital plight. "First of all, it's Tom's partner you'd be dealing with, not Tom. And second of all . . ." She drifted off for a moment, uncertain of how to finish. "I'd feel funny about bothering him at home."

"Why would he think you were bothering him? He's your friend," Lynne reminded her.

"I know," she said vaguely. Her mind filled with an image of him standing on her porch, his tall, rangy body just beyond her reach, the golden light from the window playing across his chiseled features, the breeze tousling his blond hair. Gazing at him, she'd experienced resentment and remorse, curiosity and yearning...and fear. Fear that her life was in danger, fear that he knew, fear that she was tempted to turn to him for assistance.

Whatever tangled emotions existed between her and Tom, she did trust him professionally. If anyone needed the aid of an overprotective ally, it was Lynne. "I'll call his office first thing in the morning," she promised.

"Thanks, Jodie." Lynne gave her another hug and then waltzed out of the kitchen. Jodie listened to her footsteps as she ascended the stairs. Then she sagged against the counter and closed her eyes, feeling every last ounce of energy drain from her.

She was glad to be able to help her sister, glad to do what she could. But now that Lynne's current crisis was temporarily under control, Jodie's thoughts reverted to her own crisis. Lynne would get her divorce, with a cushy settlement and full custody of her children—and Jodie would never get to see it happen because she'd be dead, slain by some demented reader from Philadelphia whose kids had complained because her home-made frozen fruit pops, prepared with a recipe from the "Penny-Wise" column, didn't taste as good as store-bought frozen pops—or for some equally petty reason.

Jodie could fend off the terror, but she couldn't keep it from returning. She could be tough and supportive when it came to her sister, but not when it came to herself.

She loathed feeling weak. She loathed admitting that she wanted someone to be tough and supportive for her. She loathed it so much she'd insulted a man whose only mistake had been to hint he wanted to be that someone.

Chapter Four

"Tom?" Lilian's voice crackled through the intercom box. "Mrs. Duryea is here. She's on her way to Jerome's office at this very moment."

Tom glanced up from the file he'd been pretending to read. Ever since he'd arrived at the office he'd been waiting to hear his secretary speak those words. He knew Jodie's sister had an appointment that morning with Jerome DeLucca. What he didn't know was whether Jodie had accompanied Lynne to Manhattan.

Jodie herself had scheduled the meeting. She'd telephoned Tom the morning after his trip to Orangeburg and asked if his firm's divorce specialist would consider taking her sister as a client. When Tom had mentioned the firm's fees Jodie had remained unfazed. All she'd said was, "Lynne needs the best representation she can find. Her husband is threatening to take away her kids. She needs the absolute best, Tom. Can your partner come through for her?"

Tom couldn't say for sure that Jerome was the absolute best, but he was damned good. He'd told Jodie so.

"Great. Who do I talk to to make an appointment?"

"I'll connect you to Jerome's secretary in a minute," Tom had said, then floundered. He'd wanted to fill that minute with a statement of some sort regarding how much he respected Jodie's strength and courage, how much he hoped she'd forgive him for his unintentionally oppressive concern when it came to her safety—and how much he'd like to take her out, romance her, kiss her.... But his own courage hadn't matched hers, and instead he'd said something along the lines of "You ought to come to the office with your sister. She's going to need some moral support, Jodie. Even with a topnotch lawyer handling her case, divorce is a messy, painful procedure."

"I'd love to come to the office with her," Jodie had said. "Unfortunately, there's this column I've got to write."

"You could take off an hour or so, couldn't you?" he'd asked, hoping he didn't sound pleading. "It's really not such a long trip." It was, in fact, a trip Tom himself wouldn't mind making often, if only Jodie gave him a sign that he would be welcome in her world.

"I don't know. I'll have to see what I can work out."

He'd wanted to say something more while he'd had her ear. He'd wanted to warn her to be careful. He'd wanted to promise he wouldn't overwhelm her with his warnings. He'd wanted to tell her that all through a surprisingly restless night he'd lain in bed thinking of her, picturing her luminous eyes and her long, lovely legs.

"I'll connect you with Jerome's secretary," he'd said.

Now her sister was here. His gaze traveled from the contents of the file spread before him to the thick oak door across the office from his desk, and from there back to the intercom box at his elbow. Drawing in a deep breath, he pushed a button on the box and asked Lilian, "Did Mrs. Duryea come alone?"

"No—another woman is with her. Bethany just led them into Jerome's office. Now she's coming out—"

"Who?"

"Bethany. She's going to the coffee machine and filling the china coffeepot—"

"Okay." One reason Tom adored his secretary was that she never failed to supply him with the information he needed. "How many cups is she putting on the tray?"

"Three."

"Okay. Thanks, Lilian." He released the button, sprang from his chair and strode out of his office. Lilian was stationed at her desk just outside his door—the lion at the gate, he frequently teased her, always with gratitude. Her word processor was humming and her desk was piled with documents to be attended to, but her attention was riveted to Jerome's secretary, who was still at the coffee machine arranging a wheeled service tray for her boss and his guests.

Without glancing at him, Lilian asked, "What's going on over there, Tom? What makes Mrs. Duryea so special?"

"The woman with her—she had short black hair?"

Lilian nodded. "Yeah, and her earrings looked like bunches of grapes."

Tom entertained a mixture of delight and apprehension. It made no sense that he should be keyed up about seeing Jodie. They'd spent a somewhat pleasant, somewhat bizarre couple of hours together a few days ago, that was all. She'd written him a kind, sensitive note, and he'd visited her, they'd had dinner and he'd left. And now she was at Black, DeLucca, being billed a small fortune for the privilege of having Jerome resolve her sister's marital plight. This was no cause for anxiety.

Bethany had finished filling the matching china sugar bowl and was wheeling the tray toward Jerome's office. Tom sprinted across the room, weaving deftly among the other secretaries' desks to halt Bethany before she reached her destination. "You'll need just two cups," he said.

Bethany blinked at him in bewilderment. She was young and pretty; if not for Tom's strict adherence to the principle that one should never become involved with the people one worked with, he might at one time have asked her out. The longer she'd worked at the firm, however, the more Tom had come to realize that she was much too literal, too unoriginal for his taste.

"There are three people in there," she said, gesturing toward Jerome's door.

"There are about to be two," Tom explained. "I'll take this." He lifted the third cup and saucer from the tray.

"But Mr. DeLucca told me to get coffee for three," she insisted.

"He was mistaken." Tom placed the cup on the counter by the coffee machine, then escorted Bethany back to her desk. "I'll bring this in," he said, pushing the tray to Jerome's door.

"But—but you're a lawyer," Bethany argued.

Tom only smiled and opened Jerome's door. "Hi, Jerome," he greeted the massive older man, who had wedged his bulk into an upholstered armchair that stood at right angles to the matching sofa on which Lynne and Jodie sat. Tom's smile faded as his pale eyes met Jodie's glittering dark ones. She returned his steady stare, her expression revealing not the slightest nervousness. Her features were as clean and angular as he'd remembered, her chin as stubbornly set, her hair as lustrous and alluringly tousled, her lips as temptingly soft. She was dressed conservatively in an ivory-colored blouse and pleated grey slacks that, to Tom's regret, hid her legs even though they emphasized their glorious length. Dangling from her earlobes were bubbly purple beads that did indeed resemble bunches of grapes.

Tom held her gaze for as long as he dared—which wasn't long. Then he turned sheepishly to Jerome. "I hijacked this tray from Bethany," he said. "I wanted an excuse to come in and say hello to Mrs. Duryea and her sister."

Jerome let out a booming laugh. "Well, of course, Tom. After all, we lawyers don't have anything better to do than charge a fortune to serve coffee."

"It's *very* good coffee," Tom joked, shooting a grin at the women.

"It had better be," Jodie muttered. "You didn't even bring the right number of cups."

"I was hoping you'd join me for coffee in my office," Tom said in a deceptively casual tone. "That would give Jerome and your sister a chance to discuss her case."

Jodie gave him a probing look. "I thought I ought to be here to help Lynne through that particular discussion."

"Oh, no," Lynne interjected, waving off her sister's concern. "Mr. DeLucca and I will be just fine. Why don't you run along and visit with Tom? You told me you were looking forward to seeing him."

Jodie's frown conveyed supreme irritation mixed with a touch of embarrassment. She shoved herself to her feet and stalked to the door, leaving Tom with the impression that her reason for leaving Jerome's office had less to do with wanting to be with Tom than with not wanting to be with her blabbermouth sister. Still, her obvious annoyance notwithstanding, Tom was thrilled that she wanted to see him.

He hastened across the room to open the door for her. "We'll be in my office," he informed Jerome and Lynne before ushering Jodie out. He refrained from taking her arm as they meandered past the scattered secretarial stations. But he stayed close enough to her to catch a whiff of her perfume, to appreciate the dynamic line of her jaw, to get an intimate look at her left earring. Definitely grapes.

After tossing a quick smile at his unabashedly curious secretary, he held open the door to his own office. Jodie stepped inside and skimmed the room with her gaze. It was smaller than Jerome's office, in part because Jerome was a senior partner in the firm and in part because he truly needed the sofa and the coffee table, with its discreet yet convenient box of tissues, to make his clients feel comfortable enough to talk freely about their disastrous marriages. Compact though it was, Tom kept his own office impeccably neat. The floor-to-ceiling bookcases held leather-bound tomes; his desk was appointed with an onyx-and-brass pen stand; a couple of tasteful still lifes decorated the walls.

"Have a seat," Tom invited her as he circled the desk to his chair. He gathered up the loose pages on his desk and inserted them into the file, which he set aside. Then he gazed across the desk at Jodie, who lowered herself into one of the two leather chairs reserved for clients.

She returned his stare for a moment, then said, "I was about to have some coffee."

"Of course." He pushed the button on his intercom. "Lilian? Could you bring us a couple of cups of coffee, please?"

He heard something that sounded like a cross between a snicker and a snort, but Lilian dutifully said, "Right away, Mr. Barrett."

He turned back to Jodie. She was eyeing the file folder inquisitively. "You were in the middle of something."

"It can wait." He leaned back in his chair, his edginess beginning to wane. "How've you been?" he asked.

"Just fine. And you?"

He hadn't intended his question to be a clichéd conversational gambit. He'd wanted to find out whether Jodie had received any further communications from her homicidal correspondent in Philadelphia and if so, what she was doing about them. Perhaps she knew that was what he was getting at and she'd deliberately steered him away from the subject.

"Fine," he remembered to answer. "No relapses of the flu. But now I know that the next time I get sick, I can toss some ice cubes into a steaming pot of homemade chicken soup and all the fat will congeal around them."

"Not all of it, but a lot," she confirmed, smiling. "That trick was in a very old column, Tom."

"The woman who lives across the hall from me shared that little Penny Simpson tidbit. Through my own efforts, I've learned how to make automobile bingo cards for your kids when you're going to take a long car trip and how to make stale rolls edible by placing them inside a wet paper bag and sticking them in the oven for a few minutes.''

"You've been reading 'Penny-Wise,''' Jodie deduced.

"At some sacrifice," he noted with a grin. "I've had to buy a second newspaper. The *New York Times* doesn't run your column."

"They don't accept anything from the syndication companies," Jodie complained. "They consider it below them." She fell silent as Lilian knocked on the door and then entered carrying a tray with two ceramic mugs of coffee, a pitcher of cream and sugar. She set the tray down on Tom's desk, then left. "How come Lynne and her lawyer get china and we get this gas-station-giveaway stuff?" Jodie asked as she lifted one of the mugs.

"You aren't a client," Tom teased.

"Oh? Who do you think is paying Mr. DeLucca's bill today?"

Tom frowned. "You are."

"Unless your partner wins a huge divorce settlement from Hank, I'll have to pay his retainer. Lynne hasn't got any money." She sipped her coffee.

It took Tom several seconds to digest this news. Jodie was so vibrantly young, so disorganized, so—so feminine. She had enough to do just taking responsibility for herself. He simply couldn't imagine her having to support her relatives, too. He helped his mother out financially, but then, he was a lawyer, earning an enormous income—and he was a man.

A man of his generation, he reminded himself. He mustn't assume that, just because women like his old girlfriend from high school wanted to be doted on, so did all women. Many women supported their families nowadays. If only Jodie wasn't quite so slender in build, if only her eyes weren't quite so poignantly radiant, if only Tom didn't sense such an exquisite vulnerability lurking behind her fearless facade. If only her pen name were Margaret Thatcher or Betty Friedan or Jackie Joyner Kersee—anything but Penny Simpson.

"You shouldn't have to pay for this," he said quietly.

"Is Mr. DeLucca willing to represent Lynne for free?" she countered, arching her eyebrows and smiling impishly.

Tom had no trouble detecting the challenge in her voice. "I'm sure Jerome will find a way to work his fee into the settlement," he mumbled, silently chastising himself for his reactionary response to her generosity toward her sister. Just because he liked Jodie and was attracted to her—just because he found himself wanting to take care of her—didn't mean she couldn't take care of anyone else.

"Have you received any more death threats?" he blurted out. He needed to know. He needed to make certain that if she was going to expend her resources protecting her sister she at least had the common sense to protect herself.

Her smile became ironic. "Not a word, Tom. Call off the dogs."

He refused to let her make him defensive. In truth, he was relieved to learn she was no longer in danger. "That's wonderful!"

"I told you you were overreacting the day I got the letter," she chided him. "It was just some crackpot. I've gotten lots of other crackpot letters since then—"

"Oh, no! From whom? What did they say?"

She laughed. "I got a letter from a lady in Albuquerque expounding on the virtues of iguanas as pets, and I got a letter from a reader in Boise who suggested that if everybody planted their front yards with corn instead of grass, we could defeat world hunger. And I got a letter from a housewife in New Hampshire who said I ought to devote an entire column to the link between rock music and cancer.''

"What link?'' Tom asked, nonplussed.

"How the hell should I know what link? I get this sort of junk from readers all the time. If I took it seriously I'd wind up spending most of my time worrying about the fate of the human race. It's scary to think that people like that are allowed to vote.''

Actually, Tom considered that fact pretty scary, too. But right now Jodie was the sole object of his worry. Even if she was apparently out of danger, her bravado continued to worry him, and her stubbornness and the fervent glow in her large, haunting eyes. "I wish you weren't so blasé about this,'' he said, hoping he wasn't coming across as didactic. "Your sister doesn't have any trouble accepting help from you, Jodie. I don't know why you have so much trouble accepting help from me.''

"My sister *does* have trouble accepting help from me,'' Jodie flared. "The problem is, she has no alternative. She depends on others because she can't take care herself. I can. Not that there's anything here to take care of,'' she added quickly.

"It isn't a sign of weakness to accept help.''

She pursed her lips. "If I wanted help, Tom, I would accept it. I don't want it, so I won't accept it. Please stop trying to be my knight in shining armor. I'm perfectly safe.''

"Nobody in this world is perfectly safe.''

"What a cheering thought." She glanced at her watch and stood. "Lynne must be done by now."

"When she's done my secretary will signal us," Tom said, scrambling to his feet as well. He didn't want Jodie to leave, not until he established a truce with her. He'd done nothing to apologize for, but he couldn't bear the thought of her walking out of his office angry.

Instinctively, he positioned himself near the door to block her escape. "I'd like to have dinner with you," he declared. It wasn't in him to be suave and clever, so he opted for bluntness.

She checked her watch again. "It's ten-thirty in the morning."

"I didn't mean now," he said, daring to take a step toward her, carefully positioning himself between her and the door. "I meant a date."

"Like our last date?" She smiled sadly. "You must be a glutton for punishment."

"I'm a glutton for brainy women with long legs," he admitted.

She seemed taken aback by his flattery. Her gaze flew around the room, buying her time to collect her wits. Then she shook her head. "I was awful last time, Tom. I blew it royally. I lost my temper, I was rude—"

"And I'm willing to give you another chance," he said, with exaggerated benevolence.

She laughed in spite of herself. "Oh, Tom... It's just that I—I think we're a really lousy match."

"I think—" continued his approach "—we've got possibilities."

"All you want is someone to fuss over."

"No, Jodie." He was inches from her. "I want much more than that." He inhaled her perfume again, faint yet exotic. Her skin looked so smooth, her lips so tantalizingly soft, so close to his. He couldn't tell her what he wanted; he couldn't even tell himself—other than that he wanted a woman as imbued with confidence and energy and spirit as Jodie was, as strikingly attractive, as smart and funny—and challenging. He wanted that challenge. He welcomed it.

He leaned toward her, to touch his mouth to hers, but before he could she ducked her head. "Don't," she whispered.

He inhaled sharply and backed off. She kept her face averted, furling and unfurling her fingers at her sides.

"I like you, Tom," she confessed, her voice low and enticingly husky. "I mean—I could like you a lot. But I just—don't think it would work out, okay? I think it would turn into a big fiasco."

"Maybe it wouldn't," he suggested. "Why not take a chance?"

"Me? Take a chance?" She pretended to be shocked. "Someone as cautious and self-protective as me?"

Tom was usually slow to anger, and the abrupt flare of rage that shot through him took him by surprise. "Yes, you," he retorted, suffering from both physical and mental frustration. "You're willing to take chances when some murderous thug threatens you, but when it comes to going out with me, you're suddenly ready to measure the risks and back off. You've got your priorities all screwed up, Jodie."

"Well, well," she snapped. "Thanks for that little thumbnail psychoanalysis. Why don't you criticize my driving while you're at it?"

"You're a terrible driver," he said, still fuming.

"Great. Maybe when you get tired of milking divorcées and their sisters for thousands of dollars, you can get a job as a traffic cop. You can spend your life issuing tickets and giving speeches to drivers about how you're citing them for their own good.'' Moving in long, smooth strides, she stormed out of his office and slammed the door shut behind her.

Tom let out a sigh. Why did she have to be so damned obstinate? Why did she have to equate caring with control and domination? Why couldn't she be just a little more open and flexible and concede that when a man cared for a woman, it brought him joy to be able to take care of her?

Penny Simpson had always understood that. She'd always let Tom know how much she appreciated his support, his willingness to watch over her. "When we get married I'll make you so happy," she used to promise, nestling in his arms and closing her eyes. "I know I can lean on you, Tom, and that means everything to me."

Why couldn't Jodie be like that, just a little bit?

And why, since she obviously couldn't be like that, was Tom unable to put her out of his mind?

"I'm feeling a lot better," Lynne announced as Jodie drove sluggishly through the heavy midtown traffic, swerving around stalled cars and double-parked delivery trucks. A taxi lurched alongside her car and the driver gave her a glowering look as he and she both braked at a red light. Instinctively, she rolled up her window.

She wished she could tell Lynne that she was feeling better, too, but she wasn't. The cabbie wasn't a felon, yet his menacing scowl was enough to throw her nerves into such an uproar she'd felt it necessary, in spite of the summery weather, to raise a glass barrier between him and herself. She'd lately developed the ludicrous habit of circling her car before she opened the door, inspecting the dashboard for evidence of tampering. She had no idea exactly what she was looking for. Dangling wires? Wads of plastique? A bundle of dynamite with a ticking alarm clock attached to it? The fact that she didn't know what a car bomb looked like only proved that these inspections were a waste of time. But she couldn't bring herself to stop doing them.

She double-checked all her locks before going to bed every night. At the office, she eyed her mail with dread, refusing to relax until Helen had read the final letter in the daily stack. Not one of them contained the merest hint of a threat, and Jodie consoled herself with the understanding that she was completely on top of the situation.

So why was it that Tom could rile her so easily? Why did she lose her temper with him whenever he raised the subject of that single, insignificant letter? Part of her reaction, she acknowledged as she accelerated onto the West Side Highway, was that she was so strongly attracted to him. In the days since she'd last seen him she had almost succeeded in forgetting how handsome he was. But the moment he'd invaded his partner's office that morning, she'd been forced to confront the fact that he was the best-looking man she'd had the privilege of laying eyes on since the night she'd dragged Helen to a Mel Gibson double feature at a local movie theater a few months ago.

But Tom's appearance alone hadn't been what she'd reacted to that morning. What really troubled her, she admitted dolefully, was that the moment she'd seen him she'd felt *safe*. She wasn't in any danger—of course she wasn't—and yet . . . In Tom's presence, she'd felt as if no one could harm her. She'd felt secure. She'd felt she could drop her guard and rely on him to protect her.

And that was the one thing she didn't want. Maybe he thought she took her notions of independence to an extreme, but she'd learned by observing the women around her that the minute you relinquished your autonomy and let a man take over, you were lost.

"...Another thing I liked about him," Lynne was saying.

"Huh?" Jodie dragged herself out of her troubling ruminations. "Who?"

"Jerome DeLucca," Lynne answered. "He's so big. I mean, Hank isn't exactly a shrimp, but can you see him going nose to nose with someone like DeLucca? The man is built like an NFL pro-bowler."

"A superannuated one," Jodie pointed out. "He must be at least ten or twelve years older than Hank."

"I'm not saying we ought to let them slug it out in the ring, Jodie. This is supposed to be a civilized legal proceeding. All I'm saying is, picture Hank sitting in the witness box, with the Incredible Hulk bearing down on him, intimidating him and bombarding him with questions. Hank would wilt in no time flat. He's real tough when he's dealing with people who are smaller and weaker than he is, but put him in a courtroom with Jerome DeLucca, and the poor guy'll agree to anything."

"I hope you're right," Jodie muttered. "DeLucca's charging a hell of a lot to make Hank wilt."

"I know I've thanked you for that," Lynne hastened to say, "but I'll thank you again, Jodie. I couldn't have afforded this myself. I'm really indebted to you—"

"Don't be indebted to me," Jodie grumbled, wishing her spirits would improve. Just because she was vexed by Tom didn't mean she should be short-tempered with Lynne. "Once you're divorced and raking in the alimony, you can pay me back."

"Once I'm divorced...." Lynne repeated the words, weighing each one. "I can't believe this is actually happening, Jodie. It's like a whole new beginning for me. I'll be making all the decisions, raising the kids my own way, answering to no one but myself. I'm going to be as strong as you are, Jodie. And I'm not going to be scared."

Be stronger than me, Jodie thought, as she headed west across the George Washington Bridge. *Even if you get a weird letter from an anonymous fiend that frightens you to your soul, be stronger than me.*

TWENTY MINUTES LATER, they arrived at Jodie's house. "Have you got enough money to pay for the baby-sitter?" Jodie asked Lynne before letting her out of the car.

Lynne pulled out her coin purse and looked inside. "I've got a couple of dollars. I don't think that'll cover it."

Sighing, Jodie pulled her purse from the floor beneath the dashboard and fished around inside it. Although smaller than her tote bag, her purse was just as crowded and she had to push aside a half-consumed roll of breath mints, two pairs of sunglasses and a paper-clip chain to reach her wallet. Lynne might be neater, but at least Jodie had money.

She handed her sister a five-dollar bill, then revved the engine. "I've got to get to work," she said. "I may be late tonight. I've got to write a column and fax it in."

"Should I make dinner?" Lynne asked.

"Sure. If I'm not home by six, though, just make something for you and the kids. I'll probably stop at House of Cheng on my way home."

After thanking her again, Lynne got out of the car and waved Jodie off. Tearing down the snaking mountain road toward town, Jodie tried unsuccessfully to shake off her bad mood. If only Tom weren't so downright attractive—if only he weren't so godawful *nice*.... If only she didn't experience the uncharacteristic desire to dump all her problems on him and let him make everything better with a kiss....

If only she hadn't wanted his kiss so much.

This line of thought was not doing her much good. She turned on her radio to a country-western station, sang "I Go To Pieces" along with Patsy Cline and decided that she felt worse.

Maybe she ought to stop now and pick up lunch. She and Helen could split an order of mushu pork—except that Helen always insisted on making her midday meal something healthy, like plain yogurt and fruit. She was so insufferably sensible.

Anyway, Jodie didn't have time to stop. She'd get to the office, send out for a sandwich and work through lunch. She had to get her column written by the end of the day or she'd miss her deadline. Merely thinking about it inspired her to press harder on the gas pedal.

She careered off the main road and onto the drive that cut through the industrial park, not bothering to slow down for the speed bump, which bounced her a good two inches off her seat. She had the road to herself; most people had arrived for work hours ago. She veered around a bend, then skidded to a stop when she saw a police car and a police van parked in front of the building that housed Penny-Wise, Incorporated's offices.

"Nothing to be afraid of," she said aloud, though her voice shook. Gnawing on her lower lip, she cruised slowly into the parking lot. She spotted Helen's car parked in its usual space and the familiar cars of the people who worked for the consumer-products testing company that shared the building with Penny-Wise. That was it, she bolstered herself. The police had come to visit the consumer-products people. Whatever their business might be, it had nothing to do with her column.

Jodie wished she could believe that. "Please," she prayed under her breath, "don't let it be Helen. Don't let me find out that something bad happened to her." Drawing in a short, tremulous breath, she swung out of her car. The sharp stench that filled her nostrils brought burning tears to her eyes.

"Yuck!" she grunted, covering her nose and mouth with her hands. The stink was so strong she could almost taste it. Holding her breath, she dashed to the building and inside.

Helen and two uniformed police officers were standing in the hallway talking, but they fell silent at Jodie's arrival. Then Helen announced, "Here she is."

"Ugh! What's going on?" Jodie groaned, trying not to gag. "What's that horrible smell?"

"Skunk," Helen told her.

"I've smelled skunk before," Jodie argued. "It never smelled that bad."

One of the two police officers explained, "You've probably smelled it from a distance or after the passage of a day. This was a freshly killed skunk."

A freshly killed skunk. Jodie felt her coffee returning on her, but she swallowed it back down. "What skunk?" she asked faintly.

Helen gave her a long, meaningful stare. "I had the windows open in my office, Jodie, and less than a half hour ago the smell started wafting in. I went outside and found a dead skunk just outside the doorway."

"A dead skunk." A prank, Jodie thought frantically. A practical joke. A fraternity hazing ritual. A commentary on the work of the consumer-products testers.

"We've already talked to John, Shirley and the other people upstairs," Helen reported, reading Jodie's mind. "But you know they usually use the side door by the stairway. In light of the letter you received last week, I think it's safe to assume that this dead skunk was intended for you."

"What letter?" Jodie asked, faking ignorance.

"The letter you received containing a death threat," one of the police officers answered. "Your assistant has already filled us in on it, Ms. Posniak, but we were unable to find it in your office. You haven't thrown it out, have you?"

"No." Thanks to Tom Barrett, Jodie hadn't discarded it. "I think I left it on my desk somewhere," she said, beckoning Helen and the policemen to follow her down the hall. En route to her office she asked, "Does it really take two police vehicles to take care of one dead skunk?"

"The van belongs to the animal warden," one of the policemen explained. "He's going to perform an autopsy on the skunk."

"An autopsy?" As panic-stricken as she was, she couldn't help finding something perversely comical about the idea. "Why on earth would anyone want to do that?"

"Ms. Posniak," the other policeman said, his tone patronizing, "if this skunk was left by the same person who issued a threat on your life, it would be useful to find out precisely how the skunk was killed."

"You mean, if it was poisoned we can conclude that I'm slated for poisoning, too?"

"Well, actually—"

She laughed at the sheer lunacy of the concept. "Whereas, if the skunk was shot," she continued, "I can safely expect the nut to take target practice on me. Or let's say the autopsy reveals a malignancy in the skunk. Maybe my friend in Philadelphia is planning to expose me to carcinogens."

"Philadelphia?" Helen and the police officers asked in unison.

"That was the postmark on the envelope. I saved it, too," Jodie declared with unjustifiable pride.

"You did?" Helen's eyes widened. "I can't believe you'd do something that prudent, Jodie."

Jodie refused to rise to her taunting. She led the others into her office and rummaged through the mess on top of her desk, trying not to scatter her notes for that day's column. Unable to find the letter there, she yanked open one desk drawer and then another, pawing through their contents and attempting to remember where she'd hidden the damned thing. At last she found it behind a stack of graph-paper pads in the bottom left-hand drawer. "Here," she said, attempting to smooth out the wrinkles before she presented it to the police officers. "Given that Helen's already told you about this, I assume she's also told you that in my line of work I hear from screwballs all the time."

While one officer unfolded the letter and perused it, the other answered, "Yes. She's also told us that this is the first time you've heard from someone who specifically threatened your life."

"Whoever wrote that didn't specifically threaten my life," Jodie pointed out. "All she said was that my days are numbered. For all I know, they could number in the millions."

"You see?" Helen complained to the officers. "She never takes anything seriously."

"I do take things seriously," Jodie argued. "I take that putrid stench outside seriously. As a matter of fact, I think we can write an excellent column on how to combat skunk spray. I've heard that tomato juice works—"

"Jodie," Helen reproached, her expression stern. "Please be serious. People don't leave a dead skunk on someone's doorstep as a friendly gesture."

"On the other hand," Jodie argued, "you won't get much pleasure out of life if you live in fear all the time. I can't rearrange my life according to some psychopath who wants to give me a cheap scare."

"We'd like to hold on to this letter, Ms. Posniak," one of the policemen said. "If you get any more letters of this nature, telephone the precinct and ask to speak to me—I'm Sergeant Ludwig—or Officer Rodriguez here. And, of course, if anything else of a sinister nature occurs—anything like this dead-skunk business—you let us know." The officer handed Jodie a card with his name and the precinct house telephone number on it. Then he eyed Helen. "You make sure she does," he said.

Helen nodded and tossed Jodie a sanctimonious look. Jodie would bet good money that as a child Helen

was always the kid the teacher asked to watch her classmates and report on troublemakers when the teacher
had to leave the room.

"Be careful," the policeman named Rodriguez said
as he walked to the door. "We'll give you a call when we
get a report from the animal warden."

The bizarre image of a veterinarian wearing a white
surgical coat, latex gloves and a clothes pin on his nose
as he performed surgery on a dead skunk provoked a
weak grin from Jodie. She thanked the officers and
waved goodbye as they headed down the hall. Then she
shut her door and sagged against it. Alone inside her
office, she surrendered to a choked sob.

"You're okay," she whispered to herself, even as her
knees trembled and her heartbeat thundered inside her
skull. "You're okay. This is just a tasteless joke. If
someone really wanted to hurt you, they would have
done it by now."

She staggered back to her desk and collapsed onto her
chair just before her rubbery legs gave way beneath her.
Then she buried her head in her hands. It wasn't only
the ghastly thought of the dead skunk that upset her; it
was the realization that, if the letter and the skunk were
connected, whoever had it in for her was no longer in
Philadelphia. UPS didn't deliver dead skunks. Jodie's
enemy had to be somewhere close by.

She couldn't figure it out. What had she ever done to
hurt anyone? Was it her fault that some idiot hadn't
been able to pull off the soufflé? Should she be held
liable if certain cockroaches proved to be immune to her
boric-acid roach killer or if her suggestions for baby-
shower gifts fell flat? Or if some snotty kid could tell the
difference between store-bought granola and the inexpensive homemade stuff?

And even if she could be blamed for such mishaps, was that any reason to intimidate her with death threats and dead skunks?

She could tell herself she wasn't frightened. She could swear on a mile-high stack of Bibles that she wasn't—but that wouldn't alter the truth. She was terrified, and she hated it.

If only someone could make everything better. If only someone could see her through this crisis, someone strong and stalwart and trustworthy. Someone who wouldn't make her feel any weaker and more helpless than she already felt.

With a quiet moan, she lifted the telephone receiver and dialed Tom's number.

Chapter Five

By the time Tom arrived at Jodie's house he was drained. He'd left Manhattan at a quarter to five; so, unfortunately, had hundreds of thousands of commuters who lived in the bedroom communities northwest of the city. Not once did the clogged traffic exceed ten miles per hour across the George Washington Bridge and up the Palisades Parkway. The only difference between Tom and every other driver on the road was that the others probably had a pretty good idea of what would be waiting for them when they reached their destination.

Tom didn't. No matter how hearty Jodie had managed to sound when she'd called him, the very fact that she *had* called him implied that she was scared witless.

"Would you like me to come to Orangeburg?" he'd asked once she had informed him about the skunk.

"Right now?" Her tone had been heavy with disbelief.

He'd sighed. Even if she'd begged him to drop everything and race to her side at once, he couldn't have. He had finished reviewing the Huddleston file over lunch, but he was scheduled to take a deposition from John Huddleston himself in twenty minutes, which would probably last late into the afternoon. "After work, Jodie. I'll leave the city as early as I can, okay?"

"You don't have to come," she'd said with false confidence.

"Maybe I don't have to, but I want to. I'll drive up after work."

"All right." She hadn't fought him, hadn't sworn that she could handle this situation by herself, hadn't berated him for making a fuss over nothing. Her swift capitulation proved to Tom how frightened she was.

He was frightened, too. He'd phoned her from his apartment, where he'd stopped briefly after work to change his clothes, check his mailbox and get his car, to find out if any other horrors had befallen her during the afternoon. She had assured him everything was fine, but when he'd said he was coming to Orangeburg anyway, she hadn't objected.

Maybe she just wanted to see him, he thought. Maybe when he arrived at her house she'd waltz outside to greet him with a hug and one of her fruit smoothies.

Or maybe she'd be hysterical.

Jodie's aging Plymouth wasn't in sight when Tom steered up the driveway alongside her quaintly ramshackle house. He pulled to a halt and climbed out. The front yard was littered with toys—a junior-size baseball bat and ball, a pink doll carriage and a Hula-hoop. Through the house's open windows he heard someone shouting, "If you two don't calm down this instant I'm turning off the TV!"

Hoping for the best but bracing himself for the worst, he strode up the walk and onto the porch. He rang the bell and heard its chime, along with a babble of television cartoon sounds, through the screen door.

After a minute Jodie's sister arrived. She'd changed from the conservative dress she'd had on that morning into jeans and a T-shirt. Viewing Tom through the screen, she broke into a smile. "Tom! Hi! What brings you up this way? I hope it isn't business."

Tom hesitated. Lynne's greeting implied that she knew nothing about the skunk. He experienced a rush of joy at the understanding that in her moment of panic Jodie had turned to him for comfort, instead of to her own sister. Then he admonished himself not to take so much delight in the fact that Jodie was in enough trouble to have turned to him for comfort at all.

In any case, he wouldn't tell Lynne what Jodie apparently didn't want her to know. He smiled vaguely and said, "I came to see Jodie."

"She's not home yet," Lynne said. "I don't know when she'll get here. She said since she didn't get to her office this morning, she might have to wind up staying late to finish her column."

Tom didn't like the idea of her remaining after hours all by herself in that sprawling industrial park. "Let's telephone her office," he suggested, keeping his tone level so he wouldn't alarm Lynne. He found it odd that, although Lynne appeared to be the elder sister, Jodie was the protective one, housing her sister, covering her legal expenses and refusing to burden her with her own crisis.

Lynne gave him a sly smile, and he realized that she had misinterpreted his impatience about Jodie's absence. Or maybe she hadn't misinterpreted it. Maybe he was eager for her to get home because he wanted to kiss her even more than he wanted to protect her.

"Come on in," Lynne said, holding open the screen door. "I'll give her a buzz."

Tom entered the house and followed Lynne down the hall to the kitchen. He had no sooner entered the room when Jodie's pigtailed little niece darted in through another door and barrelled into him. What she lacked in size she made up for in speed; the impact sent him staggering.

"Sarah!" Lynne shrieked. "Watch where you're going!"

Sarah glared tearfully up at her mother from the tile floor, where she'd landed on her rear end. "Well, I woulda," she mumbled, rubbing her elbow, "but I didn't know we had company." She turned her dark, brimming eyes up at Tom and eyed him accusingly.

"Excuse me," he said, even though she'd been the one at fault. He squatted down next to her and checked her elbow. "Anything broken?"

"Uh-uh," she said with a dramatic sniff.

"You aren't going to need a new elbow?"

"Whaddya mean, a new elbow? How could anyone get a new elbow?"

"Well, I don't know. We could make one out of pipe cleaners or something."

"Pipe cleaners?" She started to giggle, and Tom immediately fell in love with her. He had never been the sort to gush over children, but this little girl, with her soulful eyes and dark hair and pugnaciously set chin, reminded him very much of her Aunt Jodie.

After helping Sarah to her feet, he turned to discover that Lynne was holding the telephone receiver to her ear and listening. A few seconds elapsed and she hung up. "Jodie must have left the office," she reported. "No one's answering."

"Then she's on her way home," Tom said, refusing to consider any grimmer explanations for her failure to answer. "I'll go outside and wait for her."

"You're welcome to wait inside if you want," Lynne offered. "I'll call off the charging elephants."

Evidently, Sarah understood that she'd been insulted. She scowled at her mother and grabbed Tom's hand. "Let's go outside," she declared, dragging him toward the doorway. "Do you know how to fix doll carriages? Mine's broken and my daddy never fixes anything."

Tom suffered a pang of sorrow for the little girl. Although her mother appeared reasonably cheerful in the wake of her meeting with Jerome DeLucca, Tom knew that divorce was a traumatic step—and that the children of the divorcing couple were often the most severely traumatized by it.

"See?" Sarah said, dragging him down the porch steps to the lawn, where her doll carriage stood. She turned the carriage on its side and pointed to one of the wheels. "It's stuck. It won't turn."

Tom fiddled with the wheel. "It looks like there's some rust here," he explained, pointing out the corrosion on the axle. "We'll have to clean that off and then lubricate the wheels. You shouldn't leave this outside, Sarah. When you're done playing with it, you ought to put it someplace dry."

"Where?" Sarah complained. "At our house we had two garages, but Aunt Jodie only has one. She says we can keep our stuff in the cellar, but it's scary down there. It's all dark and messy and Peter says there's spiders."

Tom could easily believe that Jodie's cellar was messy. "Well, you'll have to work something out," he said. A typical tax lawyer's solution, he acknowledged silently. Tax lawyers rarely found themselves zealously arguing cases in court. They spent the bulk of their professional lives in conference rooms, working things out.

"Hey, Sarah!" A boy's voice boomed through one of the screened windows. "*Smurfs* is on."

"Oh!" Sarah let the carriage drop. "Gotta go," she said before racing into the house.

Tom chuckled and set the carriage upright on the porch. He considered cleaning up the rest of the yard, but refrained. This wasn't his home. He'd let the Happy Housekeeper pick up the clutter.

If she ever made it home, he thought, his grin fading. He lowered himself onto the porch step and tried, without much success, to gaze anywhere but at the road. Closing his eyes, he pictured Jodie's sister standing in the kitchen, holding the telephone receiver to her ear and waiting in vain for her sister to answer. What if Jodie had been hurt? What if whoever had left the skunk had come back for Jodie? The creep obviously knew where she worked. She wasn't safe there—

His ruminations were halted by the percussive sound of automobile tires spitting loose pebbles on the driveway. He opened his eyes and his vision filled with the welcome sight of Jodie's Plymouth approaching the house. Grinning with relief, Tom stood and bounded down the walk to greet her.

Her car coasted to a stop alongside his and Jodie turned off the engine. Tom opened the door for her and she climbed out. "Here I am, safe and sound," she declared brightly.

Tom gathered her into his arms, overcome by the sheer jubilation of seeing Jodie alive and well. He gave her a fierce hug, enthralled by her presence, her health, her grace and resilience and, almost paradoxically, the tantalizingly delicate fragrance of her perfume. Without stopping to anticipate her reaction, he buried his lips in the feathery black tufts of hair crowning her head, then cupped his hands around her face and tilted it back.

Her mouth met his without resistance. For an instant his heart stopped beating, and then it started again, strong and potent, filling his body with a glorious warmth.

Hesitantly, Jodie lifted her hands to his waist. Smiling inwardly, he moved his lips over hers, nibbling and teasing, kissing her not because he was glad she had survived the day but because she was beautiful and sexy and vibrant. With each brush of her soft lower lip against his, with each subtle movement of her fingers against his sides, he grew more deeply convinced that she desired him as much as he desired her.

Drawing in an uneven breath, she pulled back and stared at him. Her eyes sparkled and her mouth shaped an adorably bashful smile. "Well," she said huskily. "Hello."

The skin of her cheeks felt velvety against his palms. It seemed incomprehensible to him that someone so indomitable could have such soft, soft skin. "I guess," she said, her smile widening, "there's more than one way to put danger out of your mind."

"Oh?" He mirrored her grin. "What's the other way?"

"Working. You want to hear a neat trick? If you're sewing patches onto clothes, you can fasten the patch to the article of clothing with a couple of strips of masking tape to hold it in place while you sew it on. It's much faster and easier than basting the patch. The tape keeps it in position, and you can even use the tape edge to help you stitch a straight line. I devoted my column to sewing tips today."

"Sewing tips, huh." Tom reluctantly let his hands drop. He was glad that she'd had a productive day, but he was equally troubled by her chipper mood. "You must have spent a long time writing the column," he remarked. "I thought you'd be here by the time I arrived. I was worried."

"You're always worried," she teased. "That should be your epitaph: Here Lies Tom Barrett. He Was Worried."

"I'd rather not talk about epitaphs," he said sternly. "Not after today."

"The skunk?" Jodie sounded inexplicably pleased. "I heard some good news from the police—the skunk was hit by a car."

"That's good news?"

"As opposed to the skunk's having been murdered? Sure. The crackpot—assuming it's the same crackpot who wrote the letter—probably saw a dead skunk lying by the road and decided to dump it in the industrial park."

"It wasn't just dumped in the industrial park, Jodie. It was dumped on your doorstep."

"I know that," she said impatiently. "The point is, we're not talking about anything premeditated here. The crackpot saw the skunk and, on the spur of the moment, decided to try to scare me with it."

"Wonderful," Tom grunted. "Let's hope this crackpot doesn't get any of these spur-of-the-moment inspirations when he happens to be packing a gun."

Jodie exhaled and rolled her eyes. "It's a she, not a he," she argued. "Men don't read my column—you should know that better than anyone. And as far as the skunk . . . well, I thought you'd be reassured."

"What reassures me is seeing you here, all in one piece," he said. He almost added that what reassured him more than anything else was the fact that she'd let him kiss her—and that she'd returned his kiss so enthusiastically. She seemed to have resolved not to exclude him from her life, and that was more than reassuring. It was exhilarating.

But he couldn't say that. So, instead, he said, "I'm glad you don't smell skunky."

"The parking lot outside my office stinks to high heaven," she informed him, wrinkling her nose. Abruptly she glanced at the house. "Have you been here long?"

"Maybe fifteen minutes. Why?"

"You didn't tell Lynne anything about this, did you?"

"No. I gather you didn't, either."

"I don't want to upset her," Jodie explained. "I mean, with the divorce and all, she's got too much else on her mind."

Tom considered chiding Jodie about her insistence on bearing the entire weight of her predicament—and yet he respected her desire to shield her sister. He understood her protective feelings; they were oddly similar to his feelings toward her.

"So," he said. "Would you like to go out for dinner?"

Before Jodie could answer, her niece shot out of the house and down the porch steps. "Aunt Jodie! Aunt Jodie, guess what? This man is going to fix my doll carriage, and you know what else? Peter says he's your boyfriend!''

Tom would never have figured Jodie for the sort of woman who blushed, but her cheeks darkened to a deep crimson. He gently slid his arm around her waist and gave her a light hug. ''Jodie and I are friends,'' he told the child.

Jodie tossed him a quizzical look, but she didn't push his hand away. ''Friends, huh?''

''That's how you introduced me to your sister last week,'' he reminded her.

''Which was before you kissed me,'' she whispered.

She had a point. He wanted to question her about what she took their kiss to mean—and what word she'd use to describe their relationship—but Sarah intervened in a loud, demanding voice, ''Are you going to fix my carriage?''

''No,'' Jodie answered for him. ''He's going to have dinner.''

''Not right away,'' Sarah said. ''Mommy says dinner won't be ready for a while. She's cooking something and I don't know what it is, but it looks gross.''

''Lynne? Cooking dinner without being asked?'' Jodie laughed. ''This is an event.'' She started up the walk with Tom. ''When Lynne and I were growing up, my mother did all the cooking,'' she explained. ''She never let us help. She used to say that cooking was her job. So neither of us ever learned how to function in a kitchen.''

''But you invent recipes for a living, don't you?'' Tom asked, bewildered.

''That's more like chemistry than cooking,'' Jodie said. ''And I learned more about cooking during my few years with the original Penny Simpson than I did during my entire childhood. I think my mother was afraid that if Lynne and I started cooking she'd be left with nothing to do, no important role to fill. And then how could she prove to my father that she was worthwhile?''

Tom recalled everything Jodie had told him about her parents' stormy marriage. Before his father had died, his mother hadn't had a paying job, but she'd worked damned hard—preparing meals, maintaining the house, cultivating the garden, keeping Tom in clean clothes and out of trouble. Nobody had ever regarded her work as less important because it didn't earn her an income; it had been just as essential as his father's work driving a truck for a silage company, and whatever Tom could do to help, he did—especially after his father had passed away and he and his mother had moved to Carroll so his mother could take a secretarial position. She hadn't felt less important because Tom helped her with the housework; he hadn't felt less important because his after-school job bagging groceries at the local supermarket paid a paltry salary.

"A person's worth doesn't come from what they do," he observed. "It comes from who they are."

"Well, isn't that a pretty little philosophy," Jodie said dryly, as she preceded him onto the porch and inside. Heading for the kitchen, she called out, "Hey, Lynne, rumor has it you're fixing dinner."

"I'm trying," Lynne responded when Jodie and Tom arrived in the kitchen. "You hardly have any food in the house, Jodie. I'm just throwing some things together."

Tom surveyed the variety of ingredients scattered across the counter: two cans of tuna fish, a bottle of ketchup, a plastic bag of uncooked rice, several carrots, a squeeze bottle of honey and a single cherry tomato. "We could make a casserole," Jodie said optimistically, unbuttoning the cuffs of her blouse and rolling up the sleeves. She glanced at Tom. "This may take a while," she warned. "You don't mind, do you?"

He had intended to have dinner alone with Jodie, preferably at a restaurant with a romantic ambience—not that brightly lit Chinese restaurant with all those rowdy happy-hour patrons swapping baseball jokes at the bar, but a place with muted lighting and string music, linen napkins and wine-sauce entrées. A place where he and Jodie could lose themselves in the warm, lush atmosphere and could gaze into each other's eyes.

The prospect of eating at her house didn't truly disappoint Tom, though. After Jodie's kiss, nothing could disappoint him.

"Sarah, why don't you take Tom into the living room and show him how the TV works?" Lynne requested. "Maybe he'd like to watch the news while Aunt Jodie and I make supper."

Yes, Tom thought, he'd like to watch the news. He'd like to hear if the police had perchance caught some deranged idiot who'd been cruising around Orangeburg in a car with Pennsylvania license plates and a trunk full of dead critters. He'd like to learn that the idiot had been arraigned and locked up for the night, with bail set at a million dollars. He'd like to find out that Jodie was utterly safe.

Barring that, he'd like to distract himself from the possibility that Jodie and her sister were actually going to create a casserole out of the assortment of foods lined up on the counter—and that he was going to have to eat it with a smile. Grinning down at Sarah, he allowed her to take his hand and usher him out of the kitchen.

"Okay, so what's going on?" Lynne asked.

Jodie finished measuring the rice and emptied the cup into the Pyrex casserole dish she'd gotten for opening a bank account back in the days when banks gave gifts. She mulled over her sister's question, unsure of what Lynne was getting at. Had Tom, in fact, told Lynne about the skunk? Jodie really didn't want her to know. If Lynne knew, she'd either fall apart completely or try to help, and Jodie didn't like either possibility.

"I give up," she replied with a blithe shrug. "What's going on?"

"I mean, between you and Tom," Lynne clarified. She was tearing lettuce into a salad bowl at a rate of about one leaf a minute. Her mouth, in contrast, was moving at a rapid clip. "You never even mentioned him before last week, and now here he is again. I mean, is this a big thing? Are you and he serious?"

"Serious?" Jodie guffawed, but her laughter sounded peculiarly hollow. The kiss Tom had given her outdoors hadn't been overly deep or passionate, yet there had been something serious in the extreme about it. "I hardly know him, Lynne," she said. "And I highly doubt that it's going to develop into anything major."

"Why not? He seems awfully nice." Lynne methodically peeled another leaf from the head of lettuce and tore it into the bowl. "If I'm not mistaken, he's the first guy you've spent any time with since Jeff took a powder."

"You're not mistaken," Jodie muttered, returning the ketchup to the refrigerator and then pulling a jar of spaghetti sauce from a shelf.

"I never understood why you and Jeff broke up," Lynne remarked. "I mean, there wasn't a big blowup or anything. It was suddenly just . . . over."

"Do we have to discuss this?"

"I'm your sister," Lynne reminded her. "I want to make sure you don't screw up your life the way I've screwed up mine."

"Believe me, I won't," Jodie promised. "If you really want to know, there were lots of little blowups between Jeff and me. He was put off by the fact that I earned as much as he did and that I loved being Penny Simpson at least as much as I loved being his sweetheart, and that I made decisions without consulting him—even though they were decisions that had nothing to do with him. He was furious when I bought this house. I told him it was my money and my investment, but he hit the ceiling because I didn't ask him for his opinion before I bought the place."

"You should have humored him," Lynne commented. "You could have asked him what he thought and then gone ahead and bought it anyway. Men love to think we need their wisdom to help us with these kinds of decisions."

"I didn't want to humor him," Jodie snapped. "That would have been hypocritical." She didn't add that Lynne might not be filing for divorce right now if she hadn't devoted the past dozen years to humoring her narrow-minded husband.

Lynne fondled another leaf of lettuce. "So why don't you think things could work out with Tom? He doesn't seem like the sort of man who wants to be humored."

As far as Jodie could tell, all men wanted to be humored—and Tom, with his warnings and cautionary cluckings, was no exception. In a moment of weakness, she'd humored him by asking him to come to Orangeburg to help her cope with this skunk business. And then he'd kissed her. He'd circled his arms around her and held her and charmed her with a marvelous, magical kiss.

In that instant she would have promised to humor him forever. She would have handed her life over to him and said, "Protect me, defend me—just don't stop kissing me."

Merely thinking about it infused her entire body with a sensuous heat. It was scary to realize how easily she could surrender to Tom, how delightfully hedonistic it would be to cede her autonomy, to let him take charge and make everything better. It was much scarier than having a dead animal left on her doorstep.

"I think he's still hung up on an old flame," she blurted out. She hadn't consciously been thinking about Penny Simpson from Iowa, yet as soon as she spoke the words she recognized the truth in them.

Lynne grimaced. "Too bad. Do you think he's taking up with you on the rebound?"

"No." A dozen-plus years after his Penny had broken up with him, he couldn't still be waiting for his wounded heart to heal. "It's just..." Jodie reflected for a minute. "She was someone he loved a lot, and I'm nothing like her at all."

"Maybe that's a good thing," Lynne noted.

Jodie dumped the spaghetti sauce and the tuna into the casserole dish. "I think he finds me interesting," she allowed. "But when it's time for him to fall in love again, it's going to be with someone like her." Someone sweet and beautiful and demure, Jodie contemplated. Someone with traditional values and a homely manner. Someone who spent her days making the world cozier for her man—with the help of clever hints from the "Penny-Wise" column in her newspaper, no doubt.

Lynne peered curiously into the casserole dish, then returned her attention to Jodie. "So he finds you interesting," she said, crossing her arms and striking a superior pose. "If you want to hang on to him, Jodie, that's not going to be enough. Maybe you ought to bend a little—"

"Look who's talking." Jodie cut her off with a withering stare. "Every time Hank opened his mouth, you bent a little. And now you're contemplating a divorce. I'm not going to change my personality to be what Tom—or any man—wants. I'm satisfied with myself the way I am."

"Yeah, but your face lights up whenever you see him. I can see it, Jodie. You really like this guy."

Jodie shoved the casserole dish into the oven and adjusted the heat. She would have liked to shove Lynne, too. Jodie was in no mood to listen to her sister report on how obvious it was that Jodie was infatuated with Tom. "Why don't you finish making that salad already?" she grumbled, grabbing a stack of napkins and stalking to the dining room to set the table.

An arched doorway connected the dining room with the living room. Although she stubbornly refused to glance through the door to see how Tom was faring with her niece and nephew, she couldn't keep from eavesdropping on them. Above the din of the television broadcast she heard Peter pontificating on the subject of dinosaurs. "The thing about brontosaurus," he was saying, "is that he had rocks in his stomach. Really, Tom, I'm not making this up. Brontosaurus would gobble up tree limbs and branches and stuff and swallow 'em whole, and then the rocks in his stomach would grind them up.''

"That's dumb," Sarah said. "You don't believe that, Tom, do you?''

"I think he's right," Tom said.

"Of course, brontosaurus is actually aleosaurus. They changed his name or something. Now anatosaurus, he didn't need the rocks on account of he had thousands of teeth," Peter went on. "I'm kind of an expert on this stuff, Tom.''

"I can tell," Tom said.

In spite of herself, Jodie grinned. She was astonished by Tom's forbearance, and also sympathetic. When Peter embarked on one of his dissertations about dinosaurs, he could be excruciatingly boring.

As soon as she was done arranging the napkins around the table, she went into the living room with the intention of freeing Tom from the children's clutches. She found him seated on the sofa with one child on either side of him. Peter had a book about dinosaurs spread half on his own lap and half on Tom's, and Sarah was marching a phalanx of plastic ponies up and down his arm. Tom alternated his attention between one child and the other, sometimes staring at a picture in the dinosaur book and sometimes trying to snag Sarah's toy ponies with his hand.

"I've come to rescue you," Jodie announced.

He glanced up. "Thanks anyway," he said. "I don't need to be rescued. I can take care of myself.'' His knowing grin conveyed that he was deliberately imitating her words, mocking her protests of self-reliance.

"Fine," she said briskly, pivoting and marching back into the dining room. "Suit yourself.''

"How much longer till we eat?" Peter called after her. "I'm starving!"

"Fifteen minutes," Jodie predicted. "If you don't think you can wait that long, you can pretend you're a brontosaurus and eat some rocks. I've got plenty in the back yard."

"Ha, ha, ha," Peter groaned, milking each syllable for sarcasm.

Back in the dining room, Jodie exhaled. She felt bad that Tom was in the living room with her niece and nephew while she was alone, and worse that she and Tom had somehow wound up staying home for supper instead of escaping the house for a couple of hours. She felt worst of all because she understood the truth in what she'd told Lynne, and in what Lynne had told her. She could never measure up to Tom's old flame—she truly didn't *want* to—but she really liked the guy.

As it turned out, dinner *was* ready in ten minutes. The meal was accompanied by a continuation of Peter's discourse on dinosaurs. "You know, Tom, some scientists think that birds evolved from the dinosaurs. Some dinosaurs had hollow bones, just like birds do. Pretty amazing, huh, Tom? I mean, when you think a brachiosaurus could be the ancestor of a robin red-breast!"

"He said a dirty word, Mommy," Sarah said smugly.

"Just before summer vacation, my class did a whole unit on dinosaurs and I knew more than anybody else," Peter droned on. "When I grow up I'm gonna be a paleontologist. Either that or a professional wrestler. I haven't decided."

"I'm going to be a ballerina and sell ice cream," Sarah announced. "Both. I'm gonna do both."

Jodie shot Tom frequent glances as the children prattled on. He rarely met her gaze, though. He appeared to be fascinated by their nonstop babbling. "When I was a kid, I wanted to be a fireman," he told them. "We had a volunteer fire department in town, and the firemen used to hang around at the station every evening playing cards. That's what I wanted to do."

"I wanted to be a fireman when I was a kid, too," Peter said with great solemnity. "Where'd you grow up, Tom?"

"Iowa."

"Iowa! Wow. Hear that, Mom? He's from Iowa."

"Where's Iowa?" Sarah asked.

Once or twice Jodie thought of intervening, steering the discussion to a subject Tom might find more scintillating. But then his words would echo inside her: *I don't need to be rescued.* His words and her own.

After dinner, Tom helped Jodie to clear the table while Lynne herded the children upstairs for their baths. "We'll just leave the dishes to soak," Jodie told him as she filled the sink with water and dishwashing detergent. "It's a lot more efficient to clean the dishes that way."

Tom shot her a look of amusement. "Is this Jodie speaking, or Penny Simpson?"

"Penny," Jodie confirmed. "One thing Jodie isn't is efficient."

Laughing, Tom patiently held a stack of plates until the sink was half full of sudsy water. "It must be very confusing to have two identities," he said as he handed the plates to her.

"Jodie gets confused, but Penny doesn't," Jodie quipped. She smothered the impulse to ask him which of her two identities he preferred. She suspected he'd choose Penny, and the notion didn't thrill her. "You really don't have to help me clear, Tom," she said, returning to the dining room to collect the remaining dishes.

"I don't mind." He lifted the empty casserole dish. "This was delicious, Jodie. I noticed that, for all her complaining before dinner, Sarah wolfed down two big portions."

"I'm sorry the kids held you captive all evening," Jodie said, leading him back to the kitchen. She set the dishes in the sink and then filled the casserole dish with soap and water and left it on the counter. "Today was a rough day for them, I think. Lynne left them with a baby-sitter all morning—a neighbor of mine. She's very nice, but the kids hardly know her—and they *did* know that the reason Lynne was gone all morning had something to do with their father."

"How much do they know?" Tom asked. "I mean, about their parents' separation."

Jodie didn't find it odd that Tom would take an interest in Lynne's divorce. For one thing, his partner was handling it, and for another, it was in his nature to worry about the travails of helpless women. In answer to his question, she shrugged. "I'm sure Peter knows what's going on. He's going on ten years old. And both kids have witnessed more than enough fights between their parents."

"Fighting and separating are two different things," said Tom. "In fact, they're opposites. Fighting is an engagement, while separating is a disengagement."

Jodie eyed him inquisitively. "How come you're so knowledgeable on the subject?" she asked.

"I live in the real world, Jodie," he replied. "I see what goes on around me."

She focused on the glinting bubbles in the sink and meditated. Just because Tom hadn't married his Penny didn't mean he might not have married someone else and divorced her. Or, if he hadn't married someone else, he could have still had one or two intense relationships with other women. He didn't strike Jodie as a Casanova, but he was a mature, attractive man, and he'd clearly learned how to kiss somewhere.

Had he known plenty of women? Fallen in love plenty of times? Had he broken up with those women because he kept comparing them to his one true love and deciding they didn't measure up?

"...In the office," he was saying. "Jerome sometimes asks me for assistance in his cases because the dissolution of assets frequently has tax ramifications. Or I can tell from reviewing back tax records whether a spouse is concealing financial information."

"Oh," said Jodie, forcing herself to ignore her troubling thoughts. She would only make herself miserable trying to compete with Tom's Penny. It was always possible that she was blowing the woman way out of proportion. Maybe, as Tom had claimed the first time he'd met Jodie, he'd responded to the "Penny-Wise" column only out of curiosity regarding a long-lost acquaintance. Maybe he was truly over her.

"It's a nice evening," he commented. "Why don't we go sit out on the porch?"

"Okay," she said, scanning the kitchen and then following him outside.

He was right: it was a lovely evening. The air had cooled considerably as the sun slid below the horizon, and the sky was a dim blue traced with lavender clouds. Tom waited until Jodie was seated on the porch steps before lowering himself to sit beside her. He surveyed the toys strewn across the yard and grunted. "I think I was supposed to fix your niece's doll carriage," he said.

"I didn't know it was broken."

"One of the axles is rusty."

Jodie nodded. "I can fix that for her. A little steel wool, and then a coat of Vaseline."

"God bless Penny Simpson," he said with what she chose to interpret as admiration.

She sighed and twisted to face him. "Let's not talk about my work. Tell me about your day. Did you take your deposition?"

He smiled. "Yes, we got it done."

"What was it about?"

His smile widened. "You don't really want to hear about this, do you?"

"Of course I do."

He studied her for a minute and apparently concluded that she was sincere. "My client went into a partnership with several friends to buy a tenement in Newark as a tax shelter," he told her. "One of the partners was involved in some other shelters that Uncle Sam is questioning the validity of. It's all pretty dry. The best thing I can say about it is that it didn't take too long to depose my client."

"If it had taken too long," Jodie joked, "you might have missed out on a scrumptious meal and a five-star lecture on dinosaurs."

"Oh, I would have come here one way or another," Tom declared his smile growing gentle. "I just wouldn't have had time to stop off at home and pick up my mail first."

"I hope it was worth the detour," she said, noting silently that he'd also had the time to change his clothes before he'd left the city. He'd looked impressive in his business attire that morning, but now, dressed in a fresh cotton shirt and jeans just snug enough to emphasize his long, athletic legs, he looked comfortable and casual and devastatingly attractive.

"I got two bills," he admitted with a grin. "Also a letter from my mother, forwarding an invitation to my high school's fifteenth reunion."

"A high school reunion?" Jodie grimaced. "I can't imagine going to one of those."

"Where'd you go to high school?"

"Irvine, south of Los Angeles. I hated high school, though. I couldn't wait to get as far away from the place as possible. I certainly wouldn't want to go back."

"Not even out of curiosity?" Tom asked. "Don't you ever wonder what became of all the kids you used to know?"

"Most of them are probably doing time in Folson State Prison," she joked, then shook her head. "No. I wasn't very popular in high school. I was fat—"

"No! Really?"

"Well, chubby," she amended. "Everybody thought I was weird because I dressed like a freak, with strange jewelry—"

"Some things haven't changed," Tom noted with a smile.

Jodie smiled back. "I was an oddity there. I went to the prom with my cousin because none of my classmates would go with me. All I ever heard was how cute and popular Lynne was and how weird I was." She shrugged. "I lost weight in college, and now I wear whatever I like, and I don't have to rely on my cousins for dates anymore. But I have no burning interest to go back and see all those jerks again."

"Not even to show them how fantastic you've turned out?" Tom asked.

His flattery touched her, but she refused to dwell on it. "I take it you're going back to your reunion."

"If I can arrange my schedule," he confirmed. "It's in July. I'll have to see if I can squeeze in a weekend trip."

"I bet you want to see Penny," she remarked in a deceptively nonchalant tone. She almost dreaded what he would say in response, but she couldn't stop the question from popping out.

Tom shifted, stretching one leg out until his foot came within an inch of hers. His smile never wavered; his gaze never left her. "Sure, why not?"

Why not, Jodie thought morosely. He'd see his Penny and remember all the things he'd adored about her, all the wonderful things that had lived in his memory for these many years until he'd felt an irrational compulsion to write to "Penny-Wise." He'd see her and realize how lovely she was in comparison to Jodie.

Straightening her shoulders, she admonished herself to stop being so negative. No matter how attractive she found Tom, no matter what unformed hopes she might harbor about enjoying a romance with him, she would never want to change places with a passive housewife from some tiny midwestern town. Jodie was proud of who she was and happy with her life. If Tom wanted to be a part of it, fine. If he didn't, that was his problem.

He shifted on the porch again, and his foot bumped hers. "Are you uncomfortable?" she asked. "I've been meaning to buy some deck furniture for out here, but I—"

"I'm fine," he said, cutting her off, although he continued to rearrange his lanky body on the step. It occurred to Jodie that he was adjusting his position in order to move closer to her. He extended his other leg and slid his arm around her shoulders. "Now I'm even better," he said.

Her laughter was peculiarly airy. She liked the cozy feel of his arm around her, the tangy scent of his skin, the firm contours of his chest as she reflexively nestled into his embrace.

"What happened before wasn't a fluke, you know," he murmured, his lips ominously close to her temple.

"What?" she asked.

"This." He pressed his lips lightly to the silky black tendrils at her hairline. "I wanted to kiss you this morning at my office," he told her.

"Did you?" Her voice cracked, embarrassing her. She cleared her throat and grinned. "Actually, I was sort of disappointed that you didn't."

He chuckled softly. "How could I? You stormed out of my office in a rage."

"I tend to get that way when people criticize my driving," she said, recalling the spark that had ignited her anger.

"Well, then," he said, sliding his thumb under her chin and angling her face to his, "I swear I'm crazy about the way you drive." His hand slid from her jaw to the sensitive skin below, stroking, seducing. "I'm absolutely crazy about it," he whispered before covering her mouth with his.

Chapter Six

He definitely knew how to kiss.

That was the first hazy thought to drift through Jodie's mind as her lips, and then her entire body, responded to the eloquent pressure of his mouth. There was nothing particularly forceful about what he was doing, nothing the least bit pushy or demanding. He wooed her with gentleness, coaxing and cajoling, letting her know she was safe with him even as they ventured closer and closer to the edge of abandon. He traced an abstract pattern with his fingertips along the sleek skin of her throat and then let his hand trail to the nape of her neck. His other hand roamed down her spine to her waist, urging her closer. His lips continued to graze hers, inflaming her with the devastating weapon of tenderness.

Her second thought was that he had a wonderful physique. As her mouth moved with his, her hands journeyed across his shoulders, down his sides and over the lean, supple contours of his back. She savored the tensile strength of his thigh against hers, the hard angle of his knee brushing hers, the tantalizing sweep of his tongue along her lower lip. She felt a slow, luscious thawing deep inside her, a heat that spread from her throat to her breasts to her hips—and still, the unshakable understanding remained that she was safe with Tom.

She recalled her first impressions of him—his modest letter and his reserved demeanor when they'd met and her certainty that lurking just beneath his benign facade was a whirlwind of potent feelings. His kiss was similar: restrained yet provocative, tantalizing her with the profound emotion she sensed inside him, just beyond her reach.

With a hushed groan, she parted her lips. His tongue found hers, and he groaned, too. Yet his control never faltered. She comprehended that he was arousing her far more with subtlety than he could have with explosive passion. It was a strange thing, being kissed by a man who didn't seem to be plotting his next move, who nibbled instead of devoured, who left her with the clear comprehension that she could bring the kiss to an end whenever she wished.

Which was never. She couldn't imagine ever wanting to stop kissing Tom.

His tongue explored her mouth with delicate jabs and exquisite strokes, with confidence and consummate skill. She could tell he was as enraptured as she was by the way his fingers furled and unfurled against the small of her back and his heart raced against her palm as she slid her hand across his chest. His shirt was soft, the body beneath it firm and rugged, and it required enormous willpower on her part to resist the temptation to unbutton the shirt and slip her hand inside, to caress him skin to skin. Merely thinking about touching him increased the heat inside her. It spread through her flesh and her soul, melting her until she seemed to be nothing but a pool of sensation within the protective circle of his embrace.

After several minutes he drew back to look at her. His eyes sparkled with glints of green and silver in the dim evening light; his chest swelled against her hand with each heavy breath. Dazed, she stared back at him, reading in his gaze a blend of affection and desire and infinite promise. She knew intuitively that he would be as painstaking as a lover, as patient and masterful and utterly enthralling, as he'd been as a kisser.

"Come home with me," he whispered.

Assuming he wasn't clairvoyant, she realized that her expression must have revealed the erotic thoughts drifting through her mind. She was overcome by a sudden pang of shyness. She had never been coy, but then, she'd never been so transparently aroused by a man before. She felt utterly, embarrassingly exposed.

"I don't know," she said in a wavering voice.

He combed his fingers through the soft dark tufts of her hair, brushing it back from her feverish cheeks. "What don't you know?"

She sighed. What she *did* know—what they both knew—was that she desired Tom, that he desired her, that a night spent in each other's arms would probably wind up redefining the concept of ecstasy. But as much as she trusted that Tom would make a sublime lover, she didn't know whether she trusted his love, or whether love was even a part of what they were feeling for each other.

She liked him, and she felt reasonably assured that he liked her. But love...? Love entailed honoring and obeying, which she wasn't sure she was willing to do. And it entailed forsaking all others, which she wasn't sure he was willing to do.

"I don't know if I should," she answered.

He seemed on the verge of arguing with her, then resorted to the more persuasive tactic of kissing her again. He guided her back to him and covered her lips with his, and she felt the heat building inside her again, pulsing through her bloodstream, gathering in her heart, in her womb. He molded his hand around the back of her head, refusing her the chance to escape as he intensified his amorous assault on her mouth.

Not that she had any notion of escaping. Her eyes fluttered shut as she closed her arms around him. Her tongue engaged his, then let him lure it to his lips, to the edge of his teeth and deeper. She felt his smile in response, felt his growing hunger in the anxious flexing of his fingers at the nape of her neck, in the tension of his leg against hers. She sensed a matching hunger inside herself and an implacable question: Why not? If it feels this good, why not?

And then she heard another implacable question, this one spoken in a childish whine arising somewhere inside the house: "Why not? Let me just ask him, Mommy! I bet he'd—"

"Get back up here, Sarah!" Lynne shouted, her voice reaching Jodie's ears through the screen door. If Lynne was demanding that Sarah get back up, Jodie deduced that Sarah was on her way down. Downstairs. Outside.

The comprehension that Sarah might storm out onto the porch sliced through the romantic spell that had woven around Jodie and jarred her to full consciousness. She gave Tom an imperative nudge and inched back from him. In the nick of time, too; just as he glanced quizzically toward the door, it swung open and Sarah bounded out onto the porch. She had on a pink

nightgown and clutched her stuffed rabbit and a book.
"Will you read *Fox in Socks* to me?" she asked Tom.

Thank heaven for little girls, Jodie thought wryly. If
Sarah had been any older, she might have realized what
she'd just interrupted. As it was, Tom felt it necessary
to rearrange his legs on the steps and drape an arm dis-
creetly across his lap. Jodie pressed her hands to her
flushed cheeks and drew in a deep, bracing breath.
"Isn't it bedtime?" she asked, prompting Tom to catch
her eye and grin suggestively.

"I want Tom to read me this book first," Sarah said
as she grabbed his hand and attempted to haul him to
his feet. "You don't mind, do you?"

"No, of course not," he said, rising and tossing Jodie
another look, this one of amused resignation. "I can't
think of anything I'd rather do right now than read you
a book."

"You don't know what you're getting yourself into,"
Jodie warned under her breath as she followed Sarah
and Tom into the house and up the stairs.

Lynne stood at the top of the stairway. "Tom, I'm
sorry—"

He cut her off with an indulgent smile and a wave of
his hand. "I don't mind," he insisted. He seemed on the
verge of saying something more, but Sarah gave his arm
a sharp yank and dragged him into the room she shared
with her brother. Peter was sprawled out on top of his
sleeping bag, his hair still damp from his shampoo and
his chin marked with a smear of toothpaste.

"Sit on the bed," Sarah ordered Tom. "Right here—
and read the whole thing. Don't skip any pages, okay?"

"She sure is bossy," Peter muttered with a wisdom
born of experience.

Tom sat where Sarah had indicated and opened to the first page. Almost at once he began to stumble over the book's malevolent tongue twisters. For not the first time that evening, Jodie pondered the idea of rescuing him. Sarah didn't have the right to take advantage of his generous nature. He was here to visit Jodie, not her niece and nephew. He belonged out on the porch with her, attempting to convince her, in whatever heavenly manner suited him, to spend the night with him.

"Um—Tom—" she whispered from the doorway.

He paused in the middle of a stanza and sent her an impatient look.

"If you don't want to do this—"

"If I didn't want to I wouldn't," he said curtly, then turned back to Sarah and Peter and resumed reading.

She analyzed his brusque tone, wondering whether he was angry with her—and if so, why. All she'd done was to remind him that he was under no obligation to the kids. She'd wanted to offer him a chance to put down the book and cut out, to protect him from the demands of her young houseguests.

But he didn't want to be protected. If anyone ought to understand that, it was Jodie.

Sighing, she left him with the children and headed down the hall. She found Lynne gathering damp towels from the floor of the bathroom, which was still steamy from Sarah's bath and Peter's shower. Lynne glimpsed Jodie over her shoulder and winced. "I'm really sorry about the bedtime story, Jodie," she said, straightening up and dumping the towels into the hamper. "I tried to keep Sarah upstairs, but—"

"Forget it." Jodie lifted a waterlogged washcloth from the edge of the tub and tossed it to Lynne, who dropped it into the hamper.

Drying her hands, Lynne turned to face her sister. "He's *so* nice," she whispered.

Jodie nodded vaguely. Describing Tom Barrett as "nice" was about as accurate as describing him as "kind of good-looking, I guess."

"Sarah knows a good thing when she sees it."

Jodie didn't smile. What Sarah saw in Tom was a father figure, someone more kindhearted than her own father. Jodie couldn't picture Hank sitting on the edge of Sarah's bed and reading Dr. Seuss to her. If Sarah asked, he'd probably say, "That's your mother's job. She ought to spend less time crabbing about how she wants a career and more time reading to her children. I earn the money to buy the damned books—she can read them to you."

The thought depressed Jodie. "I think I'll go do some stuff in the kitchen," she said, feeling the need to be alone for a while.

She plodded down the stairs, annoyed that the euphoria Tom had ignited inside her had completely disappeared. She didn't know why it had. Surely losing him to Sarah and Peter for a few minutes was no big deal. Having Lynne give him high marks wasn't cause for sorrow, either. And yet…Jodie no longer felt crazy and giddy and ready to romp off to New York City for a blissful night in Tom's bed.

Exhaling, she plunged her hands into the murky dishwater in the sink, groping for the drain plug. The soaking had been a success; most of the dishes required little more than a wipe and a rinse. "Bravo, Penny," Jodie grumbled, stacking the plates one by one in the drying rack. "Another brilliant time-saving tip for homemakers and dishwashers everywhere."

"Maybe it'll win you a Pulitzer Prize," Tom said.

She spun around to see him standing just a few feet behind her. Blushing, she offered a faint smile. "I sometimes talk to myself when I'm doing the dishes."

"It sounded like you were talking to Penny," he teased, coming up behind her. He cupped his hands over her shoulders and pulled her gently to himself. "Any chance we could pick up where we left off?"

She looked at her wet hands, at the lingering suds streaking the sink, at the pile of dishes in the rack. His chest felt warm and strong against her back, and she reflexively leaned into him. He slid his arms forward, hugging her close. She smiled pensively. "I don't know, Tom. Somehow, doing the dishes doesn't exactly put me in a romantic mood."

"Ditto with reading tongue twisters. That book was agony. I think your niece is a sadist."

"You're not the first person to reach that conclusion," Jodie said with a laugh. She dried her hands, then faced him.

He gazed down at her, his eyes glittering with laughter and longing, his smile seductive. She wrestled with the urge to reach up and pull him down to her, to lose herself in another exquisite kiss, to forget her misgivings and half-formed doubts and enjoy herself with Tom. Once again, he seemed to read her mind, because he bowed toward her and touched his lips briefly to hers.

"I feel a little public in here," he murmured, shooting a meaningful glance toward the doorway.

Although the children were in bed, Lynne was around—and although Lynne was tactful, the house was small. "We could go back out onto the porch," Jodie suggested.

He nodded, but she could guess what he was thinking: that their privacy had already been breached on the porch and that if they wanted to guarantee no more interruptions, they would have to go to Tom's apartment. She appreciated that he didn't press the issue, because she still hadn't made up her mind whether to leave with him.

The sky had darkened to black while they were indoors, and the crickets chirped their rustic chorus in the night air. "It must be hard getting used to having your house full of relatives," Tom remarked.

Jodie shrugged. "I don't mind it."

"Even so.... It's awfully generous of you."

She shrugged again. "Lynne's my sister. She had nowhere else to go."

"Your parents?"

"They don't understand why she wants a divorce. My father thinks Hank is just swell—not terribly surprising, since they're so much alike. My mother thinks she's put up with a lot worse with my father than Lynne ever has with Hank, so she doesn't know why Lynne can't shut up and suffer like a good wife, too."

Tom meditated for a moment, then shook his head. "Lynne's lucky to have you," he said. His low, earnest tone informed Jodie that he meant his words as a high compliment.

"Maybe I'm lucky to have her, too," she returned. "Having her around reminds me..." She drifted off. Having Lynne around reminded Jodie of how destructive some relationships could be, and how vital it was for a woman not to lose her sense of herself in the love of a man.

But she couldn't say that to Tom. It would come out all wrong. "She reminds me of how great it feels to take care of someone you're close to," she concluded. "I like doing things for Lynne and the kids. I like being there when they need me."

"How long have they been living with you?"

"A couple of weeks. They moved in right after the end of the school year. Lynne didn't want Peter and Sarah to miss any school."

"What's she going to do in the fall?" he asked. "Will she enroll them in school here in Orangeburg?"

Jodie faked a panic-stricken look. "Good God, do you think I'll still be stuck with them in September?" Then she grinned. "I guess it's up to your partner DeLucca to make sure she'll be able to find her own place to live by then."

"The odds of negotiating a settlement in a couple of months are pretty slim," Tom cautioned her. "Jerome is an excellent lawyer, but he can't work miracles."

"Well, then, they'll stay here," Jodie decreed. "I won't have them living in a motel."

Tom looped his arm around her shoulders and gave her a hug. "It must be tiring, bearing the weight of all their problems."

The truth was, it *was* tiring. The house was crowded and noisy, the yard was cluttered with the children's junk and the jingles of assorted television cartoons provided an insidious layer of background music to Jodie's every activity. She spent so much time bolstering Lynne and mediating squabbles between the children that she hardly had any time or energy left for herself.

But she truly didn't mind. Being able to provide them with the support they needed during their crisis made her feel strong and capable and in control of things.

"Especially now, when you've got problems of your own," Tom added, twirling his fingers absent-mindedly through her hair.

The skunk. Cripes. That was the last thing she wanted to think about. She'd done such a good job of putting it out of her mind—and now Tom had raised the subject and spoiled everything.

No. Tom was entitled to raise the subject because he'd been the one to put it out of her mind in the first place. She hadn't deliberately avoided thinking about her troubles at work; Tom had distracted her. He'd emptied her mind of the skunk, the police, the letter, Helen's scolding—all the unpleasant things that had driven Jodie to call him that afternoon and let him know how terrified she was.

"Frankly," he went on, his fingers still toying with her hair, his gaze fixed on the moonlit yard, "I'm not as worried about your sister staying here as I am about you. If a reader can find out where you work, she can find out where you live, can't she?"

"I'm not listed in the telephone book," Jodie informed him, forcing into her voice a cheeriness she didn't feel. "We celebrities do whatever we can to hang on to our privacy."

"I'm glad you're unlisted," he said, then exhaled. "Even so, if she could find your office—"

"You found my office, too," Jodie reminded him. "It wasn't so difficult."

"Yes, but..." He lapsed into thought, his fingers drifting through her hair to stroke down along the curve of her earlobe. He fondled the tiny purple beads of her earrings for a second, then wandered to the sensitive skin behind her ear. His light touch sent a fiery shiver down her back and she sighed involuntarily. "I really think it would be a good idea for you to come to my apartment tonight," he said.

The sensual warmth his delicate caresses had provoked within her vanished beneath a crashing wave of icy rage. He didn't want her to come to his apartment for a night of love. He wanted her to come so he could protect her from the skunk woman!

"Forget it," Jodie snapped, jerking away from him.

"Jodie?" He appeared perplexed by her incensed reaction.

"You think I'd spend the night with you out of fear? You think I'd come to your apartment so I could hide from a lunatic? If I were going to spend a night with you, Tom Barrett, it would be because I wanted to make love with you, not because I was running for cover."

He frowned and raked his fingers through his tawny hair, absorbing her blunt words and her anger. "I have no problem with that. It should be pretty obvious that I want to make love with you, too."

"Not as much as you want to protect me."

"Much more, Jodie."

She shook her head and twisted away. It didn't matter how much he wanted to make love with her—she couldn't, not tonight. Not after he'd reminded her that a psychotic "Penny-Wise" reader was stalking her and that Tom aimed to be her self-appointed savior. The only way she would go to bed with him was if he was her equal, not her guardian. She could accept him as a lover, but not as a gallant knight.

He slid his hand to her shoulder and gave it a squeeze. "I didn't mean to put a damper on things," he said apologetically. "I think . . ." He mulled over his words, choosing them carefully. "I think we've got a good thing here. Ever since I met you, Jodie . . . I don't make a habit of asking strangers out to dinner, but the minute I saw you I knew..."

"You knew what?" she asked testily.

"I was attracted to you."

Right, she thought furiously, reviewing mentally the first time they'd met. The way she remembered it, he hadn't asked her out to dinner right away. He'd been all set to march out of her office and out of her life—and then Helen had rushed in, waving the death-threat letter around. And that was when Tom had decided he was attracted to Jodie. When he knew she was imperiled. When he saw her as a damsel in distress.

She ought to put a lid on her temper. She was risking something special by lashing out at Tom. He was so sweet, so smart, so incredibly sexy. She could fall for him in a big way—if only he'd stop doting on her. If only he'd stop fussing. If only he would come right out and declare, "You're tough enough to take care of yourself. I have faith in you. I won't interfere."

"Tom..." She sighed, disappointed and miserable and riven with doubt. "I think we've got a good thing, too. I'm not saying no to it. But..." She sighed again. "I can't go home with you tonight. I just can't. It wouldn't be right. Can you understand that?"

He cupped his hand under her chin and turned her to face him. His gaze penetrated her, searching. "I'm not sure I understand," he murmured. "I'm not sure you do, either. But I can respect your decision."

He drew her to himself for a light, tender kiss, then released her and stood. "I'd better go," he said, starting down the front walk to his car.

She almost screamed that it had been unfair to kiss her before he departed, unfair to rekindle the heat inside her and then turn his back on her. But she held her silence. If he wanted to torture her by leaving her with a hint of what she'd just refused, that was his choice. She could as easily torture herself by thinking about his earlier kisses, remembering the way his heart had beat against her hand, the way his breath had mingled with hers and his arms had tightened around her. Memories alone could set her soul on fire.

And a memory of the dead skunk on her doorstep could put that fire out in no time flat.

She reminds me of how great it feels to take care of someone you're close to.

He cruised south along the parkway, his eyes on the road ahead of him and his mind on the woman he'd left behind. Her voice echoed in his ears, in his heart, telling him why she was so eager to help her sister's family. *I like doing things for them. I like being there when they need me.*

Damn. If Jodie could say that and mean it, why couldn't she understand how Tom felt about her? He liked doing things for her, being there for her, taking care of her. Was there anything wrong with that?

Sure there was: Jodie Posniak was wrong with it. She was the wrong woman to feel that way about. He should have set his sights on someone like her sister, Lynne, someone able to accept help from people who cared for her, someone who didn't believe her ego was at stake if a friend intervened on her behalf.

Maybe Lynne wasn't the sort of woman he wanted, either. Lynne, after all, was about to divorce a husband who'd kept her wrapped in protective padding for too long.

The sort of woman Tom needed was one who, while intelligent and independent, didn't feel she had to prove her strength at every opportunity. He needed a woman who didn't think that leaning on the man in her life now and then meant she was an evolutionary throwback, who didn't think that if the man in her life actually *wanted* to be leaned on now and then he was an unreconstructed sexist. Tom needed a woman secure enough in her own femininity not to be threatened by the fact that some men had an innate tendency toward chivalrousness.

He needed a woman like Penny Simpson.

The thought so startled him that he almost veered off the road. Taking a deep breath, he tightened his grip on the steering wheel and paid stricter attention to the lane markings illuminated by his headlights. Once the idea had lodged in his brain, however, he couldn't dismiss it. He worked it over, weighing and measuring it, dissecting it in search of the truth.

Penny had been terrific, no argument there. She'd been the ideal high school girlfriend: pretty and bright, energetic and completely devoted to him. She'd shared her thoughts with him, and her dreams—dreams that, unfortunately, didn't coincide with his. She'd explored sex with him, nervous but willing, teaching him and simultaneously learning from him. With time and practice, they'd eventually gotten the hang of it. They'd enjoyed each other a great deal. She'd been so pure and soft and obliging, and he'd done his best to please her.

But nothing he'd ever done with Penny came close to exciting him as much as kissing Jodie had.

"Damn," he groaned, then let loose with a few more pungent curses. It made no sense that such an exasperating, stubborn woman could turn him on so powerfully. Merely thinking about her exasperated him—and turned him on all over again so intensely, he nearly swerved off the road once more.

He imagined himself returning to Carroll for his high school reunion. "Well, no, I'm not married yet," he'd tell Jay and Danny and the other guys over glasses of too-sweet punch, "but I'm seeing this fantastic woman. She dresses strangely, and she's kind of flat-chested, and her hair's too short, and she's just about the most beautiful lady I've ever met. She's got an amazing job, too: liberating housewives by teaching them how to resuscitate crushed carpet piles."

Or even better, he'd bring Jodie to Iowa with him. "Pozz-nee-ack," she'd introduce herself. "It's Serbo-Croatian." He had no idea what her ethnic background was, but Carroll didn't have too many residents with last names like Posniak. She'd be wearing a miniskirt, of course, and kelly-green stockings and phosphorescent shoes and earrings shaped like Porsches. The guys would all gape at her, and the girls... Tom laughed out loud at the picture his mind conjured. The girls would all gather around this exotic woman from New York via Southern California, and they'd say, "But, Jodie, I've tried everything to clean the stain from my linoleum floor," or "So tell me, Jodie, what's the secret to making no-stir spaghetti?" or "You know, Jodie, if you take that home-made Play-doh recipe of yours and add a little food coloring, it resembles the store-bought stuff even more!"

They'd love her. Except for Penny Simpson. Penny would probably eye her with a combination of be-musement and shock. "You've changed, Tom," she'd say. "Good Lord, but you've changed."

It was close to ten o'clock when he finally pulled into his reserved parking space in the basement garage of his apartment building. He called a greeting to the night guard, then entered the elevator and rode up to his floor. Unlocking the door, he suffered a transient pang of disappointment at his solitude. How much nicer it would have been if Jodie were standing beside him now, brimming with anticipation, eager to race down the hall to the bedroom, directly to the bed, into Tom's loving arms.

As soon as he'd locked up behind him, he hurried into the kitchen to phone her. He wasn't going to pressure her, he promised himself. He wasn't going to make her feel rotten about having turned down his invitation to spend the night with him. He was just going to telephone her, to tell her he was glad she hadn't said no to their relationship, and then he'd wish her a good-night.

He'd already lifted the receiver before he remembered that she had an unlisted telephone number and she had never given it to him.

It occurred to him, after he expelled another ripe series of expletives, that Jodie was having a corrosive effect on his vocabulary. Resolving not to curse anymore, he dialed Jerome DeLucca's number. "Jerome?" he said as soon as his colleague answered. "Did I wake you up?"

"Nah," Jerome assured him. "I love staying up late on a school night. Reliving my rebellious youth."

Tom rewarded Jerome with a polite laugh. "Listen, Jerome—just a quick favor. You don't happen to have Lynne Duryea's telephone number at home, do you?"

"I've probably got it in my briefcase," Jerome answered. "Convince me it's worth getting out of this leather recliner and schlepping all the way to the study to get it."

"I need to talk to her sister," Tom said.

"The grapes," Jerome recollected with a chuckle. "That sister of hers was something, wasn't she? I'd love to see her in a skirt someday."

You wouldn't be disappointed, Tom thought, momentarily visualizing Jodie's spectacular legs. Then he berated himself for allowing Jerome to discuss Jodie's anatomy, no matter how flatteringly. "Have you got her phone number?" he asked impassively.

"Hey, come on," Jerome criticized him. "Just because you sent me her sister for a client doesn't mean I'm free to hand out said client's telephone number. Give me a reason, Tom."

I think I'm in love with Jodie, Tom tried out, then shook his head. *I'm crazy about her legs.* No good. "I'm concerned about the woman's safety," he said truthfully. "She's being harassed by some kook. I want to make sure she's all right."

"No kidding? Is there a suit in it?"

"If there is, I'm sure she'll let me know. Be a pal, Jerome. Give me the number."

"Hang on."

Tom waited for a minute, listening to static on the line until Jerome returned with the number. Tom wrote it down, thanked Jerome and hung up. Then he dialed Jodie's house.

"Hello?"

He hadn't expected the sound of her husky, sleepy voice to have such a profound effect on him. It aroused him more than physically; it aroused his concern. He thought about her in that drafty old farmhouse on that remote, winding road, surrounded by two vulnerable children and her helpless sister.

"Are you all right?" he asked.

"Tom?"

"Yes. I just got home and I—" He sighed. She must think he was nuts, calling her like this. "I was thinking of you."

"Oh." She fell silent for a moment, then said, "Well, if you want to know the truth, I was thinking of you, too."

"Good things, I hope."

"Good things."

He smiled. Jodie didn't play games, and she didn't say anything she didn't mean. Someday—someday soon—she would work out whatever was bothering her. She would relax and accept him. He would extend his hand and she would take it without qualms.

"I had a wonderful time tonight," he said.

"Even though I blew it at the end?" She muttered something unintelligible, then laughed bleakly. "I sure have a way of doing that when I'm with you."

"You didn't blow it," he argued. "If you'd blown it, do you think I would have called you?"

"Thank you," she said, and he could almost hear her smile in her words.

"Listen, it's late, so I won't keep you. I just wanted to say hello and make sure you're all right—"

"All right?"

"Safe and sound," he said, apprehension creeping into his voice. He should have done this differently. He should have whispered that he wanted to hear her voice before he got into bed so he could spend the night spinning erotic fantasies about her in his dreams.

But he didn't play games any more than she did. He'd called because he wanted to remind her that he was close by if she needed him. He wanted her to know that, no matter where they were sleeping tonight, he was in her life and she could count on him.

"I'm safe and sound," she said coolly.

"I'm glad."

"That makes two of us. Good night, Tom."

"Good night."

He lowered the phone into its cradle, severing the connection. Then he permitted himself one last therapeutic curse. Who was it who said the road to hell was paved with good intentions? Wherever hell was, Jodie Posniak's everlasting resentment couldn't be far from it, because every time he gave vent to his concern, he seemed to be laying another paving stone into place.

Chapter Seven

Even on the best of mornings, Jodie would not have been in the mood to change a tire. And this wasn't a good morning.

The previous night had been a sleepless one. She'd lain awake for hours, kicking the sheets, punching the pillows and castigating herself for having sent Tom home alone. He had been the only bright spot in a wretched day. In his company she had been able to forget about the fact that a loony-tune was out to get her. She'd been able to banish all thoughts of the letter she'd received from some wacky lady in Laramie who claimed that pleated shades were the handiwork of Satan himself, and the missive from some clown in Tallahassee who suggested that the best way to cope with household drudgery was to reward oneself with a shot of whisky upon the successful completion of each chore.

After Jodie had endured a mail bag full of similarly cuckoo letters, a half hour of messy experimentation involving an egg slicer and fresh mushrooms, and a blood-sweat-and-tears effort to get her column written and faxed to the syndication company before deadline—to say nothing of chauffeuring her sister to Jerome DeLucca's office and back, committing herself to the payment of what would no doubt be a humongous legal bill and arriving at her office to discover Officers Ludwig and Rodriguez and a dead skunk waiting for her—Tom's presence on her front porch when she'd finally gotten home had worked on her raw nerves like a salve, calming her, charming her, illustrating the old saw about dark clouds with silver linings.

Yet she was positive she'd done the right thing in not spending the night with him. She couldn't even consider becoming intimate with him when she wasn't sure what their relationship was based on. If there was anything old-fashioned about Jodie, it was her unshakable belief that two people ought to love each other before they made love.

Or so she reassured herself time and again during her night-long battle with insomnia. But then she would roll onto her side and reshape the pillows—and she would be inundated with the absolute certainty that she did love Tom. And if she loved him, what on the earth was she doing all by herself in bed? Why wasn't she with him?

Maybe he didn't love her. Even if he did, his love undoubtedly arose from the wrong things. If she had gone to his apartment with him, he would probably have destroyed all the romance by praising her for her sensibility in letting him shelter her from the "Penny-Wise" crackpot and conferring upon him total responsibility for her safety. He would have commended her sound judgment and assured her that the situation was fully in hand—his hand. He would have approved of her decision.

She didn't want his approval. She wanted his love.

And what did she get? A flat tire.

She had spent the better part of the night eating herself up over Tom. She wasn't going to spend the morning dwelling on him, too—especially not when she was uncomfortably drowsy and her front left tire was so low her car looked almost as if it were kneeling in the driveway.

Groaning through a yawn, she tossed her purse onto the seat and loped back up the walk to the porch. Through the screen door she hollered, "Lynne? Do me a favor—call Helen at the office and tell her I'm going to be late again today."

"Why? What's up?" Lynne asked, stepping into the front hall from the kitchen, where she'd been fixing the children breakfast.

"I've got a flat tire. I've got to change it and then go to a service station to have the damned thing fixed. Tell Helen I'll be in as soon as I can."

"You can't change a tire dressed like that," Lynne scolded.

Jodie glanced down at her outfit—a short white skirt, a black-and-white striped cotton T-shirt, summerweight gray-tinted hose and her bright red espadrilles. Granted, a white skirt wasn't the most practical attire for working on one's car. But she didn't want to use up valuable time switching her outfit. "It's all machine washable," she told her sister. "Who knows better than Penny Simpson how to launder grease and grime?"

Lynne appeared dubious. "Are you sure you don't want to call the garage and have them send someone over?"

"To change a tire?" Jodie snorted and started back down the front walk to the driveway. "I'm not going to shell out forty bucks an hour for something that simple—let alone sit around here waiting for half the

morning until a repairman arrives. I can do it myself."
Even when I'm half asleep and in a lousy mood, she
grumbled silently.

Lynne's face registered awe at her sister's expertise.
Lynne didn't know the first thing about automobile
maintenance. Hank had always taken care of her car for
her, and she had never bothered to learn how to check
the oil or add windshield-washer fluid. Jodie wanted to
teach her, but Lynne kept protesting that any such
instruction would be wasted on her—she was helpless
when it came to mechanical things.

Helpless was the word for it, all right. Jodie hoisted
her full-size spare out of the trunk, grunting under the
weight. She'd made it a point to master the skills of
automobile maintenance. She didn't want to have to
depend on some man to keep her car running for her.

It didn't take her long to attach the spare. Before
heaving the flat tire into her trunk she examined it
closely, but she found no punctures, no protruding nails
or shards of glass imbedded in the treads. Frowning, she
bolted the tire into the well, slammed the trunk shut and
headed for the local gas station.

"I don't know, lady," the mechanic told her a few
minutes later, once she emerged from the gas station rest
room where she'd gone to scrub the dirt from her hands.
"I can't find anything to fix here."

"What do you mean? The tire was flat."

"I know that," the young man said, guiding her
through the cluttered repair bays to a semicircular tub
of water that stood near the far wall. "I filled her up
with air and I can't find a leak. Come on, I'll show
you." He lifted the reinflated tire into the tub and rotated it in the water, searching for a stream of bubbles.

Jodie searched, too. The filthy water splashed with the movement of the tire but produced no telltale bubbles. The mechanic turned the tire slowly, pausing after each turn and watching the water. He took the tire through two complete revolutions; Jodie kept track by monitoring the air valve.

The air valve. If the tire hadn't been punctured, then someone must have deliberately let the air out.

No. Jodie was not going to get paranoid. "Spin it one more time," she requested, gesturing toward the tire in the tub. "There's got to be a hole somewhere."

"All right," the mechanic yielded, starting another rotation, "but I don't think we're gonna find anything. There's nothing wrong with this tire that I can see."

"Not even something that could cause a slow leak?" she asked with faint hope. "A defect around the valve stem or something?"

He shook his head and turned the tire in the tub. "We'd get bubbles from that," he noted. "Only thing I can figure is, someone tampered with the valve. You got any enemies?"

She wanted to throttle the man for having verbalized her deepest fear. "No," she said much too quickly. "I haven't. It was probably vandalism."

"Maybe," he allowed. "Just some random mischief or something."

She drove out of the gas station after paying the mechanic for his effort and merged with the sluggish traffic on the main route cutting through town. Refusing to think about the tire, she steered aggressively from lane to lane, weaving past slow-moving cars whenever she spotted an opening, stomping on the brake and the gas pedal, cursing at every vehicle that dared to cross her path. At a red light she skidded slightly trying to stop; as soon as the light turned green she lurched ahead, heedless of the car in the lane next to hers and of the disapproval the driver expressed with a resounding blast of his horn.

She didn't care what the other drivers thought. She was late for work, her desk was piled high with paperwork demanding her attention and her lab was crowded with nearly new slow cookers the consumer-testing people upstairs had donated to her kitchen. Helen was without doubt pacing the hall impatiently, and who knew what animal corpse might be bestowed upon them today?

Don't think, she reproached herself. *Don't think about it.* But it was too late. Her eyes filled with tears, blurring her vision so badly she had to pull off the road. A sob overcame her, and another one. She buried her face in her hands and wept.

The flat tire wasn't what upset her, any more than the skunk had upset her, or the nasty letter. What twisted her gut with sheer fright was the realization that if all three incidents were connected, whoever was perpetrating this campaign against her had somehow managed to learn her unlisted address. Some maniac from Philadelphia had traveled to Orangeburg and found out first where Jodie worked and then where she lived. Even at home she wasn't safe.

Oh, God, she wished Tom were here!

Startled that she would even think such a thing, she straightened up, opened her eyes and swabbed her damp cheeks with her palms. What on earth was wrong with her? If she was going to wish that Tom were here, it ought to be because she appreciated his company, not because she was falling apart. She *wasn't* falling apart. She wasn't going to let herself.

What she was going to do was analyze her situation logically and take control of it. She was going to cope. She was going to face down her dread without any help from anyone.

An insane "Penny-Wise" fan couldn't possibly have found where Jodie lived, she reasoned. Her flat tire could have been caused by a defective air valve or some teenage hell-raisers. Tonight after work she would contact a few of the neighbors and find out if anyone besides her had been victimized.

There was absolutely no link between the tire and the dead skunk. Jodie had no cause for fear.

Or perhaps one cause, she amended as she restarted the engine and eased back onto the road. In her moment of crisis, as despair seized her, she had cried out for Tom. She'd wanted him to be with her, to make it better. She'd fallen apart, let herself become weak, yearned for someone to take over and put everything to rights. Not just anyone—she'd wanted a strong, warm man, a pillar of strength and a stalwart protector.

She'd wanted Tom Barrett.

And that was a damned good reason to be frightened.

"TOM?" LILIAN'S VOICE CRACKLED through the intercom on his desk.

Tom glanced up from the partnership contract the hapless John Huddleston had entered into when he'd purchased shares in the ill-fated Newark tenement venture. On occasion Tom found himself wondering whether he would have done as well attending a Berlitz language workshop as law school; it frequently seemed as if his work as an attorney entailed nothing more significant than translating obfuscating texts and contractual jargon into straightforward English so he could figure out what the heck his clients had gotten themselves into.

Ordinarily, he would whip through a contract like this one in no time flat. Ordinarily, however, he was working on a full eight hours of beauty rest followed by an invigorating jog, a brisk shower and a healthful breakfast.

That morning, however, after an uncharacteristic bout of restlessness, he'd overslept and had to skip his sunrise run through the park. He'd rushed his shower, nicked his chin while shaving and faced his bagel with an utter lack of appetite. As a result, his brain seemed foggy and unable to focus. His thoughts kept straying from the contract, flying like homing pigeons straight to Jodie.

He meditated on her dark, lovely eyes, her silky hair, the way she'd shivered with pleasure when he ran his finger behind her ear...the way he longed to touch her, to please her all over. And then he meditated on how badly he'd botched things with her and how aggravating it was that he could botch things simply by letting her know he cared, by extending a helping hand. If she was going to be so absurdly stubborn about her independence, he might as well give up all hope for a relationship with her.

Yet, if she was going to be so wildly responsive to him, so sensual and sensitive and downright alluring, he couldn't stop hoping.

With a sigh, he pressed the button on his intercom box. "Yes, Lilian?"

"Your mother's on the phone," his secretary reported. "And you sound like you could use another cup of coffee. You aren't having a relapse of the flu, are you?"

"No," he said, clearing his throat. If he sounded that bad to his secretary, his mother was sure to think he sounded even worse. She would chastise him in proper maternal fashion for not taking better care of himself; heaven help him, she might even offer to come to New York and whip him into shape.

"I'm okay, Lilian," he assured his secretary. "I'll pass on the coffee, thanks." After clearing his throat again, he lifted the telephone receiver and said, with as much vigor as he could muster, "Hi, Mom."

"Hello, Tommy." In public she generally remembered to call him Tom, but privately she still resorted to his little-boy nickname. He didn't mind; it made her happy. "How is everything?" she asked.

"Fine. I'm up to my ears in work," he added pointedly. "What's up?"

"I was wondering if you got the invitation to your high school class reunion that I sent along."

"It arrived yesterday, thank you."

"Are you planning to come?"

"I'd like to," he told her, "but I've got to see if I can fit it into my schedule. My calendar's really packed these days."

"You work too hard," his mother complained, although he detected a strain of pride in her voice. "Would the world come to an end if you took a Friday off and enjoyed a three-day weekend here?"

"I can take *a* Friday off," he distinguished. "The question is whether I can take that particular Friday off. I'll call you as soon as I know one way or the other."

"Well, listen, Tommy—I don't want to take up too much of your time, but I had some news I thought you should know about."

He drummed his fingers on the polished surface of his desk. He was always interested in hearing news about Carroll, but not in the middle of a hectic work day. His mother knew how busy things were at the office and she usually saved her chatty telephone calls for the weekends, when he wasn't under so much pressure.

"I ran into Harriet Simpson at the market yesterday," said his mother.

Tom didn't respond immediately. Carroll wasn't so large a metropolis that a chance meeting between Penny Simpson's mother and his own should be noteworthy enough for a long-distance call during business hours.

"You know, Tommy, Harriet and I have always maintained a cordial relationship," his mother went on.

"Of course," he said quickly. Conversing with his ex-girlfriend's mother on the checkout line didn't constitute a breach of loyalty on his mother's part.

"Well, we got to talking, Tommy. She said Penny's going to be at the reunion."

"Great." He glanced at his watch and then at the contract spread across his desk, demanding his attention.

"Tommy—it's just that I thought you should know. Harriet told me she'd divorced."

"Harriet Simpson's divorced?" He wondered why his mother thought he should know that. "I'm sorry to hear it, Mom, but—"

"Not Harriet. Penny. Penny and Roger Slater. They separated over a year ago. Harriet wasn't telling anybody, I guess because there was always the chance they might patch things up. Evidently they didn't.''

"Penny," he repeated, his mind suddenly sharpening. "She's divorced?"

"Yes. Thank the good Lord there are no children involved, that's what Harriet said. She told me they were trying for several years and Penny never conceived. But Harriet said it's for the best, given how things turned out. It was never a good marriage. Penny didn't know him long when they got married, and . . . well, now this is Harriet talking, Tommy, but she said the marriage was doomed from day one because Penny never really got over you."

"Never got over me?" He suffered an irrational surge of anger. "I didn't break up with her, for crying out loud. She left me."

"She was a young, foolish girl," his mother observed. "Now she's nursing regrets. Anyway, I thought this was something you ought to be aware of before you came out here and saw her at the reunion. The reunion committee is planning a really nice party, from the sounds of it. They wrote up some details in the paper— they're going to have a band and an open bar and a midnight buffet. It sounds like it's going to be very nice."

"I'm sure it will be," he mumbled.

"Well, I'll let you get back to work. Give me a call as soon as you've got your plans worked out. If you can make a three-day weekend out of it, you know Granny and Grampa would love to see you."

"I'd love to see them, too."

"Just let me know when you're coming."

"I will. Goodbye, Mom."

"Take care of yourself, Tommy—you sound kind of run-down. Are you getting enough sleep?"

"Sure," he fibbed. "I'll call you soon, Mom. So long."

A full minute after he'd hung up, he was still staring at the bookshelves lining the wall across the room from where he sat—staring without seeing them. Staring through the dizzying swirl of emotion that crowded his brain.

Penny was divorced. She'd never gotten over him, and now she was divorced. In one month's time, if he could arrange his calendar to accommodate a long weekend, he would see Penny at his class reunion. He would see her with the knowledge that she'd never gotten over him, with the awareness that she was fifteen years older and wiser—and available.

He felt something, but he wasn't sure precisely what it was. He tried to figure it out through the process of elimination. Revenge? No, he felt no vindictive glee over the demise of Penny's marriage. As he'd told Jodie last night, he had observed too many divorce cases to wish such misery on anyone.

Excitement? No, not really. He visualized Penny in her youthful schoolgirl incarnation, a pastel, soft-focus image of feminine beauty. Seeing her at the reunion next month might somehow lead to something exciting, but he felt no particular thrill before the fact. No matter how pretty she was in his memory, he could reminisce about her in the present and feel none of the electrifying passion he'd felt last night when he'd kissed Jodie.

Curiosity? Sure, that was part of it. Curiosity and nostalgia, and . . . well, not exactly revenge but a distant relative. When Penny laid eyes on him, she would see that he'd aged well, that he was still in shape, that, if anything, he'd improved over the years. He knew how to dress now, he had his hair cut professionally and he understood the nuances of style. He was a Harvard man—whatever that was worth in Carroll—and a partner in a successful Manhattan law firm, and he had a prestigious address and a prestigious car.

Usually the trappings of power meant little to Tom. But suddenly, when he thought of seeing Penny Simpson at the reunion, the phrase *I'll show her* flashed with neon brightness inside his skull. *I'll show her what I've made of my life. I'll show her what she turned her back on. I'll show her what she could have had, if only she'd stuck by me.*

It wasn't a particularly generous sentiment, but Tom was too honest with himself to deny what he was feeling. There had been times, while he'd still been in school, when his hurt and bitterness over Penny Simpson had pumped through him like fuel, motivating him to try harder, to achieve more. *I'll show her,* he'd sworn while applying for a position on the *Law Review. I'll show her,* when he'd chosen to sign on with Black, DeLucca over a smaller, less illustrious law firm. *I'll show her how much I can accomplish without her.*

Now, for the first time since she'd ended their relationship, he actually had the opportunity to show her. It was a dream come true, being able to swoop down on his sleepy hometown village and dazzle the girl who had left him high and dry. He ought to be overjoyed.

Instead, he felt disoriented and uneasy. He wasn't sure he wanted to show Penny anything. Quite the contrary, he wanted her to show him something: how much he used to treasure docility in a woman, how much he used to welcome her acquiescence, how wonderful he used to feel when she gazed up at him with those innocent blue eyes of hers and say, "You decide, Tom. You take care of it, Tom. Whatever you say."

He *did* use to like that. He used to like feeling indispensable and heroic. But now, fifteen years later...he wanted Jodie.

Why was he obsessed by a tall, slim woman with an angular face, a pixie hairdo and a feisty personality? Why, without much apparent effort, was Jodie capable of sending his hormones—and his mind—into a frenzy? Why did he prefer yesterday evening's fantasy of bringing her to Iowa with him over his long-lived fantasy of coming face-to-face with Penny Simpson and saying, "I showed you, didn't I?"

Why, of all the women in the universe, did his heart insist that he wanted to be Jodie Posniak's hero?

"PENNY-WISE, MAY I HELP YOU?" said Jodie's secretary.

It was four o'clock. Considering how much time he'd devoted to thinking about Jodie, Tom was proud of himself for having waited so long before telephoning her. Another couple of hours' work lay ahead of him before he would be able to call it quits for the day, but he deserved a break. More than that, he desperately wanted to talk to Jodie.

"This is Tom Barrett," he identified himself. "May I speak to Jodie Posniak?"

"One moment, please."

He was put on hold for a few seconds and then Jodie came on the line. "Hello, Tom."

She sounded as weary as he felt, but he decided not to comment on it. "Hi. How are you?"

"Oh, just fine."

Her artificially cheerful tone implied that she was lying. He wanted to flatter himself with the thought that, if she wasn't fine, it was because she was tormented by desire for him. But the likelihood was far greater that she was tormented by a dead skunk. "Have you had—" he began, then stifled himself. If he started badgering her with questions about her problem, she'd probably hang up on him.

"Have I had what?"

"A chance to catch up on your work," he improvised. "I know you were really snowed under yesterday."

She laughed. "I'll never catch up," she said with spurious dismay. "Someone wrote asking how to keep mattress covers in position and I've been manipulating strips of Velcro all morning. Then I had lunch with my lawyer—"

"What lawyer?" he asked, suffering an unjustifiable twinge of jealousy.

"I told you—I'm being sued for damages by some idiot because her soufflé collapsed. The woman's nuts, Tom. She decided to increase the damages she's demanding. I didn't know you could do that after a suit's been filed."

"It's not general practice," Tom confirmed. "Are there extenuating circumstances?"

"The only extenuating circumstance is she's obnoxious. Her lawyer told my lawyer she's determined to make me pay, one way or another. What the hell is that supposed to mean? Sometimes I forget this whole thing is over a soufflé."

"People tend to get worked up," Tom noted. "Particularly when they're armed with legal representation."

"Legal representation," Jodie snorted. "If you want my opinion, the woman's a prime candidate for the funny farm."

Tom reflected for a minute. He didn't want to upset Jodie, but she *was* being badgered by a demented reader, after all. "Have you told the police about her?" he asked.

"Told them what? That I'm the subject of a lawsuit? They'd enter me into their files if I did."

"You're already in their files," Tom said, realizing at once that that wasn't a particularly consoling thing to say. "What I meant was, you might mention this woman to them as a possible suspect in the skunk matter."

Jodie was silent for a moment. "That's an idea," she conceded, surprising him with her compliance. "I'll fill them in on her. I'd love to get her off my back. My lawyer's been saying I ought to consider letting the syndication company settle with her."

"Mm-hmm."

"What's your opinion, Tom? Do you think it's a smart idea to settle with her?"

"Well..." Although loath to interfere in another attorney's case, Tom was delighted that Jodie would turn to him for advice. "Is the syndication company interested in a settlement?"

"I think so. They're the ones who hired this lawyer, after all."

"Generally speaking, negotiating something out of court is more expeditious than a protracted trial. When you figure out what a full-scale trial would cost—"

"But what about the principle at stake?" Jodie argued. "If word gets out that we settled with this pest, everybody and her aunt will be suing me every time one of my columns has a typographical error in it.''

''You might be able to negotiate the terms of the settlement so word can't get out,'' he counseled. ''Include a secrecy clause in the agreement.''

''I don't know,'' Jodie muttered. ''It still doesn't seem right to me. I mean, the principle of the thing...''

Much as he admired her ethical stance, Tom couldn't shake the understanding that Jodie's adherence to principles over reality bordered on fanaticism. If she were a bit more pragmatic, she would pick her fights more carefully. She'd settle with this pest and solve the problem of the physical harassment in the bargain. Self-reliance was a noble principle, but staying alive was better.

''I don't know....'' She sighed. ''I told the lawyer I'd think it over. I'm too frazzled to deal with it today.''

''Oh?'' *Because of me?* he thought optimistically. *Because you tossed and turned all night over me, the way I did over you?*

''I started off my morning with a flat tire and got to work late again.''

''Oh.'' He tried not to feel disappointed. ''You weren't hurt, were you?''

''No. It wasn't a high-speed blowout or anything. Just a hassle. Every day it's something. Not that I believe in astrology, but sometimes I wonder whether the planets are out of alignment.''

''People get flat tires all the time, no matter where the planets are.''

''I suppose.''

''Maybe I could cheer you up by taking you out to dinner,'' he said, checking his watch. He could handle a late dinner with her—or he could come to the office a couple of hours early tomorrow and catch up on his work. He would gladly rearrange his life around a dinner date with Jodie.

"Tonight?"

"I know it's short notice," he apologized.

"Oh, Tom..." She sighed again. "I'd really like to. I mean that."

"But...?"

"I'm so backed up. First I lost time with the tire, and then I killed two hours with the lawyer. The man wouldn't stop talking."

"We lawyers can be that way sometimes."

"Can we have dinner another time?" she asked, gratifying him immensely. Her words proved that she wasn't simply inventing excuses or slamming the door on their friendship.

"How about Saturday night?"

"As far as I know, that should be fine."

"I'll see you then," he said happily. If Saturday night went well, perhaps it would extend into Sunday. Perhaps, away from her work for the weekend, Jodie would forget her reasons for resenting and resisting Tom. Perhaps he could lure her to New York for the day. They could go to the park or take in a museum or a movie. They could go someplace luxurious for dinner, and afterward...

"I've really got to get back to work," she said, breaking into his daydreams before they ran amok. "As soon as I finish with the Velcro, I'm going to dabble with a new recipe for fried banana chips. If they come out well, I'll make a batch for you."

"Thanks," he mumbled, not terribly enthused by the prospect. "I should get back to work, too. I'll call you tomorrow."

"Okay. Goodbye, Tom."

He wound up remaining at his desk for three more hours. The longer he worked, the more tired he would be when he finally got home—and the less time he'd have to spend wandering aimlessly around his apartment, wishing Jodie were with him. Knowing that she had reserved her Saturday night for him revived his spirits and boosted his energy level. He whipped through the contract, taking copious notes on the most questionable clauses, and then reviewed his client's deposition and took more notes. When, shortly after seven, he turned off the light and emerged from his office, the only sign of life at Black, DeLucca was the purr of a vacuum cleaner down the hall in the law library, where the cleaning staff began their overnight labor.

June evenings exemplified Manhattan at its best, Tom thought, as he left the office building and headed uptown. The air was mild, warm but not humid, and the people thronging the sidewalks were outdoors by choice, taking relaxing strolls or rejuvenating jogs, browsing along the shop windows or sipping tall drinks beneath the umbrellas shading the outdoor tables of sidewalk cafés. Perhaps, he ruminated, he would take Jodie to one of the al fresco cafés instead of some swanky upscale restaurant. They'd gaze at each other across a pretty candlelit table, oblivious of the pedestrians ambling past them and the waiters circulating with their trays. Their eyes would meet and Jodie would murmur, "I trust you, Tom. I know you won't take over my life. You just want to be a part of it—and I want that, too."

Saturday night would be wonderful. In retrospect, he was relieved that she'd declined his invitation for dinner tonight. As she'd said, she was frazzled. He himself was wiped out. But on Saturday, well distanced from the stress of their jobs, they could ignore everything but each other.

Grinning at the sheer promise of such a night, he sauntered through the lobby of his apartment building, slowing only to pick up his mail, and then rode upstairs to his floor. He arrived at his apartment, shoved the key into the lock and heard through the door the muffled sound of his telephone ringing.

Maybe it was Jodie, he thought happily, jiggling the key and shoving the door open. Maybe Jodie was calling for no other reason than that she wanted to hear his voice one more time before the day ended.

Or maybe it was his mother. His joy flagged slightly at the notion. He enjoyed talking to his mother, but the memory of her call earlier that day was still fresh. He didn't want to talk about Penny Simpson, her divorce, her current single status or the odds that he would see her in Iowa. He didn't want to think about her at all.

Hurrying into the kitchen, he grabbed the phone. "Hello?"

His wish was answered. "Tom," said Jodie, then let out a strange, agonized sound. "Tom?"

His heart began to race. "Jodie? What happened? Are you all right?"

She began to sob. "Tom? I'm scared, I'm so scared—"

"Tell me what happened."

She lapsed into silence for a moment. When she finally spoke, her voice was hoarse but no longer tremulous. "I'm okay, Tom. Really. I'm okay. It's just... I'm a little bit shaken up, that's all."

"What happened?" he demanded.

"Somebody tried to bomb my house."

Chapter Eight

"Why didn't you tell me?" Lynne railed.

Jodie stared through the window at Sergeant Ludwig, who stood on her front porch taking photographs of the black scars seared into the planks. The damage the explosive had done to the porch was minimal—some sanding and a fresh coat of paint would conceal the charred patches. The damage it had done to Jodie's psyche, however, wasn't.

Sergeant Ludwig had called the bomb "a small incendiary device." Peter had called it a cherry bomb and said that such firecrackers were frequently used by teenagers to blow up garbage cans. Sergeant Ludwig had explained that this sort of bomb had relatively low heat and small range. Peter had explained that this sort of bomb made a really awesome bang.

Jodie's eyes shifted from the police officer to the driveway. She was anxious to leave, but she couldn't until Sergeant Ludwig was done collecting evidence and Lynne and the children were safely on their way to Helen's apartment. Jodie wanted to be with Tom, right now, this instant. She wanted to be with him so badly her longing frightened her as much as the bomb had.

She shouldn't have telephoned him. When Sergeant Ludwig had advised her and Lynne to clear out of the house for the night, she should have agreed to go with the others to Helen's. Helen lived in a one-bedroom apartment, but she'd assured Jodie that as long as nobody minded waiting in line to use the toilet, they were all welcome to stay with her.

"My sister and Peter and Sarah will stay with you," Jodie had resolved.

"Jodie," Helen had reproached, "not to be an alarmist, but *you're* the target, not your sister and her children. If anyone should leave your house for the night, it's you."

"Don't worry about me," Jodie had said. "You haven't got room for me, anyway. If you put Lynne on your living room couch and the kids in sleeping bags on the floor, where would I go? In the bathtub?"

"You'd be safer there than in your house," Helen had countered. "Wherever you spend the night, Jodie, it had better not be at your home. You've got to take this seriously. The flat tire, and now this—this bomb! If I have to drag you bodily out of your house—"

"You don't," Jodie had said. She had no intention of staying home alone, waiting for her next encounter with the lunatic who had greeted her that morning by bleeding her tire of air and now was firing small incendiary devices onto her porch. But she wasn't going to let Helen know how terrified she was. "I'll find somewhere else to stay, I promise. I appreciate your hospitality in putting Lynne and the children up, but I can't ask you for anything more."

"You aren't asking," Helen had said firmly. "I'm offering."

"And I'm thanking you from the bottom of my heart. But I tend to get kind of itchy when I've got to wait in line to use the toilet. I'll impose on someone else."

She'd called Tom back. He had been the first person she'd phoned after the police, and he'd pleaded with her to come to New York. She'd demurred then, but after Sergeant Ludwig had inspected the porch, heard about her mysterious flat tire and factored in the skunk and the letter she'd received from Philadelphia, he had recommended that she and her relatives stay somewhere else until the culprit was found. "The perpetrator knows where you live, Ms. Posniak," the officer had pointed out. "That alone is reason enough for you to find someplace else to live for a while."

Jodie didn't want to become an exile. She didn't want to go into hiding. However, her desire to stay alive was stronger than her aversion to laying low. "I'm not doing this because I'm scared," she'd claimed, yielding to Sergeant Ludwig's advice with great reluctance and less-than-total honesty.

She *was* scared—more than scared. When she'd heard the cherry bomb's blast through the open kitchen windows, she had shrieked, let the plate she'd been washing slide out of her hands and shatter on the floor and raced hysterically up the stairs screaming, "Get the kids! Get the kids and run!" Halfway up the stairs she'd heard Sarah crying and Peter cursing so colorfully that, under other circumstances, his mother would probably have slapped his face.

"Why didn't you tell me about the skunk?" Lynne scolded Jodie now.

"I didn't want to worry you," Jodie said limply. She felt weak and shaky. More than resenting her tormentor for shifting the site of her assault to Jodie's house, Jodie resented the creep for having depleted her of courage and self-confidence. She kept trying to throw up a shield of strength, but it kept slipping. She lacked the strength to pretend she wasn't afraid.

"Well, all I can say is, I'm glad you've got Tom to take care of you," Lynne scolded. "You apparently can't take care of yourself."

"Thanks a heap," Jodie snapped. "In case you haven't noticed, Lynne, I've been taking care of myself for years—and lately I've been taking care of you, too."

"What do you think, you're invincible? You think just because your alter-ego, Penny Simpson, isn't defeated by soap scum you can't be defeated by anything, either?"

"I *can* be defeated. I have been," Jodie conceded in a tremulous voice. "I called Tom, didn't I? I asked him to rescue me."

"Forgive me for eavesdropping, Jodie, but you told him you were going to drive down to New York for the evening. You wouldn't even let him come up here and get you."

"Because if he came to Orangeburg to pick me up, I wouldn't have my car with me. He would have to drive me all the way back here in the morning so I could get to work."

"He must have been willing to do that. You and he were arguing about it for a while."

"Because he was being silly," Jodie explained, hoping she didn't sound as querulous as she felt. "Saying he would drive up here to get me was very nice of him, but it wasn't practical. If he had to drive me back to Orangeburg tomorrow he wouldn't get to his own office until ten o'clock or later. Or else I'd have to take a commuter train in the morning, which would mean I'd have to wake up at the crack of dawn. Thanks but no thanks. I can drive myself to the city and back."

"Assuming all your tires have air in them," Lynne muttered under her breath. "I swear, Jodie, you are the most stubborn person in the world."

"This shouldn't be news to you," Jodie retorted. "You've known me for thirty-one years."

"That's right. And you haven't matured much since day one."

Jodie tried not to take her sister's insult to heart. Lynne was upset and not thinking straight, and Jodie herself was too distraught about her situation to waste energy being annoyed about her sister's foul temper. They were both under too much stress; whatever criticisms they lodged against each other today would be forgotten as soon as Lynne's divorce was finalized and Jodie's harasser was caught.

The sheer terror that had darkened her mind like a layer of storm clouds didn't start to break up until ten minutes later, when she waved off Sergeant Ludwig and her sister and climbed into her car. For the first few miles of her drive she glanced continuously, almost obsessively, at the reflections in her rearview mirror, checking to see whether she was being followed. Not until some time after she got onto the Palisades Parkway did she finally begin to unwind.

Whoever is doing this doesn't want to hurt you. Sergeant Ludwig had made that observation before he left, and Jodie clung to his reassuring words, rolling them over and over in her mind. His rationale was that anyone who could throw a firecracker onto her porch could have just as easily thrown a Molotov cocktail there, something that would have set her house on fire. For that matter, he'd explained, given the unfortunate accessibility of guns in contemporary society, the perpetrator could have shot at her through the open kitchen window if the goal had been to kill her. Her prominent position made her a juicy target, Sergeant Ludwig had conjectured. Look at the guy who achieved fame by shooting at President Reagan or that other guy who'd gone after John Lennon.

"Yeah," Jodie had grumbled sullenly. "Reagan nearly died, and John Lennon did die."

Sergeant Ludwig had reassured her of the point he was trying to make, which was that famous people tended to attract the attention of nuts. "Can you think of anyone specific who might have it in for you?" he'd asked. "Anyone with a grudge?"

Jodie had told him about the reader who was suing her over the soufflé. "So far she's gone through legal channels," Jodie noted. "She's filed a suit. She's also vowed revenge, though."

Sergeant Ludwig wrote down her name. "Would she have access to your home address?"

"Through her lawyer she might," Jodie had confirmed. "But she lives in Arlington, Virginia. The original letter that started this whole thing was postmarked Philadelphia."

"Which may or may not prove anything," Sergeant Ludwig had contended. "Philadelphia isn't so far out of the way for someone traveling from D.C. to New York. She could have mailed the letter en route. Or she could have had someone mail it for her. So could anyone else. For all you know, that letter may have been written in Vermont, or Arizona, or Minnesota. This woman is definitely worth checking out. Can you think of anyone else who might want to take revenge on you?''

"I have so many crazy readers," Jodie had said sadly.

"Anyone who isn't a reader? A relative, perhaps?"

Jodie had snorted. "I wouldn't win any popularity contests in my family, but I don't think any of my relatives would want to bomb me. My brother-in-law is kind of ticked off at me at the moment, but he's more angry at Lynne. This campaign is directed at me, not at her."

Sergeant Ludwig had nodded. "I'm going to talk to some of your neighbors," he'd said, "to see if someone might have noticed any suspicious activity near your house this evening, or last night when your car's tire was fooled with. You take care of yourself, and keep in touch."

Jodie had thanked him and wished him luck. Her community was fairly rural, the houses set well back from the serpentine road, tucked behind ancient trees and brambly hedges. Jodie got along well with her neighbors, but it wasn't the sort of place where people could wave to each other from their windows or holler a greeting over a fence. Numerous cars cruised by at night; given the road's fiendish twists and bends, few drivers other than Jodie navigated it at high speed. No one would give much thought to a car slowing down to a crawl near her driveway, which met the road in the middle of a treacherous S-shaped curve.

Still, she appreciated Sergeant Ludwig's efforts. She wanted the perpetrator nailed. It didn't matter that she hadn't been hurt physically—the emotional injury was real and painful. Feeling vulnerable and impotent was like losing a piece of her soul.

She sighed, checked her mirror one last time and decided that the cars sharing the parkway with her looked innocuous. Relaxing her death grip on the steering wheel, she turned on the radio to a soft-rock station, hummed a few bars of "You've Got A Friend" along with Carole King and then snapped the radio off, impatient with the lyrics. All that stuff about leaning on a pal when times were rough.... Now that she was no longer in a panic over what she'd left behind she couldn't seem to keep herself from panicking over what lay ahead.

She prayed for Tom not to misconstrue her visit. She doubted that he would view her arrival as a belated acceptance of his invitation to spend the night in his bed. She was in about as unromantic a mood as possible. Her nostrils still held the faint burning stench left behind by the bomb, which wasn't much of an improvement over the stench of the skunk. Her head ached and her brief interlude of frenzied shrieking right after the damned thing had exploded had rendered her throat raw and irritated. Several times during the policeman's interview she'd felt on the verge of throwing up, and although she'd managed to keep her supper down, she couldn't imagine ever wanting to eat again. She supposed she wouldn't object to a comforting hug from Tom, but if he so much as kissed her...

No, he wouldn't. He was too sensitive to make a pass at her when she was so obviously a basket case. What concerned her was that he would say something like "I told you so," or "There, there, Jodie, I'll take care of everything," or "It's about time you came to your senses and let a man handle this." If he did, if he so much as intimated any of those things, she would hate him forever.

When he'd given her directions to his building, he had instructed her to drive directly into the basement garage rather than to waste time searching for a parking space on the street. By the time she'd navigated through Manhattan's dense crosstown traffic, she was grateful for the suggestion. She couldn't have coped with a lengthy quest for a parking space after everything else she'd been through that day.

She coasted to a halt inside the garage door and turned to the glassed-in office built against one wall. She spotted Tom in the office, waiting with the garage attendant. He was dressed in casual cotton trousers and a sports shirt, and he stared intently through the windowed wall. His hair was mussed, as if he'd raked his fingers through it innumerable times, and his expression was grim. As soon as he saw her his mouth softened into a smile.

He preceded the attendant out of the office and jogged around the front of her car to her door. "Jodie," he said with impressive calm as he opened her door and helped her out. "Have you got a bag?"

"In the back seat," she said, gesturing toward the overnight bag she'd brought with her. She was relieved that Tom hadn't swamped her with an emotional greeting. If he had conveyed either passion or paternalistic concern, she probably would have turned around and driven right back to Orangeburg.

Tom removed her bag from the seat, shut the door and took her hand. Without a word, he led her through the garage to an inner door, and from there down a basement corridor to the elevator. Once they were inside and riding up, she leaned against the wall and closed her eyes.

"Tired?" he asked.

She opened her eyes and nodded. "Among other things," she said with a bleak laugh.

He scrutinized her in the elevator's bright light. It dawned on her that she hadn't checked her appearance since she'd fled her house. She still had on the striped T-shirt, white skirt and red espadrilles she'd worn all day, but what little makeup she'd applied that morning must have faded hours ago, and she'd packed her hairbrush without bothering to fix her hair first. Closing her eyes again, she tried to recall which earrings she was wearing, but she couldn't remember.

"I bet I look like hell," she groaned.

"On you, hell looks terrific," said Tom. "You do look kind of wiped out, though. Was it a difficult drive?"

She shrugged.

He slid his arm around her shoulders and gave her a light, friendly squeeze. "This is my floor," he announced, ushering her out of the elevator and down the hall. He unlocked a door and led her inside.

She took a moment to assess her surroundings. The decor of his living room was much more elegant than she had expected. Plush midnight-blue carpeting spread at her feet, and sleek pale furnishings filled the airy room. The vertical blinds had been left open to reveal a panorama of sparkling lights beyond the window. Somewhere out there was the East River; she remembered his telling her he had a river view.

She wasn't so much startled by the fact that he was rich—she'd already figured out that he was—but by the fact that his apartment was so swanky. Tom Barrett had never struck her as a particularly swanky person. He dressed tastefully, but there was nothing ostentatious about him.

His apartment wasn't ostentatious, either, she admitted. It really was beautiful. But it was so...so daunting.

"Can I get you something to drink?" he asked, guiding her to the L-shaped sofa.

"Thanks," she said with a small nod. She lowered herself onto the cushions and discovered they were much more comfortable than they looked. She watched him stroll through a doorway into the kitchen, then gazed around the room again. One wall was filled with modernistic built-in shelves holding a stereo system and a couple of small abstract sculptures. The glass table in front of her held a carved marble ashtray. Jodie had never seen Tom smoke, and the ashtray was spotless. Pretty though it was, it seemed more like the sort of object a decorator would advise a client to display than something Tom would be likely to use.

He returned to the living room carrying a small snifter filled with amber fluid. He sat beside Jodie and handed her the glass. "What is it?" she asked, eyeing the beverage dubiously.

"Sherry."

"I don't like sherry." But she took a sip, anyway. It tasted strange and dry, but it felt good going down. She took another sip.

Tom watched her. His legs were spread and he rested his forearms across his knees. He seemed oddly satisfied that she'd tasted the drink in spite of her objection. His eyes glowed and his lips curved in a grin of approval.

"I need a coaster," she said, not wishing to leave rings on his fancy glass table.

He glanced at the table, then shrugged. "I haven't got a coaster," he admitted. "Just put it down. I don't care."

"Tom—it's going to stain the table."

"I put glasses down on it all the time, and I don't see any stains."

"But still—"

"Don't turn into Penny Simpson on me," he teased, prying the glass from her hands and placing it defiantly on the table.

"I wasn't being Penny Simpson," she protested as she leaned back into the upholstery and surveyed the room one last time. "It's just that this place is so...so glamorous."

"Glamorous?" He laughed.

"It is, Tom. This carpet has to be top-of-the-line. I ought to know; I've done tons of research on carpet restoration, and this—"

"Jodie." He gathered her hand in his and closed his fingers around it. "I don't want to talk about the carpet, okay? Tell me how you are."

"I'm fine," she declared fervently, hoping to forestall any further analysis of her condition.

He looked away, sorting his thoughts. She suspected he wasn't thrilled by her statement. He probably wanted to hear her say she was devastated, so he could heal her wounds and be her champion. She couldn't say that, though. She was anxious, and she might have been devastated when she'd first telephoned him, but she wasn't devastated anymore. And even if she were, she thought crossly, she certainly would never admit it to him.

"What are the police doing?" he finally asked.

"They collected all the little pieces of the cherry bomb and took pictures of the damage. They're going to question my neighbors. I think their chief suspect at the moment is that lady who's suing me."

"Mmm." Tom contemplated for a minute, then nodded. "She sounds like their best shot."

"They plan to pursue every lead," she said. "They'll check out the flat tire—"

"The flat tire? What does that have to do with it?"

"Oh..." She sighed. "It may have gotten flat because someone deliberately let the air out. And before you start ranting and raving, Tom, let me assure you I've told the police everything there is to tell about that, too. The letter, the skunk, everything. I'm sure they'll figure it all out soon," she concluded in an impassive voice.

Tom eyed her, his expression one of gentle reproach. "I'm sure they'll figure it out, too," he agreed. "But that doesn't mean you're barred from getting a little emotional about it."

"It doesn't mean I *have* to get emotional, either," she shot back. "I hate to disappoint you, Tom, but I'm just fine."

"Jodie." He tugged gently on her hand, easing her closer. For a frantic moment she wondered whether he was going to attempt to seduce her, but he only arched his arm around her and urged her head against his shoulder. "Relax," he murmured, his tone low and lulling. "If you don't want to cry, that's all right, but you might feel better if you do. It isn't a sin to fall apart."

"I don't want to fall apart," Jodie moaned, realizing even as she spoke that the choice wasn't hers to make. Her eyes brimmed with tears, just as they had that morning when she'd left the gas station with the understanding that her flat tire had probably been the result of sabotage. A sob filled her throat, and she didn't bother to suppress it. Just for now, for a few seconds, snug within the shelter of Tom's embrace, she would cry.

He held her close, massaging the knotted muscles at the base of her neck and absorbing the tiny tremors that racked her shoulders. His only motivation seemed to be to comfort her. She vaguely recalled that his gentleness had proven a remarkably effective weapon the night they'd sat talking on her front porch. But he wasn't plying his gentleness in order to arouse her now. He was simply letting her be spineless and sloppy for a few minutes, without passing judgment or taking advantage of her weakness. He was making it easy for her to fall apart, and all her claims to the contrary, she *did* want to fall apart, just a little, just for a while.

Eventually her tears were spent. The physical effort of crying had exhausted what little energy she'd had left, and she sagged against him and let out a weary sigh. He brushed his lips over the crown of her head, then loosened his hold on her. "I'm glad you're here," he said.

"I'll bet you are," she muttered, a hint of her fighting spirit returning.

"Oh?"

"You're probably thinking, 'It's about time she got knocked down a peg and came a-runnin'.'"

"No," he asserted, digging a linen handkerchief out of his pocket and handing it to her. "What I'm thinking is, it's about time you trusted me."

•She dried her eyes and handed him back the handkerchief. His gaze was steady and sincere, his smile modest. She detected nothing smug about him, no I-told-you-so gleam in his eyes, no I-dare-you-to-deny-it tilt to his chin.

"I trust you," she whispered.

"Good." He kissed her brow again. "You really look beat. Would you like to get some rest?"

A tiny flicker of suspicion flared up inside her, then faded. The truth was, she felt as beat as she looked. "What's the plan?" she asked.

He chuckled, clearly able to translate her question. "The bedroom's all yours if you want it. I can sleep in here. Part of this couch opens up into a bed."

She suffered a pang of embarrassment—not because he'd alluded, however obliquely, to sex, but because he was so incredibly trustworthy. She felt guilty for having suspected him of anything improper. "I don't want to kick you out of your own bed," she mumbled, eyeing the couch.

He weighed her words. "Whatever you'd like—it's up to you," he said, then stood and helped her to her feet. "I'm not ready to go to sleep yet, anyway."

"I'll stay up if you want," she said.

He smiled and shook his head. "You should get some rest. Don't worry about me. I'll just watch some TV or something." Grabbing her overnight bag on the way, he started down the hall with her.

His bedroom, like the rest of the apartment, was elegantly decorated. Here the floor-to-ceiling drapes were drawn shut and the carpet was a muted tan color. The furniture was simple oak and the queen-size bed was made with patterned beige-and-blue sheets and a matching summer-weight comforter. It looked so inviting, Jodie dropped onto the edge of the mattress, kicked off her shoes and stretched out. She nestled her head into the pillow and sighed. "This feel great," she said, peering sleepily up at Tom.

He set down the suitcase and moved to adjust the bedside lamp. "Do you want me to turn this off?"

"I don't care. Leave it on. I'll have to get up eventually to wash."

"All right." He switched the lamp to its dimmest setting, then brushed a few stray tufts of hair from her brow and straightened up. "Anything else I can get you?"

"Would you—" She bit her lip and stared up at him. He looked so tall and strong looming above the bed. Running her gaze the length of him, she took in his disheveled sandy-blond hair, his sweet smile, the chest that had cushioned her as she'd wept, the large, graceful hands that had comforted her in spite of her avowed desire not to be comforted. Her gaze continued down his torso to his waist and his trim hips. He had a spectacular build. Yet lying in his bedroom, on his bed, with him standing so close to her...

She wasn't aroused. Or rather, she *was* aroused, but not in the usual way. Her body was awash in the precious warmth of trusting him, knowing that she'd found a safe haven with him and—as he'd put it—that seeking a safe haven wasn't a sin. Turning to him for this one night during the crisis didn't mean she had relinquished her identity as a self-sufficient woman.

"Would you hold me?" she asked in a small, shy voice. If wanting to be held meant she was irredeemably dependent, so be it. Just for now, until she drifted off to sleep or found the energy to wash her face and put on her nightgown, she wanted Tom's arms around her.

He smiled and lowered himself to sit beside her. After pulling off his shoes, he swung his legs up onto the bed and rested his head on the pillow next to hers. Then he gathered her into his arms.

She had been wise to ask. She needed him right now. She needed the strength of his embrace, the warmth of his chest against her cheek, the lulling rhythm of his breathing against her hair. It didn't mean she was needy, she hastened to reassure herself. It meant only that she was human.

She savored his nearness. His legs lined hers and his insteps cushioned her toes. He twirled his fingers aimlessly through her hair and she shut her eyes, drifting into a tranquil reverie, someplace far away from Orangeburg, from "Penny-Wise." Although awake and conscious, she wasn't completely sure where she was—except that she knew she was safe here, secure and content and free.

"Tom?" she whispered, leaning back into his hands and opening her eyes.

His face was inches from hers. His glittering eyes probed hers, waiting.

She wasn't sure what she wanted to say. She wasn't sure she wanted to say anything at all. What she was sure of was that she was enormously glad to be with him tonight—and that was something she could tell him without words.

Timidly, she shifted her head until her lips met his. It was a tentative kiss and he returned it hesitantly, watching her, measuring her reaction to the light contact of his mouth with hers. When she retreated he pursued, initiating the next kiss, twining his fingers into her hair so she couldn't retreat again. He caressed her lips with his, slowly, tenderly, then paused and loosened his hold on her, giving her the chance to stop him.

She didn't. She returned his unwavering gaze, supplying a tacit answer to his silent question. He stared at her, his chest rising and sinking as he breathed, his fingers moving through her hair, along the crease of her earlobe and down to the nape of her neck. He held back for an instant longer, then yielded to her unspoken request by easing her onto her back and descending to kiss her again.

There was nothing hesitant in this kiss. His tongue skimmed along the seal of her lips, coaxing them apart, and then lunged deep into her mouth. She gasped, less from surprise than from relief, the liberating relief of loving Tom and accepting his love.

She lifted her hands to his shoulders and traced their sinewy breadth. Never had anything felt so right—or so inevitable. Welcoming Tom into her heart endowed her with a confidence and courage much greater than what she'd experienced when she'd been resisting him, running from him, fearing his ability to deprive her of those very things.

She wanted to tell him, but she couldn't speak when his mouth was doing such marvelous things to hers. Instead, she slid her hands down his back, feeling its supple contours through the fabric of his shirt. When she reached the waistband of his slacks she tugged at his shirttail, untucking it. She pressed her palms against the small of his back and he groaned.

He raised his head and gazed down at her. He appeared about to speak, but the seductive motions of her fingers against the warm, smooth skin of his back seemed to rob him of the ability to talk. Groaning again, he sketched a line with his finger down the slope of her cheek to her chin, beneath it to her throat and then further, traversing the vivid stripes of her shirt until he reached her breast. He cupped his hand around the modest swell, shaping his palm to it, kneading it with his fingertips until her body responded elsewhere, everywhere. Her throat tightened, her breath caught, her heart pounded and a luscious heat gathered within the cradle of her hips.

She sighed, digging her fingertips into his back and holding him close. He continued to caress her, moving his thumb with wicked precision over her nipple until she couldn't bear the layers of clothing separating his hand from her skin. She sat up and reached for the edge of her shirt.

Nudging her hands away, Tom pulled the shirt over her head. Then he guided her back down to the pillow and touched his lips to the hollow of her throat. He nibbled a meandering path down to her collarbone, down further to the soft, pale skin above the lacy edge of her bra. She groped for the clasp and snapped it open, drawing the wispy fabric out of his way.

He grazed across her breast, gliding his lips and then his tongue over the rosy peak at its center, teasing it with his teeth and then closing his mouth around it, sucking so gently Jodie nearly began to weep again. For a brief, dazed moment she believed nothing could ever feel as good as this, and then Tom proved her wrong by shifting his mouth to her other breast and sliding his hand down across her belly, over her skirt to her knee. As his mouth performed its magic on her breast, his fingers explored her leg. He traced the oval of her kneecap through the sheer nylon, journeyed briefly down her shin, then returned to her knee and continued past it to her thigh, pushing her skirt up as he went.

At the top of her leg he halted. His hand was strong and warm against her, agonizingly close. He stopped kissing her and rested his cheek against her breast, breathing deeply.

She hoped he'd paused only to finish undressing her and himself. Fumbling with the front of his shirt, she tore frantically at the buttons, unfastening them and sliding her hands across his chest. With a roll of his shoulders he freed himself from the sleeves and tossed the shirt aside. Her touch seemed to energize him; he attacked the buckle of his belt with a purposefulness that aroused her as much as his kisses had.

She wanted to help him, but she couldn't bring herself to stop caressing his chest. It was magnificently proportioned, streamlined and athletic, adorned with a delectable dusting of gold-tinged curls. She played her fingers over his ribs, up his sides and under his arms, then down again to the firmly muscled surface of his stomach, to the now-unbuckled belt, the open zipper, the white cotton briefs stretched tight over his aroused flesh.

As her hand brushed fleetingly over the elastic of his shorts he stiffened, his struggle for control visible in the tensing of his jaw, the glazing of his eyes. He turned away from her to remove his clothes, then dispensed with her skirt, sliding it down her legs along with her stockings and panties. At last he rose onto her, settling within the welcoming circle of her arms. He set his hand loose along the surface of her thigh, her hip, her waist and arm until he reached her cheek. He stroked upward to her temple, into her hair, and guided her mouth to his.

The glorious feel of his body upon hers had primed her for this kiss. When his tongue drove against hers she arched upward, offering herself fully to him, hungry for him. Every pore in her body seemed open to him, every nerve receptive. Every sensation she experienced bore his imprint. Every beat of her heart spoke of Tom, of love, of the sweet, hollow ache of wanting him.

His aroused flesh surged against her, tantalizing her with his nearness. She cried out softly, half in joy and half in frustration. Inching back, he made room for his hand, stroking her, entering and then stroking again, playing over her moist flesh until she was desperate for him. She brought her hand between their bodies as well, forcing him to share her blissful torment.

He wove his fingers through hers and pulled her hand away. Then he fitted himself to her, his legs parting hers, his body seeking, filling her, fusing with her. As she tensed around him, he drew his hands to her face, framing it and grazing her lips with his.

She wrapped her arms around him and held him deep within her. When he withdrew she moaned, but he stifled her protest with another kiss. Then he penetrated her again, thrusting deeper, feeding the blazing pressure within her. She closed her eyes, bewitched by the fluxing tension that increased with each plunging motion of his hips. She accepted his tempo, first slow and then faster, compelling her toward a pinnacle and then beyond it.

She soared, carried aloft on joyous energy, her body pulsing in time with her heart, beating in ecstasy and love. Above her Tom groaned, a deep, guttural sound of exhilaration and satisfaction. Then lassitude overtook him and he sank down onto her. Struggling for breath, he nuzzled her throat and sighed.

Minutes passed. Jodie's hands drifted down his back, his skin damp with perspiration. He raised his head and studied her face. He looked worried. "Jodie," he whispered hoarsely. "I know you didn't come here for—"

"If you're going to apologize, don't." Feeling his body slacken, she molded her hands to his hips and held him inside her. She didn't want to lose him, not now, not when her body was still tingling in the resplendent aftermath of his love.

He remained where he was, shifting his hips to accommodate her. The mere motion seemed to ignite something inside her, and she held her breath, waiting in astonishment as her body grew unbearably tense all over again.

Tom moved against her, delivering her to another peak. She gasped and trembled beneath him, closing her eyes as her body was overwhelmed by a fresh cascade of blissful pulses. "Oh, God," she moaned, tightening her arms around him and pulling him down to her. "Don't apologize, Tom."

His low, rumbling laughter tickled her ear. "All right," he conceded. "I won't."

Slowly, carefully, he disengaged from her. She stared at him, glassy-eyed in the wake of what she'd just lived through. She had never known intimacy could be like this, so intense, so unspeakably beautiful. "I think I'm in love," she murmured, rolling onto her side so she could face him.

"You're just hot for my body."

She knew he was joking, but she was too moved to respond in kind. "No, Tom. You're the sweetest, kindest—"

"Oh, please!" He cut her off. "You make me sound like a Boy Scout."

"I bet you were a Boy Scout," she said. He'd grown up in a small, wholesome midwestern town, after all. As an adult, he was still eager to help others. She could easily picture him as a polite tow-headed youngster, standing up to the school bully and winning a merit badge for his efforts.

"Four-H," he corrected her. "Until my father died and we moved. How about you? Were you a Brownie?"

Jodie wrinkled her nose. "In Southern California? Are you kidding? I was knocking myself out trying to be cool. Being a Brownie wasn't cool."

"You would have looked great in a Brownie beanie," he teased, ruffling his fingers through her hair. "I doubt they would have let you wear little silver fish skeletons on your earlobes, though."

She plucked at her earrings, removing them, and tossed them onto the night table. "There," she said. "Now can I be a Brownie?"

Tom leaned toward her and gave her a long, loving kiss. "You can be anything you want," he murmured. He started to kiss her again, but the ringing of the telephone interrupted him. Groaning, he reached over Jodie and lifted the receiver on the bedside phone. "Hello...? Oh, hello, Lynne. Yes, as a matter fact, she's right here." He passed the receiver to Jodie and mouthed, "Your sister."

Thank heaven the telecommunications industry hadn't yet perfected the video-phone, Jodie thought with a twinge of embarrassment. What would Lynne think if she saw Jodie sprawled out naked alongside the equally naked, breathtakingly male body of Tom Barrett?

Lynne would probably congratulate her—and issue a few nagging warnings about how Jodie should be less stubborn and let Tom make a fuss over her safety.

Sighing, she lifted the receiver to her ear. "Hi, Lynne. What's up? Has Helen kicked you out?"

"Oh, no," Lynne swore, a nervous edge to her tone. "Helen has been so generous. It took us a while to get the kids to quiet down, they were so keyed up. And Sarah accidentally broke a Lladro figurine Helen had on display. She said it cost eighty-five dollars. I know it'll take a while for me to pay her back, but—"

"I'll pay her," Jodie said, not wanting to ruin her mood by listening to Lynne fret over nonsense. "You can owe me. What's another eighty-five dollars, right?"

"Well...that's not why I'm calling, Jodie. It's partly that I wanted to make sure you're all right."

"Never been better," Jodie assured her, wondering if her sister could guess how true that was.

"That's good, Jodie."

"And? What's the other part?"

"Well...it's that I can't reach Hank. I've tried calling him three times, and he isn't home."

Jodie rolled her eyes. "Big deal. What do you care where he is?"

Lynne didn't answer right away. "Peter and Sarah are his children, Jodie, and since we're not at your house I thought he should know where they are. I mean, he has a right to know where his children are, doesn't he?"

"Why does he have that right? He obviously doesn't tell you where he is. Why should you tell him where you are?"

"Well, that's just it," Lynne muttered. "I'm thinking maybe he's spending the night at someone's house. A woman's house, Jodie. I think he has another woman."

Jodie wouldn't put it past him. "So? There's one more good reason to divorce him."

"That's the thing," Lynne explained. "If he's having an affair with someone else, he can't very well say I'm an unfit mother and demand custody of the kids, can he?"

"No, he can't," Jodie agreed, eager to end the call. "Why don't you talk to Mr. DeLucca about this? But remember, just because Hank's not answering the phone tonight doesn't mean he's fooling around with another woman. He could be at a friend's house watching a ball game on TV. Or maybe there's a problem with the telephone line."

"I know, I know. But I just have this gut feeling. I think he's with another woman."

Jodie exhaled. "I wish I could talk you through this, Lynne, but it's late and you're running up a long-distance bill on Helen's phone. We'll discuss it tomorrow, okay?"

"You're definitely coming back to Orangeburg?"

"Of course I am. I've got a job, remember?" *Where do you think the eighty-five dollars to pay for the damned Lladro figurine is going to come from?* she said to herself.

"Okay. I'll try to stay calm about this. We'll talk tomorrow."

"Fine. Good night, Lynne." Jodie twisted and set the receiver into place.

"Another crisis?" Tom asked.

Jodie sighed, her impatience tempered with guilt. "Nothing that couldn't wait. She's so helpless, sometimes. I shouldn't be short with her. I really should try to be more compassionate. She's got two kids and no money, and now she thinks her husband is committing adultery. I feel so sorry for her, Tom—but I can't help thinking she'd brought it on herself. Why doesn't she just stand up to the jerk? Why doesn't she tell him to shove it and go get herself a job, if that's what she wants?"

"Because she isn't as strong as you," Tom pointed out, enveloping her in his arms. "You're right, Jodie—you should try to be more compassionate. You're lucky to be as strong as you are."

She snuggled up to him, absorbing the cozy warmth of his body. She was, indeed, lucky—for much more than her strength. Tonight, on this day when her car and her house had been violated, when someone had crossed the line from being a petty nuisance to endangering the lives of Jodie's loved ones, when not once but twice she'd dissolved in tears of rage and fear. . . .

She'd never felt luckier than she felt right now.

Chapter Nine

"Go back to sleep," he whispered.

Jodie stretched, blinked and struggled to focus her eyes. The room was awash in the faint pink light of dawn filtering through the drapes. The bed linens felt smooth and soft against her skin. She was neither awake nor asleep but in some peaceful world of contentment in between.

Gravity pulled her toward the edge of the bed where Tom sat putting on his running shoes. He wore a pair of athletic shorts, a loose-fitting tank top and white cotton socks. Once his sneakers were tied, he crossed the room to the dresser, pulled a five-dollar bill from his wallet and pocketed his keys. Jodie tried not to ogle his limber, leanly muscled legs, the rugged breadth of his shoulders, the slim contours of his hips, the clean symmetry of his face. His jaw was darkened by an overnight growth of beard. That stubble had rubbed her skin raw more than once during the night—and it scratched her again when he returned to the bed, leaned over and kissed her.

"What time is it?" she asked groggily.

"Six o'clock. Go back to sleep, Jodie. I'll be back in about an hour." One more kiss, and he straightened up and strode out of the room.

Yawning, she rolled onto her side, hiked the blanket up to her nose and closed her eyes. Her mind filled with an image of Tom jogging, his tendons flexing and his chest pumping, his body sleek with sweat. Similar to how he'd looked making love, she realized. The thought was enough to cause a voluptuous warmth to swell deep within her, a sweet echo of the wonders they had shared last night.

No question about it, she loved him. Not so much because of his prowess and tenderness in bed but because of the way he smiled afterward, the pleasure he took in bringing her pleasure. Because of his immeasurable generosity.

His generosity out of bed, too. He had accepted her into his home last night, welcoming her even after she'd given him grief for so long about how she didn't want his help. He hadn't criticized her, hadn't stood in judgment of her. He had simply been there, ready for her, willing to give her whatever she was willing to take. Without demanding an apology, he'd forgiven her for having refused his generosity for so long.

How could she not love him?

Although she wasn't sure she could bend for Tom, as Lynne had advised her to, Jodie would do her damnedest to be flexible. She swore to herself that she would try not to view his every offer of assistance as a threat to her integrity. He knew who she was; he knew her capabilities. He wasn't aiming to control her, to dominate her or sap her of strength. He only wanted to be a part of her life. She wanted that, too, more than anything.

The bed wasn't as comfortable without him in it, and after a while she grew bored lying awake under the blanket. She rose, made the bed in an uncharacteristic display of neatness and then headed for the bathroom to take a shower. She returned to the bedroom and put on the tailored slacks and blouse she'd brought with her, then folded up the previous day's outfit and packed it into her suitcase.

Thinking about having to return to her own house depressed her—and her depression had nothing to do with cherry bombs or flat tires. She wanted to stay with Tom, that was all. She wanted to be able to hang her clothes in one of his bedroom's roomy closets and leave her hairbrush on the burnished oak dresser when she was done fixing her hair. She wanted to see the top of his night table strewn with all her weird earrings, not just the fish-skeleton ones. She wanted to be as much a part of Tom's life as he was of hers.

Could she ever feel at home in an apartment like this, though? she wondered as she left the bedroom for the palatial living room with its sumptuous carpet and its million-dollar view. In the morning light she could easily see the river; it sparkled with glints of silver as its ripples reflected the sun, which had climbed above the skyline of Roosevelt Island to the east. Below her, York Avenue was a picture of tranquillity—a few dog walkers and joggers, but none of the hustle and bustle of pedestrians or the automobile traffic that would clog the road an hour from now. It was a fabulous view, posh in the extreme.

Jodie had nothing against affluence. She'd grown up in a comfortably upper-middle-class environment—of all the things her parents quarreled about, money had never been a prime subject. She earned an ample income from her column. While she wasn't extravagant, she didn't have to count pennies, either.

But poshness was something else. She couldn't figure out how a down-to-earth, milk-fed country boy like Tom fit into an opulent environment like this.

Maybe she was underestimating him. Maybe he presented himself as a good ol' son of the soil to her, while deep in his heart he was actually a hard-nosed wheeler-dealer, a suave city sophisticate. Maybe he truly had a taste for the better things in life—designer furniture and pricy knickknacks, marble ashtrays and all the rest. Maybe, after his hick-town upbringing and his father's death, he felt he had to prove something.

Disconcerted, she wandered to the kitchen, which shared the living room's gorgeous view of the East River as well as a glimpse of the 59th Street Bridge a mile to the south. Her gaze skimmed the sunny white-tiled room, with its tidy counters and spotless appliances: the two-door refrigerator—a luxury in city apartments—the built-in microwave, the wall oven and the double-basin sink with its European-style enamel-trimmed faucets.

Above the doorway hung a wall clock. Quarter to seven. He would be back soon.

A coffee maker stood on a counter, and she poked through the cabinets in search of coffee and filters. His shelves were nearly empty—for someone with a gourmet kitchen, he certainly didn't stock much food. As a bachelor, she supposed, he wouldn't be likely to prepare fancy dinners for himself on a regular basis. But if that were the case, why did he rent an apartment with a state-of-the-art kitchen?

If he rented. For all she knew, this might be a co-op or a condominium. Tom might own the place outright. He might be even richer than she suspected.

Given how little there was in his cabinets, she found
the coffee without too much difficulty. She set up the
coffee maker and turned it on, then crossed to the
breakfast table and sat. She stared out the window until the brightening sunlight began to hurt her eyes, then
turned her attention to the small pile of correspon-
dence occupying one corner of the table. Not wanting
to snoop, she shifted her gaze away, but not before the
mimeographed sheet of paper on the top of the pile
registered on her. It featured a pen-and-ink rendering of
a banner with CARROLL H.S. printed in block letters
on it, accompanied by the heading Bring Back That Old
School Spirit!

Amused by the corny message, she lifted the paper
and perused the small print at the bottom. It was an
invitation to the fifteenth-year reunion of Tom's high
school class. The time, date and place were listed, along
with the message, *If you think your classmates have
forgotten you, you're wrong. If you think we'd love to
hear what you're doing with your life, you're right.
Come to Carroll and celebrate our "Glory Days"—and
the thousands of glory days we've enjoyed since grad-
uation. Meet old friends and make new friends. Remember the past and strengthen our bonds for the
future.*

Glory days, Jodie thought with a snort. She wondered if her old high school class even held reunions; if
it did, her parents had never sent along any mimeographed invitations to her. They knew Jodie would have
no interest in returning to the scene of her adolescent
misery, not even to show all her former classmates how
well she'd turned out as an adult. Sure, she admitted, it
might be fun for a couple of minutes to show off to
them, to let them see that the chunky, clunky weirdo

who'd had to coerce a cousin into taking her to the
senior prom had matured into a reasonably appealing
lady—ten pounds thinner and not bad looking, bright
and confident and proudly independent. It might be fun
to let them know that, no thanks to them, she'd turned
out just fine. Not that she'd ever seriously consider returning to her hometown for a class party, but it might
be fun to reveal to all those people who used to think of
her as a loser that she was, in fact, a nationally famous
syndicated columnist.

Penny Simpson.

A frown creased Jodie's brow as she reread the invitation to Tom's high school reunion. Surely he didn't
want to return to his hometown to show everyone he
wasn't a loser. He couldn't have been a loser at his high
school. On the contrary, he must have been a star, the
kid voted "Most Likely to Succeed," the bright, good-
looking, hard-working golden boy who'd gone East and
made a killing. His classmates must have assumed even
then that he would wind up accomplishing great things
with his life. His return to Carroll would only confirm
what everyone could have easily predicted fifteen years
ago. Tom Barrett must have been a winner from the day
he was born. He didn't have to prove anything to anyone.

Except Penny Simpson.

She had jilted him. She'd hurt him badly enough that
a dozen years later he still hadn't completely resolved his
feelings for her. If he had, he would never have come to
Orangeburg looking for Jodie. But he had come, not
merely because of curiosity, as he'd said, and not because she'd responded to his letter with a thoughtful
note, but because he hadn't yet recovered fully from
what Penny Simpson had done to him.

Wasn't living well supposed to be the best revenge? How better to get back at the girl who'd done him wrong than by rubbing her nose in everything she'd rejected when she rejected him? The exclusive address, the prestigious job, the nifty import car. . . .

Sure, he would want to go back to Iowa to meet old friends and tell them about his rewarding career and his upscale life-style. Sure, he'd love to go to Carroll and tell one specific old friend about the glory he'd experienced in the years since she'd broken his heart.

Tom wanted to prove something, all right. And Jodie wasn't at all sure how she felt about it.

SOME MORNINGS JOGGING WAS A CHORE, tedious and fatiguing. Some mornings his shoes felt like leaden weights on his feet, his chest ached with every breath and the only thing that propelled him onward was the knowledge that the faster he ran the sooner he would be home again, his self-imposed torture ended for another day.

Today, however, jogging was a delight. His feet barely skimmed the ground; his heart pounded in sync with the pumping of his lungs. What propelled him onward was the knowledge that when he got home Jodie would be there, waiting for him.

He flew along the walkway in the park bordering the river, his senses keenly attuned to his surroundings. He inhaled the briny scent of the water; he turned his face to the sun and listened to the whisper of the breeze created by his own body as it pushed forward through the stagnant morning air. An elderly woman taking a dachshund for a walk smiled at Tom as he passed her; he shouted over his shoulder that he hoped she'd have a terrific day. The world was a wonderful place. Life was great.

His thoughts wandered to the woman responsible for his ebullient mood. Reliving the previous night in his imagination made his breath grow ragged in a way his jogging hadn't. He reminisced about Jodie's velvety soft skin, her delectably long legs wrapped around him, the dark warmth of her body absorbing him, surrounding him, stealing his soul. He shouldn't relive such moments in his mind when he was outdoors in a public park, he thought, as his body tensed in reaction to his erotic thoughts. Certainly not when he needed to concentrate his energy on the challenge of getting himself back home before seven o'clock.

If he had skipped his jog he would have been home now—maybe making love with Jodie again. He could have found other, more exciting ways to get his morning workout. But Jodie had still been slumbering when he'd gotten out of bed and he hadn't wanted to disturb her.

Last night was only a beginning, anyway. They didn't have to break any records. They could spend a lifetime of nights in each other's arms if destiny—and Jodie—allowed it.

Around the block from his building he stopped at the bakery to buy some croissants. Panting, he walked the rest of the way home, pleased with the pace he'd maintained during his workout. He ought to be able to shower, dress and sit down to breakfast with Jodie by seven-thirty, and then he would use what little time they had together for breakfast to persuade her to come back to the city tonight.

He didn't want to have to alarm her with reminders about the nasty business at her house. He hoped that by the time she arrived in Orangeburg today the police would have figured out who had been threatening her and taken the creep into custody. Tom wanted Jodie in his bed because she chose to be there, not because she was frightened.

He waved to the doorman and sauntered through the lobby to the elevator. As soon as the door slid open at his floor he bolted out and hurried down the hall. He unlocked his door, opened it and was greeted by the aroma of fresh coffee.

Grinning, he followed the smell to the kitchen. Jodie was seated in the breakfast nook, attired in dressy slacks and a stylish orange silk blouse that looked spectacular on her despite the fact that it clashed with her red espadrilles. Her hands were folded in front of her on the table and her eyes were fixed on the doorway, as if she had been watching for him.

At his entrance, she smiled mysteriously. He wanted to believe she was as thrilled to see him as he was to see her, but judging by her strange, inscrutable expression, he couldn't be sure.

"The coffee smells delicious," he said.

She nodded and forced her smile wider. "I won't pour it until you've washed up." Her tone was low, constrained.

What had happened? Why were her beautiful brown eyes shadowed with confusion? Why was her smile so enigmatic, her hands so rigid on the table? Why hadn't she leaped out of her chair and raced into his arms? Why did she seem so pensive, so distant? Why didn't she look as joyful as he felt—or as he *had* felt until he'd seen her?

She must find him repulsive, what with his hair wind-tangled, his cheeks bristly and his body dripping with sweat. He couldn't blame her for not wanting to hug him until he was showered and shaved.

"I'll just be a few minutes," he promised, returning her smile with an equally artificial one of his own. "I stopped at the neighborhood bakery on my way home, so..." Setting the bag of croissants on the counter, he gave her what he hoped was a reassuring look and left the kitchen.

In his bedroom, he stripped off his sticky clothes and tossed them into the laundry hamper. Then he grabbed his robe and hastened to the bathroom. As he showered he tried to analyze Jodie's peculiar mood. Perhaps she'd received another frantic telephone call from her sister that morning. Or perhaps the Orangeburg Police Department had called to inform her that another vicious prank had occurred at her house overnight. Perhaps whatever was bugging her had nothing to do with Tom personally.

If only he could believe that. The odds were just as good that Jodie was entertaining second thoughts about him. Perhaps his little joke about how she was hot for his body had cut close to the truth. Maybe last night had only been sex to her, and now she was going to revert to her irrational declarations about how accepting help weakened a woman and how she intended to proceed with her life without any interference from Tom. Maybe she felt guilty about having accepted his help last night and resentful about his having taken advantage of her in her moment of weakness. It was hard to believe he could have read her so utterly wrong, but with women one never knew.

Increasingly anxious, he sped through his shower, shampoo and shave. Back in his bedroom he threw on the first suit he reached in his closet, slung a matching tie around his neck, stepped into his loafers and sprinted to the kitchen.

He was mollified by the sight that greeted him. Jodie had set the table with plates, mugs and napkins. She had arranged the croissants on a serving plate and was pulling a tub of butter and a jar of jam from the refrigerator. If she truly hated him she wouldn't have created such a cozy domestic setting for their breakfast.

Sidling up behind her, he wrapped his arms around her waist and nuzzled her ear. "Good morning," he murmured, praying for any sign from her that his affection was reciprocated.

She rotated in his arms until she was facing him. "Good morning," she said, gazing squarely into his eyes. That she didn't return his kiss was an ominous sign, but at least she wasn't fleeing from him.

"I hope you didn't mind waiting for breakfast," he said.

"Not at all." She gave him a tentative hug, then wriggled out of his embrace and rummaged in the silverware drawer for a couple of knives.

He watched her with a mixture of apprehension and respect. She moved through his kitchen with poise and assurance. Maybe in her professional role as the Happy Housekeeper she'd learned to familiarize herself with other people's kitchens. Tom's kitchen was so different from hers, though—much smaller, much more efficiently laid out, much neater. He recalled the partly-refinished wooden cabinets in her kitchen, the old-fashioned table, the clown-shaped cookie jar and the whimsical dinosaur curtains. It was much more homey than his. As soon as the police straightened out her mess up in Orangeburg, Tom would consume as many breakfasts in her kitchen as she did in his. He would gladly endure the rush-hour commute to New York to be able to sip coffee with her with that goofy cookie-filled clown looking on.

"Do you jog every day?" she asked, pouring the coffee.

"Whenever I can. A good jog followed by a brisk shower really helps to get me in gear."

"Speaking of showers," she said calmly, "you shouldn't use an abrasive cleaner on a fiberglass tub, Tom. Even the mild ones will scratch the surface."

"You mean—" he waited until she'd taken her seat, then sat facing her and struck a pose of indignation "—you inspected my tub while I was out?"

"I didn't *inspect* it," she argued defensively, apparently missing his humor. "I merely noticed some surface scratching near the drain. I've written a lot of pieces on the care and maintenance of fiberglass tubs, and I think you ought to take better care of yours."

He laughed outright. "So this is what it's like getting involved with Penny Simpson, huh."

Her eyes narrowed, dark and quizzical. "I don't know," she said quietly. "You tell me."

Tell her what? he thought nervously. That if a relationship with the author of "Penny-Wise" was going to entail periodic reprimands concerning his deficiencies in the art of cleaning the bathroom, he wanted out? "What is it, Jodie?" he asked, keeping his tone gentle. "What's bothering you?"

She presented him with a wide-eyed stare. "Bothering me? What makes you think something's bothering me?"

"Are you scared about returning to Orangeburg today?" he asked. Much as he hated the thought of her living in fear, he honestly hoped that was all it was. "You're welcome to stay here as long as you want."

"I appreciate the offer," she said, reaching for a croissant, "but really, I'm not scared. And anyway, I've got to get to my office today. I'm way behind in my work."

"You could come back here after work," he ventured. "You don't have to go to your house at all."

"I do have to, if I want to pick up some fresh clothing."

He took heart in her comment. If she'd thought things through far enough to consider replenishing the contents of her suitcase, the concept of her staying another night with him must have occurred to her even before he'd brought it up. "You could probably get a police officer to escort you home for that," he suggested.

She opened her mouth, then closed it. He braced himself for the expected tirade about his overprotectiveness. "I'm sure I don't need a police escort."

"Fine." He sipped his coffee, trying to figure out how to break through to her. "Here's another idea: I can come up to Orangeburg this evening. I could drive to your office after work and escort you to your house instead of the police."

The look she gave him tore at his heart. She appeared simultaneously deeply moved and suspicious. "I couldn't ask you to do that," she argued. "All that driving back and forth—"

"Look, Jodie," he cut her off, tossing tact aside. "We're not just talking about the incident with the cherry bomb. I'm asking you to come back here because I want to be with you tonight, and tomorrow night and the night after that."

"Oh, Tom." She sighed and reached across the table to cover his hand with hers. She gave it a squeeze and attempted a limp smile.

"Is that a yes?" he asked optimistically.

"It's an I don't know. I mean...well, I can't just move in with you. You have other things going on in your life."

"What other things?"

"Well...like, Iowa. What would I do, stay here while you were flying off to Iowa?"

Where did that notion come from? He could think of only one time he'd mentioned to her the possibility of his traveling to Iowa. If he did go it wouldn't be until next month, though, and then only for three days. Why should she be troubled by that?

He traced the angle of her gaze with his own. She was staring at the reunion invitation that was lying on top of his pile of mail.

"You could come to Iowa with me," he said.

She flinched. "What?"

"Come with me." He had spoken on impulse—but then he recalled the fantasy he'd entertained the other night about bringing Jodie with him to his reunion. The more he thought about it, the more the idea appealed to him. Jodie and his mother would undoubtedly hit it off—they were both adamantly independent I'll-do-it-myself women. And Jodie would have a ball at the reunion. He wouldn't be surprised if Carroll had its own "Penny-Wise" fan club.

"No," she said firmly. "I couldn't."

"Why couldn't you?"

She fidgeted with her croissant, shredding it into crumbs and scattering them across her plate. "Tom," she said at last, "I'm not going to let you wear me on your arm just so you can face your old sweetheart."

Now it was his turn to be startled. "What are you talking about?"

"I'm talking about Penny Simpson. She's going to be at your class reunion with her husband, right? So you don't want to go there alone."

He gaped at Jodie. Was that the way she thought he considered her? As someone to exhibit at a party? "Jodie—I'd like you to come with me so you can see where I grew up. I think you'd have fun. And I'd like you with me because I'd miss you if you were here and I was there. It has nothing to do with Penny."

Jodie appeared unconvinced. "Admit it—you feel awkward having to face your rival."

"My rival? Penny's husband, you mean?" He shook his head. "Penny's divorced, Jodie. My mother passed along that bit of local gossip recently. If Penny does attend the reunion, she won't have her husband with her."

"She's divorced?"

"Yes." He thought it wise not to add the other things his mother had told him, about how Penny allegedly hadn't stopped loving him. It was thirdhand information, and even if it were true it didn't change Tom's feelings for her or for Jodie. Nothing—not even this unexpected revelation of her insecurity—could change the way Tom felt about Jodie.

He chuckled. "You're really something," he teased. "You aren't worried about some creep sending you threatening messages, but you're worried about a girl I took out in high school."

"You did more than take her out," Jodie grumbled. "You wanted to marry her."

"Fifteen years ago." He stood, circled the table and pulled Jodie to her feet. "You aren't jealous, are you?"

"Of course not," she retorted fervently. "All I'm saying is, I'm not so sure we're talking about fifteen years ago. I think you're still carrying a torch for her, and if you are, I've got a right to protect myself."

She looked so earnest, he smothered the urge to laugh at her preposterous statement. He closed his arms around her and held her, not too tight but not so loose she could escape easily. "Carrying a torch for her?" he echoed. "Whatever gave you that idea?"

"The letter you wrote me," she answered. "Before we met. If you weren't still hung up on your Penny Simpson you wouldn't have written it."

He was gratified that she didn't try to evade him. She remained within the enclosure of his arms, gazing into his face, her eyes still strangely haunted but no less beautiful for the troubling emotion in them. "I told you," he explained gently, "I wrote you that letter because I was curious. Haven't you ever been curious about people you've lost touch with over the years?"

"If I was, I would probably go to my high school reunions," she muttered, permitting herself a wry smile. "Sure, I'm curious—but not so curious I'd mail a letter out into the great unknown."

"I didn't mail my letter into the great unknown—I sent it to a post-office box," he reminded her. "I felt free to do that because you had a little blurb at the bottom of your newspaper column inviting readers to write to you. I didn't see anything particularly risky in mailing you a note. It was just . . . I wanted to know if you and Penny were one and the same. To tell you the truth—" he dared to drop a light kiss on her forehead "—I'm thrilled that you aren't. If you were, we would have met for a drink somewhere, reminisced about old times for an hour or so and then wished each other well and went our own ways. Instead, I got to meet an extraordinary woman who I seem to have fallen for in a major way.''

He kissed her again, this time grazing her lips, sipping the sweetness of her mouth. He wanted to deepen the kiss, but his body began to tighten in a splendidly painful way and he drew back, not wishing to tempt himself when he knew he and Jodie would both have to leave for work soon.

Jodie's eyes had nearly closed during the brief kiss, and as they came back into focus on his face he detected passion in them—but also doubt. ''You don't believe me,'' he charged.

''I do believe you,'' she swore, but still he saw the reservation in her gaze, the uncertainty. She pulled away, took his hand in hers and led him out of the kitchen. ''I just ... I just want to show you something,'' she explained vaguely.

He followed her into the living room, to the coffee table. She lifted the marble ashtray and presented it to him. ''What is this?''

''An ashtray,'' he answered, bewildered. What now? Was she a fanatic about smoking? No problem—she ought to assume from his morning jog that he was something of a health fiend himself.

''Why is it here?''

He shrugged. ''In case I have a guest who smokes. Do you have a problem with that?''

She answered his question with one of her own: ''Did Penny Simpson smoke?''

Good God—Jodie was taking this silliness to the extreme. Some small part of Tom was flattered that, despite her protestations, she was obviously crazy with jealousy. But really—there was no cause for it. Penny Simpson meant nothing to him.

"No," he said definitively. "Penny Simpson didn't smoke—at least not when I knew her."

Jodie examined the ashtray thoughtfully, running her fingers along its smoothly sculpted surface. "It's almost like a work of art," she murmured.

"It is, isn't it," he agreed. "I don't have too many visitors who smoke, but I leave it out because it's nice to look at."

"Your view is nice, too," Jodie commented, glancing toward the window. "More than nice—it's breathtaking. The whole apartment... Did you fix it up yourself? Did you choose the ashtray and the carpet and all the rest of it?"

Her tone wasn't precisely accusing, but she seemed to be inquiring about something much more complicated than his choice in floor coverings. "I had a professional decorator help me with it," he acknowledged, wondering whether such an innocuous admission would somehow seal his fate in Jodie's mind.

"And the kitchen," she continued. "You've got all those fancy appliances and no food."

He shrugged. "I'm not much of a cook. But the fancy appliances increase the value of the place if I ever decide to sell it."

"It's a co-op?"

"That's right."

She digested this news. "You must have spent a fortune to buy it."

"No. I have a huge mortgage." Was she fishing for information about his financial status? He would never have figured her for a gold-digger, especially not after everything she'd told him about her sister and her mother and how dangerous it was for a woman to become economically dependent on a man.

Jodie lowered her gaze to the luxuriant blue carpet at her feet. "For her," she said brokenly. "You went and bought this place for her, Tom. Didn't you."

For Penny Simpson? Jodie must be insane to think such a thing—and he very nearly said so.

But he hesitated. She wasn't insane and she wasn't joking. She was dead serious, and he owed it to her to treat her concern with the same gravity.

"I'm not sure I understand," he said.

Jodie meandered around the room, groping for the right words. "This apartment—or co-op or whatever you want to call it," she began. "It's so—so grand, and...I mean, I just keep asking myself, why would Tom go to such an effort to buy a place like this and hire a decorator to fix it up for him? Why would he display an ashtray that's probably never even been used and looks like it belongs in the Museum of Modern Art?" Reaching the window, she faltered. She stared out at the panoramic view and mulled over her thoughts. "It dawned on me, Tom—maybe you're doing it to prove something to her. Like...you decided to prove to her how far you've come since she shafted you."

He wanted to refute what Jodie was saying, but something stopped him—her proud posture, her grace, the fierce intelligence radiating from her eyes. Her noble struggle to shape her thoughts into words.

He held his silence, sensing she had more to say.

"Remember that night when we sat on my front porch?" she asked.

Oh, yes, he remembered. They'd sat on her front porch and kissed for the first time, and that one kiss had confirmed what he'd suspected—that Jodie Posniak turned him on in an amazing way, that sex between them would be utterly sensational. That was the night he'd evolved from thinking of her as an intriguing woman to contemplating her in terms of a relationship.

"I told you I didn't want to see my old classmates again," she said, reminding him that besides setting each other on fire with a few kisses they'd also had a conversation.

"And...?" he prompted her.

She turned from the window to face him. He was abruptly stricken by the recognition of how enormous the living room was—not because Jodie had been commenting on the elegant dimensions of his apartment but because she looked so terribly far away. The back lighting from the sun-filled window threw her face into shadow. Even fully clothed and silhouetted, her statuesque body was a magnificent sight.

"You said something about how I should go back to my high school just to show all my classmates how fantastic I'd turned out."

He remembered saying something along those lines—and it seemed like a reasonable observation. "You *are* fantastic," he pointed out.

"I don't know about that," she argued modestly. "But the point is, there's no one from my school days I care enough about to show anything. It's not important to me. They have no hold on me."

"And you think Penny has a hold on me?"

"Yes."

Again he considered denying her assertion. Again, the words didn't come.

"Imagine what she would say if she ever saw you here in your New York apartment," Jodie went on, gliding across the room to him. "Imagine what she'd think of the view and the furniture and this hotsy-totsy ashtray and that kitchen of yours."

He imagined. It was a difficult exercise—not because he couldn't picture Penny squealing and sighing over his apartment but because he could, so vividly—as if he'd imagined it many times before.

He had. Jodie's perception was uncannily accurate. Not in a long time, but yes, he had spent time imagining Penny roaming through his stylish home, being forced to confront, in the most concrete terms, everything she'd missed out on when she'd abandoned Tom to marry someone else. He had imagined her exclaiming over his car and sighing ruefully over his high-powered professional status. He'd imagined her talking wistfully about the excitement of his life on the fast track in Manhattan, the culture and glamour of it, the whirlwind of museums and boutiques, cafés and clubs, the yachts on the river and the social dynamism of the streets.

It hadn't been a deliberate goal of his, but he couldn't close his eyes to the truth. He'd built this life for himself not only because he enjoyed it and because he had earned it, but because he'd been embittered. He'd been dumped. He had lost in love and he'd been determined never to lose at anything again.

"Do you think..." His voice faded to a whisper, and he cleared his throat and met Jodie's searing gaze. "Do you think she'd criticize me about the cleanser I use on my tub?" he asked, desperate for an excuse to smile.

Jodie provided one by breaking into a dazzling smile of her own. "Are you angry with me for saying all this?" she asked.

He realized how much courage it must have taken her not just to reach her conclusions, but to state them with as much candor as she had. He cupped his hands around her elbows and massaged her arms, consoling her. "No. I'm not angry."

"Do you think I'm crazy?"

"No."

She seemed at a loss for words. Her eyes darted about the room. "Then you probably hate me."

"Hate you?"

"For reopening old wounds or something."

"No." He slid his hands up to her shoulders and gave her a hug. Never, not when she'd received the first death-threat letter, not when she'd called him after the skunk debacle, not last night when she'd sought haven in his home, in his bed and in his arms, had she seemed so fragile to him as she did right now. Jeopardizing her physical well-being didn't frighten her as much as jeopardizing her relationship with Tom.

Yet she'd taken the risk because she was brave and honest. "I don't hate you, Jodie," he murmured, touching his lips to her hair. "I think you're incredible."

"Incredibly dumb."

"Incredibly gutsy."

"I could love you, Tom," she whispered. The words were muffled by his collar as she hid her face in the hollow of his neck. "I could love you, but not if I thought you were still obsessed with her."

"I'm not," he vowed. "I was for a long time, but I'm not anymore. If I'm obsessed with anyone, it's you."

"Then I should probably quit while I'm ahead," she said with a feeble laugh. She stepped back and took a deep breath. "Thank you for hearing me out," she said, contrition filtering through her voice.

"Thank you for saying you could love me," he countered. "I'll hang on to that until I can get something more definite out of you."

Her smile widened and she checked her watch. "It's getting late. I'd better go."

"Will you come back tonight?" he asked.

"I . . ." She seemed to vacillate, but her smile grew when she said, "I'd like to. Let me call you when I get to Orangeburg, okay? I want to talk to the police first and see what's going on there."

"All right. Do me a favor and don't go to your house alone, okay?"

She gave him an impatient look, but she seemed more amused than irritated by his verbal finger wagging. "I'm probably going to cruise by, just to make sure the place is still standing."

"If you're going to do that, promise me you won't get out of your car." He knew he shouldn't nag, but he couldn't help himself. He couldn't bear the thought of her taking unnecessary chances with her life.

"Tom—"

"Promise."

"I'll be careful."

She turned and walked down the hall to the bedroom to get her suitcase. He followed her and pulled it out of her hand. "I'll come down to the garage with you," he said, refusing to phrase it as a question so she wouldn't have the option of telling him not to.

They rode downstairs together, her fingers laced through his. In the garage, he paid the attendant and waited with Jodie in the office until her Plymouth rolled into view on the other side of the glass wall. He placed her suitcase in the back seat and then helped her in behind the wheel. Once she'd closed the door, he leaned through the open window and kissed her.

"Call me," he said, half a demand and half a plea.

She smiled enigmatically, started the engine and revved it. The roar echoed eerily against the vaulted concrete interior of the garage. She said something through the resounding rumble, and Tom was almost convinced it was "I love you."

Before he could ask her to repeat it, she drove away.

Chapter Ten

She wasn't jealous.

In Jodie's mind, love and jealousy were antithetical. One was an outgrowth of trust, the other of distrust. She trusted Tom completely. There was nothing dishonest about him, nothing underhanded. He didn't play games or conceal his feelings, even when he knew his feelings might run counter to hers.

That was all a part of why she loved him. But just because she loved him didn't mean she had to close her eyes to reality. She took pride in her ability to protect herself, both from berserk readers of her column and from men who might inadvertently break her heart. She knew Tom would never intentionally do anything to hurt her, but still...that old flame hadn't yet burned out inside him. Jodie was certain of it.

The parkway was relatively empty traveling northbound. In the opposite direction the road was packed with commuters from the suburbs heading into New York City. Through the sparse woods to her right she caught glimpses of the Hudson River. The trees were thick with leaves, the grass bordering the woods streaked with colorful flowering weeds. It was a beautiful vista, yet Jodie couldn't bring herself to appreciate it. She felt too unsettled, her emotions seesawing between love and fear, vulnerability and defensiveness.

Tom would have to go back to Iowa for his reunion, she decided. He'd have to go back alone and confront Penny Simpson—who was now divorced, Jodie reminded herself with a doleful groan. Either the old flame would spark into a major conflagration as a result of their meeting, or it would be extinguished. Tom owed himself the opportunity to figure out whether the woman from his past was truly and permanently in his past.

Jodie owed him that opportunity, too.

Her mind drifted to thoughts of the night they'd spent in each other's arms, the splendid heights to which he had carried her with his lovemaking, the way his eyes had glowed with rapture when she'd brought him to those same dizzying heights. Afterward, when she'd drifted off to sleep, her dreams had been blissful. The soothing heat of his body next to hers, the way he'd unconsciously hugged her to himself, the perfect shape of his shoulder cushioning her head, more comfortable than any pillow she'd ever slept on...

Damn. Jodie didn't want to lose him to some old high school girlfriend. She'd fight for him if she had to. She'd let him return to Iowa and go head-to-head with his past, but if he came back to New York with the news that the old flame had, indeed, flickered back to life, Jodie would fight with everything she had. She was strong and tough. If she could deal with a cherry bomb, she could certainly deal with a pretty blond divorcée from Carroll. Penny Simpson was not going to get the better of her.

Bolstered by the thought, she pressed harder on the gas pedal. Through the car's open windows the sultry

June breeze gusted in, mussing her hair and tugging at the open collar of her blouse. If the air was this muggy at eight in the morning it was going to be sizzling by midday. She ought to go home and change into a skirt before she went to the office.

She fleetingly recalled Tom's warnings about whether she should risk going to her house this morning. He didn't really think she ought to bring a policeman with her when she returned home to change her clothes, did he?

Of course he did. He wanted no harm to come to her. His expressions of concern, which she might have found oppressive a few weeks ago, she now considered touching and immensely flattering. Worrying about her was simply Tom's way of conveying that he cared for her.

Maybe he was right to worry. Maybe she shouldn't go into the house alone. What she would do, she resolved, was just drive by the house to see if it was intact. If everything looked normal from the outside, she could sneak up onto the porch and peek through a few windows. Only if everything looked normal inside, too, would she dare to enter the house. If anything seemed amiss—a single misplaced tree branch on the front lawn, an unfamiliar paint chip on the porch railing, a crooked shingle—she'd play it safe and go straight to her office. Tom would applaud her caution.

A few minutes after exiting the parkway, she found herself cruising along the country road that wound through the hills to her house. Just before she reached the entry to her driveway she slowed to a near stop.

A car was parked in the driveway—not Lynne's station wagon or a police car, but a top-of-the-line Oldsmobile with New Jersey plates. Frowning, Jodie inched her car forward so she could survey the front yard through her windshield.

Spotting a tall, shadowy figure on her front porch, she gasped and jammed her foot down on the brake pedal. She had been positive that the maniac stalking her was a woman—men didn't read her column—but if the person standing on the porch was a woman, she must be consuming steroids by the handful.

No, it was definitely a man, one with dark curly hair, wide shoulders and an incipient pot belly stretching the cotton-knit fabric of his shirt above the belt of his cotton slacks. He shielded his eyes and spied through one of the living-room windows, then shook his head and turned.

Hank. For heaven's sake, it was Jodie's brother-in-law, not some fiendish bomb hurler. Jodie heaved a sigh of relief, then one of annoyance. While Hank wasn't the idiot who'd been trying to intimidate Jodie, she was certainly in no mood to deal with him right now.

Recalling Lynne's frantic telephone call last night, Jodie's annoyance transformed into disgust. Not only was Hank a foul-tempered, domineering jerk with an ego the size of the Sears Tower, but he was also apparently a runaround. The nerve of him, after having been out carousing all night, to show up unannounced and uninvited on Jodie's doorstep this morning!

Fueled by righteous anger, she steered onto the driveway and shut off the engine. She took a deep, steadying breath before she got out of the car—no sense antagonizing him unnecessarily. If he was, indeed, a two-timing rat, Jodie would leave that for him and Lynne—and Lynne's expensive hot-shot attorney—to work out.

"What are you doing here?" she accosted him. Not exactly a gracious greeting, but as far as Jodie was concerned, Hank didn't deserve much in the way of courtesy.

He glowered down at her from the porch as she approached him along the front path. "What do you mean, what am I doing here? Where's my family?"

"Not here, obviously."

"Where are they?"

Jodie glared up at him, unmoved. If she'd had any objectivity left about him, she would have conceded that other than his softening midsection, he was a handsome man. She remembered when Lynne had first started dating him during her sophomore year at UCLA. Jodie had still been in high school then, gawky and unpopular, and her sister had come home for a visit, towing a hunky upperclassman for whom the expression "tall, dark and handsome" might have been coined. He'd seemed surly and aloof to Jodie even then, but Lynne had gone on and on about how gorgeous he was and how he was majoring in finance and was unquestionably superb husband material. At the time, Jodie now recalled, her reaction had been that if this arrogant young man was superb husband material, she would just as soon never get married.

"Where are they?" he repeated.

"Out," she said laconically.

"Out where?"

She rolled her eyes. She might have considered him intimidating during her adolescence, but now she considered him little more than an irritation, someone who had developed a perverse knack for giving her poor sister a hard time. "Why should I tell you?" she taunted him.

"Because Lynne's my wife, that's why. Because Sarah and Peter are my children." He descended from the porch, one slow step at a time, squaring his shoulders in an effort to present himself as menacing. Jodie checked the urge to snicker at his swaggering. "And where the hell were you, while we're at it?" he continued. "Are you sleeping around these days? I won't have my wife and children staying under the same roof as someone who's sleeping around."

"Oh, please, spare me," she said, unable to stifle her laughter. "Do you mean to say you've been here on the front porch all night?"

"What's it to you?"

"What it is to me is that you've got a hell of a nerve trespassing on my property, Hank—and even more nerve slandering me. Where I spend my nights is none of your business. And at this point, where Lynne spends her nights is none of your business, either."

Incensed, Hank gripped Jodie's shoulder. "Where is she?" he roared, his eyes burning with frustration.

Jodie realized she'd pushed him too far. "Lynne is out," she mumbled. She recalled that Lynne herself had tried to contact Hank last night because she wanted to inform him of where she and the children were going to be spending the night. But he hadn't been home. And even if he'd been involved in nothing nefarious last night, Jodie refused to give him the satisfaction of revealing where Lynne was. If Lynne wanted him to know her whereabouts, that was her choice. Jodie's choice was not to tell him a damned thing.

With a nonchalance she had to fake, she pushed past him and climbed onto the porch. In the morning light, the charred splinters of the planks on top of which the bomb had exploded looked more gruesome than they had in the previous evening's gloom. Wincing at the sight, she stepped around the patches of soot and looked through the living-room window. Nothing appeared to have been touched inside. She'd be willing to bet it was safe to go in and get some fresh clothes.

Except that if she went inside, Hank would follow her in and then she would never get rid of him.

"I'll tell you what," Jodie offered, turning to face him. "Why don't you give me a number where you can be reached, and I'll pass it along to Lynne. If she wants to speak to you, she can give you a call."

"Then you know where she is?"

"Of course I do. I'm her sister."

"And I'm her husband, damn it." He stormed onto the porch and grabbed Jodie's upper arm, his long fingers nearly meeting around the slender limb.

She tried vainly to shrug off his hand. "Would you please calm down?" she snapped. "I don't like being manhandled."

"Then tell me where Lynne is," he snarled. "I've had it with you getting in the way of things, Jodie. A husband and a wife have their differences sometimes—this is something a spinster like you wouldn't understand, but a husband and a wife sometimes argue. Then they work it out—or at least, they work it out if they haven't got some old-maid sister-in-law trying to keep them apart."

"My, my," she said wryly. "I seem to have transformed from someone who sleeps around to an old maid spinster."

"I don't give a damn what you are—I just want my wife back in my house where she belongs. It's pretty clear to me you don't want that. I don't know what your warped reasons are, but I wouldn't be surprised if it's just plain green-eyed envy.''

"Envy! Of what? Having a husband like you?'' Jodie let out a snort of derision.

"Something like that,'' Hank retaliated. "You're envious of her because she's got a man to take care of her and because she's prettier than you, and because she's got a real family and a nice house with a two-car attached garage and central air. Sure, I wouldn't put it past you—you're dying of envy. But take it somewhere else, Jodie. Stay out of our lives.''

Jodie considered explaining to him that she'd never wanted to enter into his and Lynne's life in the first place. She'd never been a part of their spats when they'd lived in Houston, but then they'd moved east, closer to Orangeburg, close enough that when Lynne and Hank had had a falling out, Lynne had begged Jodie to let her come and stay for a while. It wasn't Jodie's fault that Lynne was miserable in her marriage and anxious to leave it. Jodie hadn't instigated anything; she hadn't interfered. All she'd done was extend some desperately needed emotional and economic support to her sister.

"I didn't make her unhappy, you know,'' Jodie pointed out in a subdued tone. "You did.''

"She was never unhappy until she saw how much fun you were having, earning all that money and being the famous Penny Simpson and all,'' he countered. "She was quite happy to be Mrs. Henry Duryea until she saw you raking in the bucks and spending it on ugly jewelry for yourself.''

"Then maybe she's the one who's envious,'' Jodie remarked. She knew she shouldn't mock him by throwing his illogic back at him, but he was such an easy target. "You could have let her go out and earn some money, too," she added. "It's really pretty simple, Hank. You tied her down and she rebelled."

"Spare me the feminist bull," he grumbled, his fingers closing tighter around her arm. "Just take me to my wife and I'll leave you alone."

"Give me a number where you'll be and—"

He gave her a stiff shake, shocking her. They'd never minced words with each other and they'd engaged in plenty of heated battles over the years. But Hank had never before bullied her physically. "My family isn't safe with you. Hell, sweetheart—you've got so many enemies, my wife and kids are in danger just by being in your house. I've got a right to get them out of the line of fire. And you've got no right to endanger them."

How did he know about the trouble she'd been having? A few charred scrapes on her front porch couldn't have informed him of anything as specific as her house's being hit by a firecracker. "I don't know what you're talking about," she said disingenuously. "Me? Have enemies?"

"You think Lynne doesn't tell me? She told me what's going on. She tells me these things."

"What things?"

"About the explosion," he said, gesturing at the burned boards. "And the flat tire and the rest of it. Somebody's got you in their sights, Jodie, and if you really wanted to do what's best for Lynne, you'd get her the hell out of here."

"That's exactly what I did," Jodie said. Her heartbeat seemed to vibrate against her Adam's apple, fast and hard. This wasn't right. Something didn't make sense. "How do you know about the tire and the explosion?" she asked, forcing her voice past the knot of dread in her throat.

"I just told you—Lynne tells me these things."

"When? When did she tell you about the explosion?"

"Last night."

"But she didn't talk to you last night," Jodie said, her pulse growing even louder and faster, drumming in her temples, echoing in her skull. "She tried to phone you but you weren't home. She was unable to reach you."

"I got home later," he said. "She reached me about midnight, okay? And she told me about the flat tire and the skunk and everything. I won't have you taking chances with her life, Jodie. Now be a good girl and tell me where she is and I'll get her and the kids out of this danger. I'm not going to let them get caught in the crossfire. You've got enemies, you deal with them yourself."

Something was very wrong. Not just the demonic gleam in Hank's eyes, not the bruising strength of his hold on her but something else, something that caused Jodie's vision to blur with terror and rage, that caused her breath to rattle and catch and her brain to scramble and unscramble, frantically searching for the mistake in what Hank was saying. Because it didn't make sense. It didn't.

If Lynne had reached him at midnight, she would have told him where she was. That was why she'd phoned him—to tell him that she and the children were going to spend the night at Helen's apartment.

But he didn't know where they were. And that meant Lynne *hadn't* reached him.

And if she hadn't reached him, there was only one way he could know about the attacks on Jodie.

Tom—oh, God, Tom, I need you!

She could have sworn she'd actually cried the words out loud. Yet her lips remained pressed shut, her teeth clamped around them. The only sound to emerge from her was the belabored whisper of her shallow breath as she stared furiously into the stony eyes of her brother-in-law. For once in her life she felt as if she were in extreme danger, her very life at risk—and she wanted Tom here, right now, her savior, her knight in shining armor, her gallant hero. She wanted him to swoop down, to rescue her and carry her off to safety in his loving arms. She wanted him with her.

He *was* with her. Gradually her pulse slowed and her breath became more regular. Tom was here—in her heart, in her soul. She loved him. She couldn't let herself be defeated by this confrontation with her brother-in-law, because if she did, she might never find out what the future held for her and Tom. He was her incentive. He was her strength.

For Tom's sake and her own, Jodie couldn't afford to lose. More than her life was at stake.

"All right," she said, deliberately and calmly. She regulated her breathing and ordered her heart to stop thumping so wildly. Trying not to be obvious, she wiped her hands on her slacks to dry the clammy sweat from her palms. "All right, Hank," she said. "I'll take you to Lynne."

"That's better." He refused to let go of her arm as they marched down the path to the driveway.

"You can follow me in your car," she suggested.

"Forget it. You'll take me there yourself."

The thought of having him seated beside her in her car made her queasy, but she managed a faint smile and nodded. "Suit yourself," she said as he shoved her in behind the wheel and slammed the door behind her.

Waiting for him to get settled in the passenger seat, she gazed out at her house, at the front lawn, at Sarah's rusting doll carriage and Peter's soccer ball. What if, at the end of all this, Hank did something really awful, like kill her? What if she never saw this house again? What if she was driving to her doom?

Oh, Tom, I'm so scared....

No. She couldn't die. She had to be strong so she could prove to Tom that strong women were worth loving.

Fortified by the thought, she started the engine, backed down the driveway into the road and floored the gas pedal.

Hank let out a curse as the Plymouth careered along the hairpin curves of the road. "Jodie—what the hell are you doing?" he roared.

Her answer was to tear through a low-visibility intersection without slowing down.

"For God's sake, Jodie—"

"You said you wanted me to take you to Lynne," she said, tossing him a saccharine smile. She shot through another intersection, and her driving won her a harsh blast of the horn from the driver she'd cut off. "That's what I'm doing, Hank. Taking you to her."

"Do it slower!"

"Don't you want to see your wife?" she asked sweetly. "And your darling children? You seemed so impatient, Hank—I thought I'd try to get you there as quickly as I could."

Before he could respond, she took a sharp left turn at full throttle. Hank was thrown against the door. "Jodie, I'm warning you—"

"What are you warning me?" she asked, glancing in her rearview mirror. Why weren't there any cops around? "Would you like to get out now?"

"You know damned well what I'd like."

"Here's an idea," she said, once again unable to keep herself from needling him. She shouldn't push him, she shouldn't—but she couldn't help herself. "Why don't we see if we can find a skunk to run down first?"

"Jodie—"

"We could just squish it under the tires, and then we could find a deserving person to send it to."

"Jodie—"

"Or do I already have a skunk in the car?"

"Jodie!" He bore down on her, his hand inches from the steering wheel. If he interfered with her ability to steer they'd surely crash. She didn't want to have an accident! She just wanted a policeman to pull her over for driving recklessly. Why did that old cliché—about how you could never find a policeman when you needed one—have to come true now, of all times? How much longer would she have to continue driving this way before a cop spotted her?

Another glance into the mirror brought disappointment. Not a police car in sight.

She slapped Hank's hand away and veered around a slow-moving car. "Oops," she said. "I think I'm going the wrong way." She executed an abrupt U-turn across a double yellow line, forcing several other cars to skid to a stop in order to avoid colliding with her. "There," she said placidly, her voice belying the agitated state of her nerves. "Please don't distract me, Hank."

He cursed again. "If this is your idea of a joke—"

"No. Do you know what my idea of a joke is? Discovering that someone's let all the air out of my tire.

That's a scream, Hank. And another thing I consider a first class hoot is getting an anonymous letter in the mail, containing a death threat. I've got to tell you, that sort of thing makes me laugh so hard it hurts. Especially when the letter's postmarked Philadelphia. How long a trip was it for you to mail that letter from Philadelphia, Hank? An hour or so?''

"Jodie..."

To her enormous relief, she glimpsed a police cruiser pulling out of a Dunkin Donuts parking lot one block ahead. She couldn't let it enter the flow of traffic ahead of her—if it did the driver might not notice her. Stomping with all her might on the accelerator, she sped down the street, weaving maniacally past cars left and right, pushing the needle toward seventy. Hank threw his hands up in front of his face, unwilling to witness the inevitable crash.

There wasn't a crash. Jodie streaked past the doughnut shop ahead of the cruiser, which immediately began beaming its flashing blue lights. Jodie could not imagine a more welcome sight.

Letting out her breath, she slowed down and pulled off the road, the cruiser following directly behind her. Before the policemen could emerge she sprang from her car and raced to the black-and-white cruiser. "Thank you, thank you!" she hollered at the perplexed pair of officers, who gaped at her through the windshield.

"Uh...lady—" the driver of the cruiser emerged first, pulling his ticket book from his back pocket "—do you know how fast you were going?"

"I don't care! I just wanted to catch your attention! This man—this man, he—he..." She faltered as her body succumbed to a final surge of adrenaline. A cold shudder ripped down her spine as she pointed to Hank, who was sitting sedately in her car and attempting to look as puzzled as the policemen.

"Yes?" The officer with his ticket book drawn took Jodie's elbow and led her over to her car. "What about this man?"

"He's responsible for everything," she ranted, then drew in a deep breath, hoping to quell the tremor in her voice. "My flat tire and the skunk and the bomb...."

The policeman gave her a quizzical look, then bent over and addressed Hank through the open driver's side window. "Who are you?"

"The name is Henry Duryea," Hank said smoothly. "I'm her brother-in-law. The poor dear seems to be having an episode of some sort."

"I'm *not* a poor dear, and I'm *not* having an episode!" she fumed, then bit her lip to stifle herself. Lord help her, she sounded like a raving lunatic—which, no doubt, was exactly what Hank wanted. Taking another deep breath, she said as demurely as she could, "That man is my brother-in-law, I won't argue it. However, he's behind a campaign of terror—"

"A campaign of terror, huh," said the policeman gripping Jodie's elbow.

His partner moved around the Plymouth to the passenger door and opened it. "Would you mind stepping out of the car, sir?"

Hank got out and handed the policeman some identification from his wallet. Jodie tried to convince herself that it didn't matter how sanely he behaved or how insanely she behaved, as long as the police brought them both down to the station house. Once there, the officers would be able to pull out the reports Sergeant Ludwig had filed concerning the skunk incident and the bomb scare.

"Less than twelve hours ago," she said in what she considered a rational tone of voice, "the police were at my house collecting evidence of a bombing."

"A terrorist bombing?" the policeman holding her asked.

"Call it whatever you want. That man—my brother-in-law—set the bomb. He wants to kill me."

"I do not want to kill you," Hank railed, frowning at Jodie over the roof of her car. "I have no interest whatsoever in killing you."

"Then what do you want?"

"I want my wife and children back. She's hiding them from me," he informed the policemen.

"All right, now," said the officer standing with Hank. "What do we have here? A kidnapping, a bombing and what else?"

Jodie let out a low, shaky sigh. What difference did it make? She might spend the next twenty years of her life in a padded cell in the nearest loony bin, but at least she would be alive. Maybe, if she was truly lucky, Tom would be waiting for her when she got out.

"Why don't you bring us both down to the police station?" she implored. "We can all sit down and straighten this entire matter out."

"I have no intention of going to the police station," Hank protested. "I'm a husband and a father, and I have a right to see my family."

"Okay, sir," said the other policeman in a placating tone. "Frankly, I think the lady's finally making some sense. Why don't we go to the station house and untangle this thing." He motioned with his head toward the cruiser. "You take her, okay?" he said to his partner. "I'll follow along in her car with the brother-in-law."

"Thanks a heap," muttered the policeman holding Jodie, indicating that he considered her something of a booby prize. "Did you leave your keys in the ignition?"

"Yes."

With a farewell wave to his partner, he led Jodie to the cruiser and helped her onto the back seat. "I'm not going to have to cuff you, am I?"

"No," she said.

He eyed her dubiously, then locked the back door and got in behind the wheel. Jodie stared at him through the metal grid separating the front and back seats. "Thank goodness we already had breakfast," he muttered as he started the engine. "Something tells me getting a statement from you is going to take all morning."

"I refuse to make any statements without my lawyer present," Jodie said belatedly.

"Swell. Who's your lawyer?"

"Tom Barrett."

TOM ARRIVED AT THE POLICE STATION an hour later. It had not been a propitious time to be summoned from his office; he had a meeting scheduled for that afternoon with an investigator from the IRS to present John Huddleston's case regarding the shares he'd purchased in the Newark apartment building, and he'd wanted to spend the morning preparing his argument and assembling the evidentiary documents. But when Lilian had informed him that Jodie Posniak was on the line he'd pushed everything aside, thrilled by the prospect of hearing her voice. Before pressing the button to connect them, he sent up a prayer that Jodie had called to tell him she had decided to return to the city tonight—

or better yet, that she had decided to go the whole distance and declare out loud that she loved him.

What he didn't expect was to hear her say, "Hi, Tom—I'm at police headquarters in Orangeburg, and I'm not sure but I think I may be under arrest."

"Under arrest? For what?"

"Breaking about two hundred traffic laws. Also, I know who tried to bomb my house—but I don't know how to prove it, Tom, and they said I could call a lawyer and I..."

Say you love me, Tom silently urged her. In her current predicament, wanting to hear her utter those few precious words was inexcusably selfish on his part, but he had never wanted anything so badly.

"I need you," she concluded.

That was good enough for now. "I'll be there as soon as I can," he promised.

As soon as he'd hung up, he'd called in one of the junior associates to finish compiling the Huddleston data, then dashed out of the office, caught a cab to his apartment and from there drove up to Orangeburg. Unsure of what he was walking into, he entered the police station warily and asked the desk sergeant where he might find Jodie Posniak.

"She's in the commissary," he said. "It's down the hall and to the left."

The commissary? Scowling, Tom thanked the sergeant and strode down the hall, passing a large squad room and several closed doors, following the sound of laughter. Turning left, he stepped through an open door into a cozy lounge furnished with a couple of circular Formica-topped tables and folding metal chairs, a bulletin board covered with notices and cartoons, a cracked Naugahyde sofa and an old refrigerator. Candy and soda vending machines lined one wall, and a coffee maker and a small microwave stood on a counter on the wall opposite. A crowd of uniformed police officers stood clustered around Jodie, who had positioned herself by the microwave and was lecturing the officers.

"Anything, really," she was saying. "Once you've got your English muffin base and cheese, any topping will do. Chopped olives, tomatoes, chives, tuna fish, a slice of ham... But I'm telling you, a toaster oven works better. Microwaves are great for certain things, but they tend to make cheese rubbery."

"So, wait—like, shouldn't there be tomato sauce on there somewhere?" asked a silver-haired officer with an impressive-looking chevron on her sleeve.

"If you want. Tomato sauce juices it up. But you could also use a little mayo and a slice of turkey."

"With the cheese?" someone else asked.

"With the cheese. The cheese is the best part."

Several officers nodded. A couple jotted down this pearl of wisdom on their note pads.

Jodie scanned her attentive audience, smiling. Through the crowd she spotted Tom and her eyes lit up. "Oh—excuse me, everybody. My lawyer has arrived."

On cue, the officers stepped apart, opening a path between Tom and Jodie. She hurried across the room to him and enveloped him in a powerful hug. Although he felt inhibited by the throng of onlookers, he gingerly closed his arms around her.

"What happened to you?" he asked. "Why are you here?"

"Oh, it's a big mess," she said cheerfully, loosening her hold on him. "It'll take forever to explain." She turned back to the officers. "So listen, folks," she addressed them. "I'll send over a toaster oven. Really, they're inexpensive and they do all kinds of things a microwave can't."

"Jodie," Tom whispered sternly. "I thought you were under arrest. If you offer the police department a gift, it might be construed as a bribe."

"I'm not under arrest," she assured him. "And anyway, if I give them a toaster oven, I'll get a receipt from them. This is a charitable donation—I can write it off my taxes. Isn't that right?" She grinned sheepishly at a middle-aged officer standing beside her. "Mr. Barrett is a tax specialist. He *is* my lawyer, though."

Totally at sea, Tom slid Jodie's hand through the bend in his elbow and escorted her out of the lounge. "Jodie, what the heck is going on here?" he muttered. His joy at seeing her was tempered by the knowledge of the important work he'd left behind. "Why did you telephone me if you weren't under arrest? I've got a million things to do at the office, and I dropped everything because I thought—"

"Oh, Tom, I'm sorry." She nudged a door open, peered inside and discovered an empty interrogation room. She pulled him in and closed the door behind them. "I *was* arrested," she swore, leaning her hips against the table at the center of the room and gazing solemnly at him. "When I phoned you I was officially under arrest. But they dropped all the charges against me when I finally convinced them that Hank was the one who'd been harassing me all this time."

"Hank?" Why did that name sound familiar? "It turned out to be a man?"

"Some man," Jodie grumbled, then bit her lip and looked away. "Hank's my brother-in-law."

Bit by bit, her voice laced with genuine sadness, she related to Tom everything that had happened: how she'd detoured to her house that morning and found her brother-in-law there, searching for his family; how when he'd talked to her, he'd slipped up just enough to incriminate himself; how she'd driven like a she-devil in order to gain the attention of a police cruiser. "Hank is sick, Tom," she concluded. "I mean...the extremes he was willing to go to to get Lynne back—it's sick. If he wanted to get her back, why didn't he just agree to her terms? Why didn't he say, 'Sure, get a job, have some autonomy if it'll make you happy'?"

"Apparently he *is* sick," Tom concurred. "He wasn't being rational about it."

"They have him under observation now," Jodie told him. "It's a mess. Lynne is overflowing with sympathy for him. She says she can't possibly think about divorcing him if he's mentally unbalanced. There's been some talk of dropping the charges against him if he undergoes intensive psychiatric treatment."

"Is he willing to do that?"

"I think so. It's what Lynne wants." She hesitated, tracing a wiggly line across the scratched surface of the table. "As his victim, though, I've got to agree to drop the charges."

Tom studied her face. Her eyes were dark and luminous, alive with hidden thoughts. "Will you?"

"You're my lawyer. Do you think I should?"

It wasn't like Jodie to defer to Tom's judgment, and he wasn't sure how to respond. "I'm not really your lawyer, Jodie. You've got a local attorney, haven't you? The one representing you in that suit over the soufflé."

Jodie issued a brief, mirthless laugh. "The soufflé. The ninny who brought that suit against me was the police's prime suspect. A detective from her local police department visited her this morning and grilled her for two and a half hours while I was being threatened by my own brother-in-law here in Orangeburg." Jodie let out a long breath and shook her head. "Yeah, I think I'll agree to drop the charges. It's the only humane thing to do. I don't want to see Hank go to jail. All I want is for Lynne to be happy."

"That may be beyond your ability at this point," Tom observed gently.

Jodie shook her head again. "As a matter of fact, I think she's already happier than she's been in a long time. She says Hank is in a weak, dependent state and needs her desperately, and she wants to help him. She says the prospect of helping him survive this emotional crisis gives her an understanding of her own strength. Can you believe it?"

"Yes," Tom said simply, drawing Jodie into his arms. "I can believe it."

Jodie rested her head against his shoulder. "I couldn't have gotten through this without you," she murmured.

Once again she seemed to be deferring to him—and once again, he wasn't certain how to react. He pulled back and peered into her face. "How did I get you through anything?" he asked. "I was in New York City assembling documents for a hearing before the IRS."

"You were in my thoughts. The whole time. I just kept thinking about you and how much I wanted to stay alive for you—and for us. I don't know what's going to become of us, Tom, but—"

But I love you, he coached her. He almost said it himself. *I love you, Jodie—and whatever becomes of us will be good.*

"I just—I kept reminding myself of how much you mean to me and it kept me going. I know that sounds really stupid, but—"

"Oh, no," Tom assured her, kissing the crown of her head. "It doesn't sound stupid at all." He wanted to tell her he loved her. But she seemed so vulnerable to him right now, so open and susceptible. To speak such highly charged words might overwhelm her. It was difficult enough for her to accept that Tom had in some way helped her through her ordeal. Here, in this stuffy, windowless room in a police station, it didn't seem proper for him to burden her with deep confessions of love, as well.

"Anyway," she went on, "it worked. I would get scared, and then I'd think of you and I'd feel brave."

"But of course you never *really* got scared," he teased, touching his lips to her brow again. "Not the intrepid Jodie Posniak. She's never been scared a day in her life."

She grinned at him, but her eyes weren't smiling. They remained profoundly dark and disturbing, shimmering with questions and confusion. "I don't like being scared, Tom," she whispered. "It's awful."

"Especially for someone who isn't used to it." He brushed her lips with his, then acted to lighten her wistful mood. "Now that the danger is past, how am I going to convince you to spend the night at my apartment?"

"Twist my arm," Jodie said, then steered Tom's mouth back to hers for another, deeper kiss.

He returned it eagerly, happily—and yet a small part of him held back, wondering whether she was kissing him from love or more from need. Wondering whether she would feel stronger soon and then resent him for no other reason than that, once upon a time, she had needed him.

Wondering whether he could ever get used to loving a woman as complicated as Jodie after having lived most of his life believing that love was as simple as reheating leftover rice or bringing a limp carpet back to life.

Chapter Eleven

"Don't go."

It was a plea she would never have said aloud if she were fully awake. But she was drowsy and dreamy, snuggled cozily under the blanket with Tom. The sensation of him rolling away jarred her from a lush slumber; she reflexively reached out to prevent him from leaving her.

The sound of her voice startled her and she opened her eyes. Her vision filled with the glorious sight of him still in bed beside her, his head propped up with his hand so he could gaze down into her sleepy face. His hair was disheveled, his jaw bristly, but his eyes were as clear and bright as gemstones, sparkling through the shadows. "Have you got a better idea?" he asked, smiling mischievously.

"Lots of them," she murmured. She cupped her hand around the back of his head and pulled him down for a deep, soul-stirring kiss. She felt his body hardening against her, and her own growing soft and fluid in response. She shifted her legs around his hips and he groaned, nearly succumbing.

"Jodie," he whispered, his voice gravelly with passion and humor. "I never took you for a temptress."

"Oh?" She pretended to be insulted. "And why not?"

"A temptress would realize that grapes are for peeling, not for hanging from her ears." He kissed the tip of her nose, then lifted himself off her. "Let me take my jog, lady. If I don't keep this body in shape I'm not going to be able to keep up with your insatiable demands."

She feigned a punch, then joined his laughter. "Insatiable demands?" she repeated incredulously.

Tom swung off the bed and tucked the lightweight cover around her. "I'm not complaining about your demands, Jodie," he said as he donned his running clothes. "For that matter, I'm not complaining about your insatiability, either. But every now and then a man's got to come up for air."

"Some air," she grumbled. "It's probably a hundred degrees outside."

"More likely around seventy or so. I like jogging in Orangeburg—summer mornings aren't as muggy here as they are in the city." He smoothed the edge of his tank top into the waistband of his shorts. "Do you want me to crank up the air conditioner before I leave?"

"No. If you're going to sweat, I should, too."

"What you should do is go back to sleep," he chided her affectionately. He finished tying his sneakers and gave her another light kiss. "I'll be back in a while."

She watched him leave, his long legs carrying him in energetic strides out of her bedroom and down the hall. He'd spent enough nights at her house to have mapped out a picturesque five-mile jogging route along the serpentine roads of her neighborhood. That he had—that he felt that much at home in her house and her town— thrilled her. She was glad he preferred jogging here, because otherwise he might insist on their spending every night at his apartment. For Tom, staying overnight in Orangeburg meant contending with an agonizing commute to the city in the morning. Yet he endured the deadly rush-hour traffic without complaint. Surely Jodie could endure his abandoning her for his daily workout without complaint.

On the other hand, she had discovered after numerous failed attempts that it was impossible for her to fall back asleep once he was gone. Whether they were at his apartment or her house, she simply couldn't remain in bed once he'd left it. Without his heat and weight next to her, the blanket seemed misshapen, the pillows lumpy, the mattress vast and barren. She had grown too accustomed to having him with her. In a few short weeks she had gotten hooked on his very existence.

She had become dependent on him, damn it.

She ran her hand over the sheet where he'd lain and felt the lingering warmth left by his body. Smoothing the linen's wrinkles, she sighed. Before Tom, she had always assumed that for a woman, being dependent on a man meant relying on him to change her tires and counsel her in finances, expecting him to support her and shelter her from harm. She hadn't realized that it could mean counting on him for happiness and comfort, for his company and his gentle smile and the consummate ecstasy of his love.

She wondered how much longer he would be around. She had better overcome her dependence on him, and soon. Everything was bound to change after this weekend; by next week, she might not be able to count on him for anything but a goodbye.

Her spirits dampened, she rose and trudged to her closet for her bathrobe. It wouldn't help to wish he wasn't going, to reach out through a haze of sleep and beg him to stay. He *had* to go—for her sake as much as his own.

A half hour later, she was showered and dressed, her hair blow-dried and her earlobes adorned not with grapes but with miniature gaming dice. The house seemed unnaturally still. She had become dependent on the constant noise and bustle of Peter and Sarah, too, she realized. Now that they were back in New Jersey with Lynne, Jodie was having a hard time getting used to having the house to herself. It seemed strange to be able to walk down the hall without tripping over one of Sarah's dolls, to find the stairs no longer littered with baseball cards and dirty tube socks, to glance out the kitchen window and see a yard devoid of scattered toys. Without Lynne and the children to distract her, Jodie had even had time last weekend to finish lacquering the kitchen cabinets. While she'd done that, Tom had worked outside on the porch, sanding the charred gouges in the planks and then coating them with fresh paint. It didn't match the surrounding paint, which was faded and stained, but at least the cherry bomb's damage wasn't visible anymore.

She prepared a pot of coffee and put two bran muffins into the toaster oven to warm. Tom liked baked goods for breakfast. Jodie was a corn flakes person. Wasn't that midwestern of her, she thought glumly as she filled a bowl with cereal and then nibbled a few dry flakes from the box.

Lord, look at her—mooning and stuffing her face with dry cereal just because Tom was going to attend his high school reunion the following night. Just because he was going to put in a couple of hours at his office today and then catch a cab to LaGuardia, fly out to

Council Bluff and rent a car to drive eighty or so miles to Carroll. Just because he was going to immerse himself in the nostalgia-gilded beauty of his rural Great Plains hometown, visit with his relatives, catch up on the local goings-on and buy his mother a new vacuum cleaner. "The one she has is nine years old," he had told Jodie, "and every time I go out to Carroll she asks me to take it apart and oil it for her. I'd just as soon treat her to a new one."

Tom's three-day jaunt to Iowa was nothing for Jodie to mope about. She had no reason to be depressed about the fact that tomorrow, some time around 6:00 p.m. central time, he would be moseying over to the banquet room at the Holiday Inn to drink a toast to his old high school chums, to relive the good old days and renew the old ties. To see his old girlfriend.

"He *has* to go," Jodie intoned under her breath—as if speaking the words could persuade her of their inherent truth. She had avoided thinking about his departure all week, but she couldn't avoid it any longer. Tonight, for the first time since she'd fled to his apartment after the bombing, she was going to spend the night without him. If she couldn't fall back to sleep when he left for his jog, she sure as hell wouldn't be able to fall asleep when he was a thousand miles away. It was going to be a long, long weekend.

She heard the thump of the front door shutting and hastily manufactured a smile for him. He bounced into the kitchen, his skin shining with perspiration and his shirt plastered to his chest, revealing the masculine contours of his torso in a tantalizing way. Jodie deliberately turned so she wouldn't have to view him.

He moved directly to the sink, twisted the cold-water tap and splashed a liberal handful of water onto his overheated cheeks. "Whew!" he groaned, then cupped his hand beneath the spout and doused his face again. "It's hot out there, Jodie."

"It's going to be hotter in Iowa," she warned, unable to empty her mind of thoughts about his impending departure.

He pulled a tumbler from a cabinet and filled it with water. "Maybe I ought to forget about buying my mother a vacuum cleaner and buy her an air conditioner, instead," he said before draining the glass in three efficient gulps. He refilled it, this time to sip instead of guzzle.

"Your mother doesn't have an air conditioner?" Jodie asked.

"She's got a couple of window fans. She claims they do the trick, but I don't believe her." He drank a bit, then shrugged. "I suppose I'll find out this weekend whether she's right."

"You could get her an attic fan," Jodie suggested. "Something to draw the hot air up and out. They're efficient and much less expensive than air conditioners."

"That sounds like a quote from 'Penny-Wise.'" Tom chuckled, set his glass in the sink and gave Jodie a damp kiss on the cheek. "Five minutes," he promised on his way out of the kitchen.

In fact, it took him fifteen minutes to shower, shave and dress. Fifteen minutes during which Jodie attempted with little success to elevate her mood. If she remained sullen and sulky, Tom would consider his old flame much more pleasant company in comparison. Jodie had no doubt the woman would be pleasant. She couldn't picture Penny Simpson as a bitter divorcée. In Jodie's mind, Penny was young and pretty, sweet and accommodating. She was the girl all the guys wanted and all the girls wanted to be. She wasn't an oddball, like Jodie. She was everything Jodie had never been—except for Tom's lover. They could both lay claim to that particular honor.

Hearing his footsteps as he descended the stairs, she filled two cups with coffee and pulled his muffins out of the toaster oven. "Mmm," Tom grunted as he entered the kitchen, tightening his tie around his shirt collar. "It smells delicious."

Jodie splashed some milk onto her corn flakes, which didn't smell the least bit delicious, and took her seat at the table. She jabbed at the flakes with her spoon, stirred them, smashed a few into yellow crumbs and then lowered her spoon, unable to muster any appetite. Tonight, she promised herself, while Tom was winging westward in a 727, she would pick up some take-out at House of Cheng, and tomorrow morning, while Tom was buffing his shoes in preparation for his big evening, she would pig out on leftover sesame noodles for breakfast.

"I don't like this," Tom said, breaking into her ruminations.

She glanced up at him. "I know, they aren't as good as the muffins from your neighborhood bakery," she apologized. "But I bought them fresh—"

"The muffins are fine," he corrected her, methodically spreading butter onto one which he'd cut in half. He set down his knife, lifted one muffin half to his lips, then shook his head. "What I don't like," he explained, "is how sad you look."

"I'm not sad," she argued.

"I didn't say you *were* sad," he equivocated. "I said you *looked* it." He reached across the table to take her hand. "What's the problem, Jodie?"

"No problem," she insisted. "I was just thinking about how I'll probably have leftover Chinese food for breakfast tomorrow."

He studied her at length, plumbing her eyes with his perceptive gaze. "I don't have to go, you know."

"Don't be ridiculous."

"I'm not being ridiculous," he swore. "There's no law that says I have to."

"You've already got your ticket," she reminded him.

"Well, heavens—you're right. I've *got* to go. I paid for the darned thing with my blood, didn't I."

His sarcasm was tempered by a charmingly dimpled smile. Jodie remained solemn, though. She fidgeted with her spoon, then dropped it and took a long drink of coffee. "You have to go, Tom," she said, setting down her mug with a dull thud.

"Then come with me. It's not too late. We can get another ticket. If we can't fly you into Council Bluff, I'll trade my ticket in and we'll fly through Des Moines or Sioux City. Somewhere there must be an extra seat on a plane to Iowa."

She shook her head. "I don't want to go, Tom. I want you to go alone. If you don't…" She sighed. What she was doing was so right, so responsible—why did it make her feel so miserable? "If you don't go, it will always hang over you," she said, swallowing the tremor in her voice. "You'll always wonder, 'What if the love wasn't really dead between me and Penny? What if the feelings were still there?' If I went with you, Tom, you wouldn't be giving your relationship with Penny a fair chance."

"My relationship with Penny had a fair chance fifteen years ago," he reminded her, his tone level and earnest. "She and I each gave it what we could. And it didn't work out. It's history, Jodie." He squeezed her hand. "It should be obvious to you by now that I'm not the sort of guy who lives in the past. If I did, I'd have a toaster oven, not a microwave."

She appreciated his attempt to leaven their conversation with humor, but she couldn't bring herself to share his smile. "I know you don't live in the past, Tom. But I also know that if you don't go back to Iowa and see Penny Simpson, you'll spend the rest of your life wondering about what might have been."

"What might have been is irrelevant."

The last thing she wanted was to pick a fight with him. Surely Penny Simpson wouldn't fight with Tom; she would simply smile and nod and say, "Of course, darling—you're absolutely right." But Jodie and Tom had always been honest with each other, and Jodie wasn't about to change that. "It isn't irrelevant, Tom," she maintained. "If you hadn't been searching for Penny Simpson you would never have found me."

"Jodie." He weighed his words carefully, as aware as she was that they were venturing across an emotional mine field, one they'd managed to avoid ever since the first morning after they'd become lovers. "Yes, when I initially found you it was because I was looking for Penny. But I told you—that was simple curiosity, nothing more. I wish I could convince you—"

"You don't have to convince me," she told him, lifting her eyes to his, discerning the brooding emotion in their multicolored depths. "You have to convince yourself."

He sighed and looked away. His inability to meet her gaze proved to her that her observation had hit home. It was a target she'd hoped to miss. She would have given anything to be wrong, to have misread Tom completely. But she knew she hadn't. She knew he'd lived the past dozen years of his life with memories of Penny Simpson, sometimes bittersweet ones, sometimes just plain bitter ones. He'd made major choices because of her. He'd designed his life-style around her. Just as a clam might create a pearl out of the irritating presence of a grain of sand, so Tom had created a superlative career, an elegant home, a stellar success of his life in an attempt to assuage the irritating presence of Penny in his memory.

Jodie was too forthright not to acknowledge that. So, to his great credit, was Tom.

"All right," he conceded, returning his gaze to her. "I'll go back to Iowa and convince myself, if that's what you want."

"That's what I want."

He stood and pulled her out of her chair. Then he gathered her into his arms for a quiet hug. "I've got to hit the road if I'm going to make it to the office by nine," he said.

She nodded, her forehead rubbing against his chin.

He took that as an invitation to kiss her brow. "I'll call you tonight, okay?"

"No. Don't call me until after the reunion," she requested. "I don't want to know until you know."

Apparently he understood what it was she felt he had to know. "I'm going to miss you, Jodie," he murmured.

She closed her eyes and angled her face to his, kissing his lips. "I'll miss you, too," she whispered, wondering whether she would miss him for three days or forever.

He tightened his hold on her for a moment, then released her and offered a gallant smile. "Wish me a safe trip," he said as he crossed the room.

Jodie trailed him into the hallway, where he picked up his briefcase. "Have a safe trip," she said in compliance, ushering him to the door and holding it open for him. "Good luck."

He dropped a final kiss of farewell onto her lips and then strolled down the walk to his car. She stared after him, conscious that she should be cleaning the kitchen, that her own office awaited her, that Helen would be there, armed with a stack of letters querying the role of baking soda in a modern woman's universe, requesting granola recipes, pleading for help.

Sometimes help was easy, she thought, hovering in the doorway long after Tom had backed his car down the driveway and driven away. Sometimes a woman could help herself. Even in matters of life and death, Jodie pondered, her gaze journeying from the vacant driveway to the repaired porch—even in matters of life and death, a woman didn't have to be helpless.

But matters of the heart were quite another thing. No matter how much you loved a man, if the circumstances weren't right, if his heart wasn't free, there wasn't a damned thing you could do but wait and hope and try not to think too much about how utterly helpless you were.

WHAT TRULY AMAZED HIM was that a woman like Jodie, who had so very much going for her, could be so insecure.

A few weeks ago she'd single-handedly taken on her arguably psychotic brother-in-law and emerged un-scathed. Not only had she been strong enough to save her own life, but she was strong enough to forgive Hank. And she was strong enough to continue helping her sister. She telephoned Lynne every day, inquired after Hank's therapy, counseled Lynne on how to organize herself for her job search and checked up on the children. Last Saturday, while Jodie had been in New York with Tom, she had asked him to go with her to a toy store so she could buy Peter an addition to his Lego castle set and Sarah a new, rust-free doll stroller. She had arranged for the store to ship the toys to New Jersey and enclosed a note informing the children that they were not to open the boxes until their mother landed a job—"which I know will be soon," she'd op-timistically added as a postscript.

She was a whirlwind, a dynamo, a spellbinding woman. She was sexy and smart and unflinchingly truthful. So what was she afraid of?

A flight attendant stopped her cart by Tom's seat to remove the empty soda can and untouched plastic-wrapped sandwich he'd been served twenty minutes ago. "We're about a half hour out of Chicago," she alerted him. "If you want anything more to drink now's your last chance."

"No, thanks," he said.

She cleared his tray table and smiled. Tom glimpsed the unoccupied seat next to him. Jodie could have been sitting there, he thought. She could have been beside him, holding his hand and working up a list of air-travel tips for her column. She could have flown all the way to Iowa with him, and kept him entertained during the monotonous drive from the airport through the farmland to Carroll. She could have explained to his mother the elementary physics behind an attic fan—in fact, if he knew Jodie, she could have installed the attic fan herself.

The following night he could have taken her to the reunion, and she could have seen for herself that Penny Simpson was definitely not a rival for Tom's affections.

Penny never really got over you. He heard the words in his mother's voice, an eerie message allegedly passed along from Penny to her mother to his mother to him. *Penny never really got over you.*

What would it be like to see her? He leaned back in his seat and closed his eyes, trying to visualize their meeting. What if she was angry and resentful? What if time and mournful experience had left their marks on her? What if her once-lissome body was now plump and misshapen, and her once golden hair was now streaked with gray—or, even worse, artificially bleached? What if she latched on to him and spewed invectives at him, blaming him for her ill-fated marriage and her woebegone existence? What if she cried that he owed it to her to make good on a promise he'd expressed years and years ago, before he'd matured into the man he was today?

He would put his arm around her and offer his sympathy, that was what. He would tell her he was sorry things had worked out badly for her and he wished her happiness in the future. He would say that life had turned out differently from what either of them could have foreseen fifteen years ago when they'd marched across the football field in their caps and gowns and accepted their diplomas and gazed toward the future with stars in their eyes.

Ah, but what if she wasn't bitter? What if she was still the nubile young woman he'd remembered her to be? What if her years stuck in a rotten marriage hadn't left any mark on her at all? What if her eyes were still wide and blue and lovely, and her smile lit up the sky? What if seeing her brought back memories of their first date—bowling and an ice cream afterward—and of the hours they'd spent studying together at the table in his mother's kitchen, and of the way Penny had looked in her pink satin prom dress, with tiny pink flowers woven into her hair? What if he remembered only the balmy spring afternoons they'd spent lying on their backs on the grassy hill behind the Simpson house, staring at the sky and fantasizing about how many children they would have and what street they would live on? What if he remembered the first time they'd made love, their unpracticed bodies taut with nervousness and excitement, Penny giggling as he'd related to her his embarrassment when he'd gone to the drug store to purchase contraceptives, and then her giggles fading into deep sighs as they learned in their fumbling way how to bring pleasure to each other....

What if he saw Penny and remembered only the good things? For there had been so many good things, so many.

"Ladies and gentlemen, we're beginning our descent to O'Hare International Airport," came the metallic, disembodied voice of a flight attendant. He launched into a rote lecture about returning to one's seat and fastening one's seat belt and Tom opened his eyes and focused on the miniature houses visible through the patchy clouds beyond his window.

He had good memories of Penny Simpson, wonderful, irreplaceable memories of growing up with her. But that was all they were: memories. Moments from his past.

Remembering made him grateful for what he'd had with her. But that was then, not now. And all he could think of was that the seat next to him was empty and Jodie should have been in it.

Jodie. The woman he loved.

JODIE CONSIDERED PHONING Lynne again, then decided not to. When she'd called a couple of hours ago, Lynne had been in a state of near hysteria. According to Lynne, Hank's therapist wanted Hank and Lynne to work with a marriage counselor, and Hank balked about that until Lynne complained that seeing a counselor would cut into her job-hunting time, at which point Hank heartily endorsed marriage counseling. This naturally made Lynne impatient about the progress Hank was—or wasn't—making. The therapist pointed out that therapy wasn't an overnight cure, that they would both have to give it time and that with the possibility of criminal charges being reinstated against him, Hank didn't have too many options available to him.

And then, Lynne had wailed, as if things weren't awful enough, the lid of a plastic container had slipped during a dishwasher cycle and melted on the heating element, stinking up the kitchen.

Jodie had wanted to discuss her own malaise with Lynne. She'd wanted to unburden herself a little, but Lynne had been in no condition to offer any moral support. So Jodie had given her sister a pep talk, suggested that she zipper all plastic items inside a mesh bag and put them on the top rack when she ran them through the dishwasher and then said goodbye. She'd fixed herself a fruit smoothie, carried it out to the porch and sat on the steps, swatting away the mosquitos and staring out at the twisting road abutting her property, telling herself over and over again that sending Tom to Iowa had been the most loving thing she could do.

If only she were weaker, she could have thrown a tantrum and demanded that he stay. If she were weaker, she could have begged and groveled and sworn that she needed him more than any old flame in Iowa did. She could have clung to him and not let go.

But that wasn't like her. She loved Tom. Loving him meant freeing him to find out where he belonged and with whom. Some time within the next few days he'd have his answer, and she'd have hers.

The evening was humid, the air sticky and the crickets raucous. Sitting on the porch step reminded Jodie of the first time Tom had kissed her. She felt like crying.

With a shudder, she went back into the house, turned on the television and stared at the screen. She watched police officers chase colorful drug dealers, detectives vault over parked cars in hot pursuit, lawyers perform their own hazardous sleuthing. *Aren't they brave?* she thought churlishly, wondering whether the characters were fueled by love or just plain stupidity.

Bored and restless, she turned off the television and went upstairs. After washing, she slipped a nightgown over her head and stared at her empty bed as if it were the enemy. She was plumping the pillows when she heard the sound. At first she thought it was just an acorn hitting the roof overhead, but then she heard it again, a clear, rhythmic rapping. Then the doorbell sounded.

Lynne, Jodie thought with mixed feelings. If Lynne had fled from her husband again, Jodie would feel genuinely sorry for her—and from a selfish standpoint, her misery could surely use some company tonight. Pulling on her bathrobe, she hurried down the stairs to let in her sister. She swung open the front door and her greeting died on her lips.

Tom stood on the porch. He had on the business suit he'd been wearing when he'd left her house that morning, but his blazer was creased, his tie hung loose and his collar was undone. His face was illuminated partly by the hazy half moon, partly by the light seeping through the screen door from the front hall, but mostly by the radiant smile that shaped his lips. Bewildered, Jodie peered past him. His car was parked in the driveway.

She directed her gaze back to him, and his smile widened. She must be dreaming—except that she hadn't even gotten into that big, lonely-looking bed, let alone fallen asleep. No, this had to be real. Tom Barrett was definitely standing on the other side of the screen door, looking irresistibly handsome and grinning so brightly she almost needed sunglasses to look at him.

"What are you doing here?" she asked.

"Well, that's a real nice hello."

"Forgive me, but I'm a little bit confused." She was a lot confused—practically stupefied. Some tiny, irrational corner of her brain cautioned her not to open the screen door, because if she did he might disappear and then she'd know for a fact that she had dreamed this moment. "Aren't you supposed to be in Iowa?"

"That's an interesting way of phrasing the question," he countered. "I was *scheduled* to be in Iowa, but somewhere along the way, it dawned on me that I was *supposed* to be with you."

Jodie's puzzlement deepened and her frown seemed to amuse Tom enormously. "You were *supposed* to go to your reunion," she said, realizing at once that she sounded like an imbecile. Why was she telling him this? Why was he here? What in heaven's name was going on?

He took it upon himself to open the door and step inside. After removing his blazer, he tossed it over the newel post and arched his arms around Jodie. She moved willingly into his embrace, but the joy of being held by Tom couldn't erase her bewilderment.

"Aren't you happy to see me?" he asked, sensing her subtle resistance.

"I don't know," she muttered. She gave him a brief hug, then extricated herself from him and put a safe distance between them. "First tell me what happened."

He issued a deep, contented sigh and gazed around him, Jodie's skepticism having no effect on his high spirits. Still beaming, he took her hand and led her to the stairs. They sat side by side on the second riser, his formally trousered leg pressed along her nightgown-draped one, his polished loafers looking huge next to her dainty bare feet.

"What happened," he said, "was that I got as far as Chicago and then turned around and came back."

He sounded terribly pleased with himself, but she couldn't fathom why he should be. "Why?"

"Because I missed you."

Jodie felt a shaft of sheer elation pass through her at his affectionate words. But she fought off the sensation. Tom's return to the East Coast couldn't be explained away as simply as that. "You were only going to be gone for a couple of days," she reminded him. "You could have telephoned me if you wanted to hear my voice."

"I wanted more than your voice," he said. Despite his buoyant smile he seemed utterly serious. "I wanted *you*. I wanted you with me. I didn't want to go out there and waste three days worrying about what's going on between you and me. I wouldn't have enjoyed myself. That wasn't what I wanted."

"But...what about your mother?" Jodie asked. She knew she was avoiding the real issue, stalling for time, waiting for her reputed stores of strength and bravery to replenish themselves. "Didn't you want to see her?"

"Sure, I did. And I will, maybe in a month or two. I phoned her from O'Hare after I'd rearranged my flight, and explained that I couldn't make it this time. I told her to go and pick herself out a new vacuum cleaner and send me the bill."

"How nice," Jodie grumbled. "I bet she was really touched."

He chuckled. "She was annoyed. She said she liked her old vacuum cleaner just fine and didn't want to have to learn how to use a new one. She also told me that if I didn't come out to see her in a few weeks, she'd come to New York to see me. Which would also be okay. Either way she'd get to meet you."

"What do you mean, either way?" Jodie asked warily. "I'm not going to Iowa."

"Then I guess my mother will have to come here. I'm not going to Iowa without you."

Jodie had to be dreaming. None of this made sense. "Tom, if you want me to meet your mother, fine. But what does that have to do with your reunion? That was the main reason you were going out there, wasn't it?"

"The main reason I was going out there was to see Penny," he declared, pulling her hand across his knee and clasping both his hands around it.

She eyed him apprehensively. Now they were getting down to it; now came the moment of truth. "Then why aren't you doing just that?" she asked, bracing herself for the probability that she was going to loathe his answer. "Why aren't you in Carroll getting ready to see her?"

He examined Jodie's hand, tracing the delicate bones of it with his index finger. "It occurred to me somewhere along the way that I really had no interest in seeing her. I have nothing much to say to her—a few minute's worth of small talk, but nothing that could justify being away from you for three days. The more I thought about it, the more I realized that I'd probably wind up telling her all about you. I'd bet a year's income she's an avid reader of 'Penny-Wise.' I'd tell her about how you figure out your recipes and experiment with rug repairs and get letters from weirdos...." He drifted off, momentarily lost in thought. Then he shook his head. "What's the point in that? Why should I be halfway across the country talking about you when I could be here with you, instead?"

"But maybe you wouldn't have talked about me," she asserted. "Maybe you would have seen her and the earth would have stopped spinning. Maybe you would have fallen head over heels all over again."

"Impossible," he murmured, lifting her hand to his mouth for a kiss.

The warmth of his lips against her palm sent a shiver of longing up her arm and through her body. She wanted to believe him, but she couldn't. "You'll never know, Tom," she said, her tone laced with mournfulness. "You'll never know because you ran away." She pulled her hand from him and stood, then paced the front hall, anxious and upset. "You fled before you had a chance to prove to yourself that you were really over her. Maybe you ran away because you were afraid to find out the truth. And now you'll never know."

He watched her, his eyes narrowing. "I *do* know," he said resolutely. "I didn't have to go to Iowa to know. I didn't have to travel all that distance and shoot the breeze with a bunch of old acquaintances to prove anything. I love you, Jodie—and that's not the sort of thing you prove or disprove. It's something you know, deep inside. And I know it."

She stopped pacing and faced him. His words were stark, candid, stunning in their lack of pretense. She loved him, too. She loved him enough to have given him the chance to test his love—and to leave her, if their love failed the test. Her greatest fear was that he'd evaded putting their love to the test because he'd been afraid it wouldn't survive.

But perhaps his test was different from hers. Perhaps his test had involved trusting her when she'd gone off to face her tormentor alone the morning after her house had been bombed, trusting her to defend herself, to take care of herself. At the time she'd believed that it was her love for Tom that had given her the strength she'd needed to triumph over Hank. But maybe she'd been only half right. Maybe her strength had come from *Tom's* love for *her*.

He gazed at her, his expression inviting, but she held back. "What about your curiosity?" she asked. "Weren't you curious to see Penny?"

As always, he was honest. "Yes, I was curious. I still am. But that's no reason to hurt her."

"Hurt her?" Jodie scowled. "How could meeting with her at a class reunion hurt her?"

He exhaled, aware that she wasn't going to accept his unvoiced invitation and return to the stairs. Instead, he stood and crossed the hallway to her. He held her gently, letting his hands rest against her waist, and met her piercing gaze with his. "Don't you see?" he said, explaining as if to a child. "There I would have been, going on and on about this fantastic woman I'm in love with, a woman who's bright and strong and independent, who's made a career of solving other women's problems. I'd have told Penny about how talented you are and how generous, and about how housewives all over the country depend on you. I'd have told her how crazy I am about you, and how lucky I am to have found you. And what would she had said? 'I'm divorced, Tom. I made a mistake. I shouldn't have walked out on you. I haven't been nearly as lucky as you.'" He slid his hands up Jodie's sides to her shoulders, still holding her far enough from him that they could gaze into each other's eyes. "Why should I hurt her that way?"

Jodie felt a few tears beading along her lashes. So many people would have been thrilled by the opportunity to hurt someone who'd hurt them as deeply as Penny Simpson had hurt Tom. So many people would have welcomed the chance to take revenge.

Not Tom. He was too decent, too good, too bighearted. His staunch refusal to inflict pain on the woman who'd brought him so much grief proved beyond a doubt that Penny no longer had any hold on him.

"I love you, too," Jodie whispered, closing her arms tightly around him and touching her lips to his. "You're the most wonderful man in the world."

He grinned. "Why do I sense another Boy Scout speech coming on?"

Jodie grinned, as well. "You aren't a Boy Scout," she assured him. "You're much too sexy."

"Oh, so now you're defaming Scouts everywhere by implying they aren't sexy."

"Tom!" She laughed, but beneath the humor she was utterly serious and she wanted him to be, too. "Don't make jokes," she pleaded. "I'm trying to tell you something I never imagined myself telling a man."

"That you love me?" he asked, growing serious, as well.

"That I love you and I missed you, Tom. The minute you said goodbye this morning I started missing you. The thought that you were going to be gone for three whole days..." She closed her eyes, aware that she was confessing something even more intimate than her love. "It scared me, Tom—but it's true. I need you. I think I'm even dependent on you. I was beginning to wonder how I was going to survive this weekend without you."

Tom bowed his head and kissed her, slowly and deeply. "You would have survived," he told her. "Don't you know how strong you are?"

"I'm stronger when you're in my life."

"Then that's where I'll stay," he promised. He kissed her again, folding his arms tightly around her, holding her as if he had no intention of ever letting go of her again. After a few rapturous minutes, however, he did. His eyes sparkling with mischief but his voice thick with passion in the aftermath of their kiss, he said, "Tell me, can I earn a merit badge by helping a little lady up the stairs?"

She smiled, as well. "That depends on what you do with her once you get her up there."

"Mmm." His smile became marvelously seductive, letting her know exactly what he planned to do with her. Sliding his arm around her shoulders, he started up the stairs with her.

"You do understand that you are never to refer to me as a 'little lady' again," she warned him, snuggling into the warm arch of his arm.

"Yes, ma'am."

"And I'm perfectly capable of climbing up these stairs without any help from anyone."

"Understood," he whispered, pausing to nuzzle her hair. The warmth of his breath seeped down through her body, causing her breath to quicken and making her wonder whether she really could get all the way to her bedroom without Tom beside her.

Then again, without Tom beside her, getting to her bedroom would not be a particularly pressing goal. But he was here, exactly where she wanted him to be. Exactly where she needed him to be.

He would be here forever, she knew. And her need for him would never lessen.

And that was just fine with her.

Six exciting series for you every month... from Harlequin

HARLEQUIN

The series that started it all

Tender, captivating and heartwarming...
love stories that sweep you off to faraway places
and delight you with the magic of love.

◆

Harlequin Presents®

Powerful contemporary love stories...as individual as the women who read them

The No. 1 romance series...
exciting love stories for you, the woman of today...
a rare blend of passion and dramatic realism.

◆

Harlequin Superromance®

It's more than romance... it's Harlequin Superromance

A sophisticated, contemporary romance-fiction
series, providing you with a longer,
more involving read...a richer mix of complex plots,
realism and adventure.

HARLEQUIN

American Romance®

Harlequin celebrates the American woman...

...by offering you romance stories written about American women, by American women for American women. This series offers you contemporary romances uniquely North American in flavor and appeal.

◆

HARLEQUIN *Temptation*

Passionate stories for today's woman

An exciting series of sensual, mature stories of love...dilemmas, choices, resolutions... all contemporary issues dealt with in a true-to-life fashion by some of your favorite authors.

◆

Harlequin Intrigue®

Because romance can be quite an adventure

Harlequin Intrigue, an innovative series that blends the romance you expect... with the unexpected. Each story has an added element of intrigue that provides a new twist to the Harlequin tradition of romance excellence.

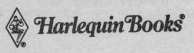 *Harlequin Books®*

PROD-A-2R

You'll flip . . . your pages won't!
Read paperbacks *hands-free* with

Book Mate · I

The perfect "mate" for all your romance paperbacks

Traveling • Vacationing • At Work • In Bed • Studying • Cooking • Eating

Perfect size for all standard paperbacks, this wonderful invention makes reading a pure pleasure! Ingenious design holds paperback books OPEN and FLAT so even wind can't ruffle pages — leaves your hands free to do other things. Reinforced, wipe-clean vinyl-covered holder flexes to let you turn pages without undoing the strap . . . supports paperbacks so well, they have the strength of hardcovers!

Pages turn WITHOUT opening the strap

SEE-THROUGH STRAP

Reinforced back stays flat.

Built in bookmark

BOOK MARK

BACK COVER HOLDING STRIP

10˝ x 7¼˝. opened.
Snaps closed for easy carrying, too.

Available now. Send your name, address, and zip code, along with a check or money order for just $5.95 + .75¢ for delivery (for a total of $6.70) payable to Reader Service to:

Reader Service
Bookmate Offer
3010 Walden Avenue
P.O. Box 1396
Buffalo, N.Y. 14269-1396

Offer not available in Canada
*New York residents add appropriate sales tax.

BM-GR